'Look at me,' Jason commanded. She could not. Each moment she was

power he seemed

her of all will to r

she did not lift h

holding her immo

cupped her chin w

head. 'That's bett

devil full in the fac

Little idiot! Com

reality. Is it so terrible for me to want you with your feet on the ground and by my side?'

The laughter was suddenly gone from his voice and sunburnt features, and she grew weak as his face drew closer. She tried to struggle against the arm that imprisoned her so closely, but her limbs refused to respond. As he slowly lowered his mouth to hers, she clamped her lips tightly together, resisting him in the only way left to her. Yet even that failed. The moment he realised her intent, she expected force to provoke an answer from her, but Jason had no intention of doing anything that would make her run from him in fear, and imparted into that long-drawn-out, passionate, heart-stopping, numbing kiss, many, many years of knowledge—and Melisande knew that she was lost!

Valentina Luellen was born in London in 1938, and educated in Gloucestershire and London. She began writing at school—mainly because she loathed maths! It took her twelve years of writing before she had a book accepted, but she has now had over 40 stories published. Historical romances are her favourite to write, because she loves researching into so many different countries, learning about customs and costumes and the way people lived hundreds of years ago.

Valentina Luellen and her husband moved to Portugal six years ago when he became seriously ill. There his health began to improve and they now live in a renovated farmhouse on the Algarve with their 21-year-old son, 21 cats, two Portuguese dogs, and around 100 trees—almonds, olives, figs, plums, lemons and oranges—most of which they planted themselves.

Valentina Luellen has written 22 Masquerade Historical Romances. Recent titles include *Where the Heart Leads*, *The Passionate Pirate*, *The Devil of Talland* and *The Devil's Touch*.

MY LADY MELISANDE

Valentina Luellen

MILLS & BOON LIMITED
ETON HOUSE 18–24 PARADISE ROAD
RICHMOND SURREY TW9 1SR

First published in Great Britain 1987
by Mills & Boon Limited

ISBN 0 263 75908 3

Set in 10 on 10½ pt Linotron Times
04–1187–82,800

Photoset by Rowland Phototypesetting Limited
Bury St Edmunds, Suffolk
Made and printed in Great Britain by
Cox & Wyman Limited, Reading

CHAPTER ONE

MELISANDE PRESSED HER nose against the windowpane, but the teeming rain obliterated all vision, and heavy, ominously black clouds, no matter where she looked, threatened to shorten yet another dismally grim summer day. Summer! It was more like the middle of winter. The sun had not shone for weeks, and here it was June. Local farmers were complaining at the ruination of their crops, children huddled in doors because it was too wet and miserable to play on the village green. Washing hung on the line forever wet! Summer!

Her precious herbs were being washed away by the stream at the bottom of the garden, which now overflowed from days of continuous rain, as were the flowers she had so diligently planted to bloom over the next three months. All her hard work for nothing, and she had better things to do. There was the running of the house, now that the housekeeper had taken offence at not being paid for the past six months and had left. Thank goodness the cook had remained faithful, or she might have ended up doing that job too, Melisande mused. She had to recognise that, although the old woman had been with them for many years, it was not so much loyalty as the free roof over her head and the food and clothes provided, however, that had determined her course of action.

The rain lashed at the panes with increased fury, and a belligerent wind rattled the chimneypots and roof-tiles, threatening to dislodge them. There would be many a house in the village in need of repair by the morning, she thought, drawing heavy velvet curtains across the window to shut out the draught. Not seven o'clock on what should have been a fine June day, when she should have been walking in the garden, enjoying the scent of roses and picking brightly-coloured blooms to adorn the living-room, and here she was about to light a candle!

Where was her sister? Lucy had been gone from the house all afternoon, seizing the opportunity afforded by the absence of their father and elder sister to disobey him yet again and go to the village, where she had recently become acquainted with a young man. Of course their father did not approve. He never approved of anyone Lucy wanted to know, and despaired of Melisande because she had no interest whatsoever in becoming a wife and mother. Lucy's adventurous spirit wanted to soar free. She hated the confines of the house, their father's restrictions, the life he planned for her. She had a passion for the sea—a craving to cross the wide expanse that separated England from France and return once more to the place where their mother had been born. Melisande often wondered, but would never have offended her sister whom she loved dearly by saying so, if the desire was but another excuse to avoid an existence which did not appeal to her.

She herself was quite content to stay in the huge, sprawling house set on the outskirts of Kingsclere, a small farming community set in the midst of rolling Hampshire hills of great beauty. She had no ambitions to marry a wealthy man, as did her elder sister Priscilla. She was the only one who had no ambitions—but she had her dreams. Whenever there was a spare moment, which did not come often these busy days, she would curl up in a comfortable chair in her bedroom and lose herself in a book. She loved tales of the past, of knights and princes and deeds of valour. Why was the world not like that now? Why did she and her sister have to marry strangers because it was their father's whim? Why could they not select the men with whom they wished to spend the rest of their lives? Did it matter if he was not rich? It did to their father, who would not relinquish the past and accept that they were no longer the prosperous de Vere family who had once been the most important people in the county.

With a sigh, Melisande rose and surveyed herself in the mirror on the wall. She was pale and tired and, alas, not beautiful like Priscilla or even pretty like Lucy. The long hair which hung almost to her waist was too fiercely red, even for these days in the reign of Queen Elizabeth. Her eyes were too large, set amid high cheekbones that often made her look too bony; and they were neither blue nor violet . . . She was slight of figure, although she was filling out now in her eighteenth year. Pulling in the waist of her blue gown, she tightened it upwards over her breasts, turning this way and that as she scrutinised herself. Priscilla's hand-me-downs did little to improve Nature.

There was nothing about her appearance to denote that she was the daughter of a once rich and prosperous Huguenot family of merchants who had fled from the appalling persecutions in France in 1572 and found a safe refuge in the English countryside, where they had continued to grow more wealthy in peace and harmony with their new neighbours. Those good days were far behind. Her mother was dead, her father near penniless, and his three daughters without a hope of making good marriages, for there was no money to provide suitable dowries. Yet still Edwin de Vere insisted that these would take place. Instead of selling the house—which they now only used in part, less than six rooms out of sixteen—and using the money to settle in a smaller property after repaying all their debts, he had preferred to retain his lavish lifestyle in order to keep up appearances, selling paintings and other valuables to purchase whatever was necessary to entertain the prospective suitors who came to court Priscilla. As the eldest she would marry first, then Lucy, and finally Melisande. She prayed the day would never come, although she wished Priscilla well in her hunt for a rich husband. It was all she wanted out of life.

It must end soon, Melisande thought, as she curled once more in the chair and took up her book. There was scarcely anyone in the village who did not know of their true circumstances now—the housekeeper would have seen to that. If Priscilla did not marry soon . . . But how could she without a dowry—unless her suitor were so enamoured by her beauty that she captivated his heart as well as his resources. And then he would have to marry her before he realised what lay beneath the charming smile and the soft voice . . . Her sister's temper was vicious, her tongue as shrewish as that of any market fishwife. Many a time both Melisande and Lucy had cringed at the wrong end of it, but as she was the one who must marry first, and if her husband was well-to-do and could ease the family problems, her tantrums had to be tolerated. Melisande knew that was the way her father looked at it, at least. She herself often thought her elder sister deserved a sound spanking.

She concentrated on her book of verse, and soon the rain and wind faded from her hearing as she grew more absorbed with the descriptive prose, sighing softly as she was transported to bygone days when chivalry was all that mattered. Men still fought duels now, but only over trivialities. The court of Queen Elizabeth in London, so she had heard, was renowned for its scandals and the foppish men each vying in some way to outdo the other with the magnificence of his clothes or the boasting of some great achievement. Intellect seemed to be of little importance, although great men like Francis Drake and Hawkins stood out from the rest, risking their lives on the Spanish Main to bring honour, not to mention vast fortunes, back to their Queen.

Mostly all that mattered to the fawning courtiers was to cluster about the ageing monarch, now in her sixty-second year, like bees around a honeypot, seeking her favours, a smile, a word that would establish them as being accepted into the élite circle at her side. One day, Melisande had promised herself, she would go to London. Not to see the Queen or to attend the court, for both were far beyond the realms of possibility with her meagre circumstances, and she had little interest in either. But to go to the theatre, to watch one of the plays of the young William Shakespeare. Now there was a man whose greatness spoke for itself in every line he wrote! Even the Queen had attended his performances and highly praised his talent. Royal patronage had quickly assured his success.

She was brought abruptly back to reality as the door behind her slammed and a shower of icy raindrops descended over her neck and shoulders. The book dropped unnoticed to the floor, as she sprang to her feet and wheeled about to face the dripping figure in the act of removing a sodden cloak.

'Lucy! Where have you been until this hour? Thank goodness Father has not yet returned, or you would have been found out and locked in your room again,' she said, quickly moving to one side as a second shower headed towards her. 'Do be careful! You are soaking the floor.'

'I—I am frozen! Oh, this wretched weather.' Lucy's teeth were chattering so badly that she could scarcely speak.

Melisande gazed in dismay at the hair plastered about her face, the inches of mud round the hem of her skirts and clinging to her shoes. 'Get out of those things at once before you catch a chill.'

'Don't be angry, Sandy,' Lucy pleaded, as she struggled to free herself of her clothes. Only she was allowed to call her sister anything other than Melisande. They shared a close relationship, which neither seemed able to have with their elder sister. 'You sound like Mother.'

'If she was here now, she would be very angry, you know she would. Going out in such weather to meet a boy! And against Father's strict instructions that you have nothing more to do with him.' Melisande feigned annoyance as she helped her sister, frowning fiercely as she extricated her from the dirty shoes and rolled down equally splattered stockings. 'What an amount of mud! Did you walk all the way to the village?'

'And back. I cut across the fields in the hope that I would be home more quickly, but they are waterlogged —and the bridge is out. Father won't be back tonight.

He'll have to stay in Burghclere.' Lucy's brown eyes became positively wicked as she divested herself of the last of her extremely uncomfortable clothes and pulled on the woollen robe Melisande held out. 'Perhaps, by morning, Priscilla will have accepted that idiot son of Lord Haslett."

'Lucy, that isn't fair! He—he may be a little slow witted, but . . .' Melisande protested.

'But he's rich, and that's all she cares about. All Father cares about, too. I heard them talking before they left. If she accepts him, Lord Haslett has promised to forgo the dowry and pay Father's outstanding debts. That's how desperate he is. And Father will agree; you know he will. He's desperate too, and then it will be my turn to be fobbed off on some . . . some . . .'

Lucy's pretty plump features wrinkled into an expression of disgust and Melisande's heart went out to her. Neither relished the prospect of the marriages ahead of them, yet nothing could prevent them. Their father's word was law! Oh, to be independent, Melisande thought. To have money of my own, to be my own mistress, to choose my own husband! The thoughts surprised her, and she realised that Lucy's wild spirit was threatening to invade her own peaceful little existence and make her dissatisfied with what she had. She was content with the house and her books, to sew and read, and play for her father on the virginals . . . one of the few valuable items they still possessed. Perhaps, when Priscilla made a good marriage, he would relent and accept the love of his two remaining daughters as being sufficient for his needs. He was growing old, and he would be lonely without them.

'You are shivering.' Melisande rolled the wet clothes into a bundle, pushing the shoes into the middle of it. 'I'll go and make you a hot drink.' Their father, although they could ill afford it, always kept a bottle of brandy in his study. She would slip a few drops into some hot milk for her sister, only too aware how likely she was to catch a chill over the slightest thing, and she had just been out in the wind and rain for hours. 'Do you love him?'

'Kit—Christopher?' Lucy blushed. 'I don't know. Yes, I think so.' The hesitation in the answer made Melisande wonder.

'And he?'.

'He talks to me like a sister. I don't think he even thinks of me in that way.' Lucy did not seem offended by his lack of affection.

'But how can you stand that?' Melisande asked. Was it love or infatuation, or another of Lucy's ways to escape from the house and their father, and from Priscilla's constant complaining about their impoverished mode of living?

'I don't ask him to love me . . . I want only to be with him, to share his company, to listen to his voice. Oh, Sandy, how happy I am when I'm with him!'

'How can you be? He gives you nothing,' insisted Melisande.

'How wrong you are! Just to be with him is sufficient for the moment. He is such a clever young man, too. I am never bored listening to him. His father was one of the poor brave men killed when the Spanish Armada tried to invade England. Like me, he loves the sea. That drew us together from the start. He understands how I feel, my longing to go back to see where Mother was born. He says he's never known a girl who wanted to go to sea before.'

Melisande said nothing, although she did not like her sister's choice of words, 'for the moment'. Was she using this young man to achieve her aim: to run away from home and the dull future she refused to accept?

'He's apprenticed to a pilot, and one day he may have his own ship and sail the sea like Francis Drake. He could become famous—and rich! I wish I were a man, so that I could go with him! I'd never come back to England.'

'I thought I was supposed to be the dreamer in this house,' Melisande said with a smile. 'Off to bed with you now, and I'll bring you some milk. What was that? Did you say that the bridge was out? It can't be . . . Father's back.' She grew quite pale at the thunderous knocking at the front door, clutching the bundle of wet clothes tightly against her chest. She had hoped to dispose of all traces of Lucy's secretive excursion before morning, and now, it seemed, it was too late.

'Father would not knock at his own front door. Who would be out in this weather?' Lucy looked quite alarmed.

'You were,' Melisande reminded her. Quickly she pushed the bundle under her bed, re-arranged the covers and pushed her sister towards the door. 'Go to bed. I'll see who it is. Perhaps someone from the village has been taken ill. You know how they always come here for some of Mistress Annie's herb possets.' Sixty-year-old Annie Lampton was their cook, and renowned for her medicinal herbs and knowledge of healing.

'But you can't open the door—with Father away.' Lucy was aghast at the suggestion. 'We could be robbed!'

'They would find little here to make them rich overnight. Go to your room and lock the door. They sound very insistent, and I cannot leave them standing outside in this terrible weather. We have little to offer except our hospitality. Mother would never turn anyone away from the door.'

Ushering Lucy into her room, Melisande proceeded down the narrow stairs to the front door, holding the candle aloft to guide her past the last remaining portraits of their ancestors, who watched her progress with unwavering stares. Sometimes she felt as if they were somehow alive, watching her every move, listening to each word. Lucy had an almost morbid interest in them all and would often stand before one of the dour faces, deliberating whether she had inherited any of their attributes. To Melisande's way of thinking, none of them looked as though he possessed a quarter of the wilfulness and determination of her sister. How different the three sisters were.

Priscilla, now twenty, thought only of a fine house and servants to wait on her. She had always been spoilt as a child, doted on by their father who no doubt saw when he looked at the lustre of her long black hair, the richness of her blue eyes, and the flawlessness of her skin, the prospect of marriage to not only a rich, but perhaps a titled young man. She would grace any home, and was most skilful in all the accomplishments that a wife should know.

Lucy, at nineteen, was as rebellious as she had been from the age of fourteen, when their mother had died. As their circumstances had become more difficult, the knowledge that the only future ahead for her was marriage to some man who would wed her only because she was young and healthy and would provide him with a large family did nothing to curb that wild streak.

One year her junior, Melisande had accepted the unfortunate change in their circumstances when it happened and tried to make the best of it. It had begun only one short year after the death of their mother, when, driven by his determination that his daughters should always have the best of everything, their father began to speculate heavily. The financial crisis, when it came, crippled them. Gone were the days of parties and balls. No longer were they invited to visit the grand houses of the nobility in the outlying districts. Friends dwindled . . . as did the prospects for each of the girls. There were no more bolts of the finest velvets and silks to make dresses for them all; she had not had a new one in over eighteen months, relying on the generosity—when the very rare fit seized her—of Priscilla to give her a gown she no longer required. Some she was able to alter for Lucy, whose figure was more ample than her own, but mostly she had to take them in drastically at the waist and bust for herself. What did it matter? Who was there to see her nowadays?

The brass knocker on the front door thudded repeatedly, and she quickened her steps, only to draw back again in a moment of indecision. What if her sister was right? This was a night for footpads and highwaymen, and she remembered that, only the week before, a carrier transporting wine to Reading had been stopped by force and left for dead in a ditch.

'For the love of heaven, is there no one awake in there?' The words shouted outside were barely audible as the wind whipped them away.

Without further hesitation, Melisande swung open the heavy door and was almost bowled over by the raging gust that swept into the tiny hall. A shape rose before her, cloaked, wet, muddy, cursing vehemently . . . it staggered past her, carrying something . . . She gave a cry and slammed the door, and turned to face the man who had entered, an unconscious young woman cradled in his arms.

'Devil take you, girl, you took your time! I'm all but drowned, and my ward needs a doctor. Where is your master? I would ask his hospitality for the night. My coach is off the road a mile or more back, and I can go no further . . .' A pair of grey eyes that instantly made Melisande think of the menacing stormclouds outside fastened on her, gleaming with anger as they surveyed the slender figure clutching a candle, who was floundering for words as she realised he had mistaken her for a servant. Why should he not? Her appearance, with her hair all in disorder and in a well-worn dress, was not that of a lady. 'Have you lost your tongue? Do you not understand what I am saying?' The girl in his arms moaned, and an oath exploded from his lips. 'She needs a warm bed. Fetch your master at once!'

'He—he is not at home this evening.'

'Dear heaven, what kind of place have I come upon! Gently, little one, gently.' The harsh tone softened as he altered his hold on the girl, and Melisande drew in her breath in alarm as she saw the blood on the sleeve of his coat where the cloak had fallen away . . . and on one side of his face, too. It was a hard face, darkened by wind and sun—that of a sailor, almost, she decided, yet his voice was that of a gentleman, and his clothes, despite the rain which had saturated them, had been tailored with flair and elegance.

'We . . . There are plenty of rooms, sir, but—but the servants have not yet returned from my master's town house in London and we are not ready for visitors . . . Come . . . I know where your ward will be comfortable,' she added quickly, as the man glowered at her in a most unfriendly fashion.

She led him up the stairs, holding the candle to one side so that he would not trip on the uneven stonework. It should have been repaired long ago, but there was no money to engage the stonemason, to whom they were already in debt for repairs to another part of the house. The door of Lucy's room began to open.

'Stay there,' she hissed to her, not wanting the appearance of her sister to add to the confusion. Why had she been so silly as to confirm this stranger's suspicion that she was only a maid? His manner was overbearing, and Priscilla would never have stood for it. Yet it was of little importance; she could explain the mistake later when the unfortunate girl was settled in bed. 'Please put her in here; this is a very comfortable room.' She opened the door of Priscilla's room and quickly lit another candle beside the bed and a second on the small writing-table against a far wall.

'You are quite safe now, Amanda. Help me off with her clothes, girl, quickly,' the stranger ordered, gently depositing his charge on the bed after removing her sodden cloak, and Melisande moved to obey as if she were genuinely the servant he believed. He sounded the kind of man who did not repeat himself. And he was not inexperienced where women were concerned, she thought, noting the ease with which he unfastened the rich brocade gown and tossed it aside with a careless gesture that made her purse her lips as it settled on the floor, and water began to ooze on to the polished wooden boards.

'Is she hurt?' She unfastened the ribbons of the girl's chemise, and was about to pull it off when she realised he was still bending over the bed. A half smile touched the lean mouth at the look she directed up at him and he drew back, allowing her to complete her task without his help, and retired to stand near the window while she fetched a nightgown from the closet and managed to get the limp form into it. 'There. She will soon be warm. Is she hurt?' she repeated again, tucking the bedclothes firmly in. The girl looked terribly pale, and the fair hair clung to her cheeks, but there seemed to be no sign of injury.

'Exhausted. We must have walked for miles. At least, I suppose it would seem like that in this atrocious storm. Your master is away, you said?'

'Visiting friends in Burgclere—Lord Haslett. He was expected home tonight, until the weather worsened. It will not be possible to fetch a doctor.'

'And whose house am I in?' the man demanded. He had been eyeing the furniture about him with a keen gaze. Priscilla's was the best of the three girls' bedrooms. As the eldest, she maintained that she should have first selection of everything, and that was how it had been. Bed-linen, curtains, furniture—attention. What would she say when she discovered a strange girl in her bed? Melisande wondered. But she had to go somewhere, as did the man watching her with narrowed gaze as though he were puzzled.

'The house of Lord Edwin de Vere. No doubt you have heard of him?' Why had she asked that? If he had heard of her father, it would not be anything to the good.

'The name is familiar, but how I came to know it escapes me for the moment. Have you someone to look after my ward while you show me to a room? You may not be aware that I am also dripping wet and in need not only of a bed, but something warming to drink.'

'I shall make you both a spiced posset . . .' Melisande began, and the stranger gave a snort of indignation as if the suggestion was repulsive.

'For Amanda, most certainly, the poor child needs it. For myself, I was thinking more of a large brandy. I am sure your master would not object to your giving me something to restore life to my frozen bones.'

He most certainly would, Melisande thought, dreading her father's reaction when he discovered that his precious brandy had been tampered with. But it was in a good cause, and she had also promised Lucy some. Lucy! She would have to sit with the man's ward until Melisande could return.

'Please excuse me. I will fetch someone.' She could not leave the room fast enough. There was something very disturbing about the way those flint-like grey eyes watched her.

He was pacing the room in an impatient manner when she returned with her sister. His gaze immediately fastened on Lucy's still wet hair and the robe she was clutching tightly about her, but he made no comment. For a moment, he bent over the bed to reassure himself that his ward was comfortable, frowning as he laid a hand against one of her cheeks. The girl's eyelids flickered but did not open, and as he drew back, Melisande saw his lips tighten.

'She is in good hands,' she said, hoping to reassure him.

He nodded, and followed her in silence to her room. As he began stripping off his wet clothes, she quickly excused herself and went down to the kitchen to heat some milk. When it was ready, she collected the bottle of brandy and a glass from the study and took them upstairs.

'Go away!' She heard the petulant tone even before she opened the door and stepped into Priscilla's room. Lucy, standing beside the bed, appeared quite taken aback as she looked down into the flushed cheeks of the girl, who had made a remarkably speedy recovery the moment her guardian had gone. 'I don't want you here with me. I'm not a child.'

'I have brought you some warm milk,' Melisande said, ignoring the outburst, and put it down on the small table within her reach. 'How are you feeling? Your guardian was very worried about you. Shall I fetch him?'

'No! I don't want to see him—or you. Go away, both of you. I want to be alone.' Delicate hands clenched into tight fists on the bedcover.

'Very well, you shall have your wish.' Melisande turned back to the door, motioning Lucy to follow her. 'You are a very rude, ungracious young woman—and ungrateful.'

'Sandy, she is naturally upset after such a terrible experience,' Lucy protested, loath to leave her, despite her manner. Besides, she was dying with curiosity to know who she was. Such fine clothes must have been made in London.

'Where is he? Where's Jason—the monster who brought me to this—place?' Her hazel-flecked eyes surveyed the clean but worn counterpane and the heavy curtains about the bed with obvious contempt. She was accustomed to better things about her, Melisande supposed, but how dared she look down her nose at what she was offered now! It was better than being out in the rain, soaked to the skin.

'In a room further along the passage. He is hurt, you know. Don't you care?'

'Hurt—him!' The girl gave a shrill laugh that betrayed the agitation raging inside her. It was clear that she did not like her guardian at all. 'Nothing ever hurts him! He is made of stone.'

That was not the impression Melisande had formed as he had stood by the bed, looking down at his ward. He cared for her very much. Jason—a strong name for a strong man! The girl was very pretty, she thought, studying the oval face framed by curly fair hair. Perhaps he was too strict a guardian in his efforts to protect her against the suitors who would come calling. There was nothing wrong in that. There was a wilfulness in her expression, a determined line about the firm young mouth that reminded her of Lucy. Both were fighting a domination of their spirit.

'I can see you have suffered no ill-effects from the

accident, and we shall leave you to rest. May I know the name of your guardian?' Melisande enquired.

'Dacre. Jason, Lord Dacre. I am Amanda Cummings.'

'Lord Dacre . . . Why, he owns that big estate just before Basing, doesn't he?' Lucy asked, suddenly in awe of such distinguished guests.

'Whispering Wood.'

Melisande saw that her sister's avid curiosity was well aroused, and so, quickly bidding goodnight to their guest, she ushered her out of the room. She herself had much to do before she could retire. She would have to sleep with Lucy, but the great old bed was big enough to hold all three sisters—and several more, when the need arose. In days past, when there had been parties and bells at the house, as many as seven girls had climbed exhausted between the sheets after hours of dancing.

'Sandy, it's Lord Dacre! And Priscilla isn't here. What a catch he would be for her,' Lucy exclaimed, as they moved towards her room. 'No wonder he took you for a servant . . . I expect he has a different one for every task. He's so rich, and he has been received at court by the Queen herself. And he's a friend of Francis Drake.'

'How do you know all this about him? I can't even remember hearing his name,' Melisande asked, and her sister's cheeks glowed with colour. 'Christopher?'

'He knows everyone. He's apprenticed to Lord Dacre's ship, *Moonwynd*. He was in the fight against the Spanish Armada, you know. His father was killed, and he took command of the ship and sailed her right under the guns of the Spanish . . . Exciting! Can you not imagine it?'

'It sounds horrible! So many men were killed, Lucy; how can you find that exciting?'

'Oh, you don't understand! Where are you going with Father's brandy?'

'Lord Dacre has a desire to warm his frozen bones; he will be wondering where I am. Quickly, fetch me Father's best robe.'

'But . . .'

'He's a guest, and his clothes are soaking wet. We must provide him with something to wear. Whatever will he think of our hospitality? I'll fetch towels, and some salve for his face.'

A few moments later, when she knocked on her own door and cautiously entered, it was to find Jason, Lord Dacre, seated on the edge of the bed, clad only in a pair of tight-fitting breeches. He was scrutinising the portrait on the far wall. Would he question the resemblance, Melisande wondered, as his attention came slowly to rest on her. She was the image of her mother—the same flame-red hair and strangely coloured eyes, and skin that bore an almost ivory sheen.

'I thought perhaps you could use this.' She watched the grey eyes consider the loose gown she laid across the end of the bed. Did anyone ever know what thoughts were in his mind, she mused, as she poured a liberal amount of brandy into the glass and handed it to him. His expression betrayed nothing, and the eyes . . . so distant, and yet when they looked at her, it was as if the ground was moving beneath her feet. He thanked her for the brandy and then, to her dismay, downed it in one swallow and held out the glass to be replenished. She dared not hesitate. 'May I bathe your face, and your arm?' She indicated the ugly cut on his right forearm, which had bled profusely. He nodded, and sat in silence while she ministered to him, not making a sound or indicating in any way that she might be hurting him.

She had never been alone with a man before, let alone a half-naked one, and her cheeks were beginning to burn long before she had finished. She could feel herself becoming clumsy under his gaze . . .

'Is there anything else I can do for you?' she asked with all the naïvety of an eighteen-year-old girl who had no experience of men, and a pair of eyes fastened on her and slowly inspected her from head to toe, the wicked light gleaming in them like the embers of a fire just reawakened.

'My dear girl, I have just walked a mile or more in abominable weather, I ache like the devil, and I have a damnable headache! I have no inclination to be entertained, interesting though I would probably find it.' And then, as she stared at him, cheeks now flaming, wondering what on earth she had said to provoke such a reply, he gave a crooked grin and added, 'If a serving-wench in London has said those words to a man, it would mean she was offering her services for the night.'

'How dare you!' She sprang back from him, eyes widening in horror. 'I meant no such thing! You . . .' Words failed her. Gathering up his wet clothes, she fled from the room.

'How dared he presume! The arrogance of the man!' Melisande said furiously. 'To think that I would . . .'

'Oh, Sandy, you of all people,' Lucy gasped. She was sitting up in bed, her arms clasped about her knees, her eyes wide with shock at what she had been told. 'I would have slapped his face.'

'Perhaps he is used to having women throw themselves at him,' she replied dourly. 'I suppose you would call him handsome.'

'Handsome, very eligible and very rich. He is a catch for someone.' As Melisande turned towards the door, Lucy asked, 'Where are you going now?'

'To dry their clothes. They will be leaving in the morning if the weather has improved.'

'Priscilla will be furious if she misses him.'

Melisande had no doubt as to the truth of those words. Lord Dacre was indeed a most inviting prospect for any woman seeking a husband. Not only wealthy, but quite young—she judged his age to be somewhere in the early thirties—and exceedingly good-looking, but she would never have said so to Lucy, for fear her comments were misinterpreted. While bathing his arm, she had been acutely conscious of the darkly tanned chest and the firm shoulders, the sinewy muscles flexing as he moved. She had seen several scars, but had not dared to look at them too closely for it would not have been proper. As it was, she knew she should have woken the cook and had her remain in the room while she ministered to him. Her fingers had trembled as they gently wiped the dirt and blood from his cheek, and once again she found those grey eyes searching her face.

She arranged the clothes as well as she could in the kitchen, grimacing as she examined the mud clinging to the velvet gown. In the morning, she would do her best to brush it off before she returned it. For a moment her fingers caressed the material and the fine lace adorning the sleeves and stomacher. It was no use to be envious of what another possessed, or she would soon grow to be like Priscilla, ambitious for money and position, without love. Melisande did not care if the man who came into her life was without a penny, so long as he loved her. That was all important—to be loved. Better never to marry than to have her dreams destroyed.

A shutter began banging somewhere in the house, and it took her ten minutes to discover the offender in one of the upstairs rooms that were now not used. Dust-covers, like silent ghosts, covered the furniture to bring back memories of her childhood. This had been the play-room, where, before the devastating change in their circumstances, they had enjoyed blissful, innocent days and lacked no comforts. The room that had once rung with happy laughter now was an empty shell, containing no more than an old chair, the window seat with faded, well-worn cushions and a trunk containing old toys. Melisande often came up to this room when she had a spare moment, to sit and remember happier times, to weave about her, as she fondled an old doll whose hair was still as golden as the day it had been given to her, a dream world where poverty and unhappiness did not exist. When she returned below, to the sound of Priscilla's whining voice and constant complaining, of Lucy's angry tones raised against their father in rebellious comment, that world remained with her, to shield her from what lay ahead. Sometimes she thought it was the only thing that prevented her from losing her own temper and telling both her sisters how ungracious and spoilt they had become.

It was not really Edwin de Vere's fault that they had no money. He had only been trying to keep them all in the style to which they had become accustomed since the day they were born, and to make good marriages for them. Their mother, too, would have wanted it, although Melisande suspected she would have gone about the whole thing in a far more subtle manner.

She had been a gentle woman of great intelligence, who rarely raised her voice whatever the provocation. If she had possessed a temper to go with her magnificent fiery tresses, Melisande had never witnessed it. She suspected she had, for she herself possessed one, and at times, when her blood began to boil at the turmoil and discontent raging throughout the old house, she barely contained it. On these occasions she would often slip away to her little sanctuary and forget the realities of the outside world, to withdraw into the one of her own making, one of peace and beauty.

Outside the house, the wind continued to howl with great fury and the rain had not abated. Her father and Priscilla could not make the journey home in such weather—their host would not allow it—but if for some reason they did, they would be wet and miserable and in need of something hot to drink. She would remain up a while longer. The room smelt damp and musty, but she hardly noticed it as she set the candle down on the floor and sat in the chair, drifting away from the wildness of the night into a land of sunshine and light . . .

Melisande awoke with a start as the shutter banged suddenly behind her, and the candle flickered and almost went out in the draught. Leaping up, she secured it again, but the fastening was old and the wood worm-eaten so that it would not hold. She pulled the chair against it, shivering. How long she had been asleep she did not know, until passing the brass clock in the hall, she discovered it was almost midnight. No use to wait further, she decided. Locking the front doors, she returned upstairs to check on the two visitors, who would surely be asleep now after their frightening experiences. Amanda Cummings lay on her side, one arm beneath her head and her fair hair tumbled about the pillow. Another example of someone who had everything, not content with her lot, Melisande mused. She was not the kind of girl she could ever call a friend. Perhaps, in a strange way, lack of money and position would turn out to be a blessing in disguise.

A movement inside her own room, where she had supposed Lord Dacre would be sleeping, made her pause outside the door. A muffled oath followed, and the sound of something crashing to the floor. What was happening? Was he ill? Or drunk! She had left the brandy bottle behind. With some reluctance, she knocked.

'Is anything wrong, sir?'

No answer. No sound from within. He obviously did not want to be disturbed, and if he had indeed been drinking, that was the last thing she wanted to do. And then, as she turned to go, a faint voice and two words that sent her headlong into the room without a moment's hesitation: 'Help me.'

Jason Dacre half sat, half lay alongside the bed. The noise she had heard had been the table overturning. The bottle of brandy she had brought—and with a sinking feeling she noted it was almost empty—had rolled across the floor to the window. The glass had shattered in the fall, and tiny fragments were scattered everywhere. She came to a halt as his gaze fastened on her. His eyes were glazed and he seemed to have difficulty in focusing. Drunk! She ignored the hand which went out to her.

'For the love of heaven, girl, don't stand there . . . Help me on to the bed.' When she did not move, he tried to raise himself. His face contorted in pain, and the blood ebbed from the dark cheeks so swiftly that Melisande grew alarmed. Drunk—or ill? Now she was not sure, but he had sustained no serious injuries to bring him to such a state. Only the contents of the bottle could have done that, yet she relented and went to help him. The hand that closed over her arm was surprisingly strong, considering his condition, and she winced as his fingers bit painfully into her soft skin.

'You must help me,' she protested, as his full weight leaned against her. She was aware of the warmth of his body, of the handsome features only inches away and of the grey eyes fastened on her mouth. 'I cannot lift you myself; you are far too heavy.'

'A pretty wench like you should have had plenty of experience in such matters,' came the mocking reply, and she almost dropped him back on the floor in disgust.

'Some men have great difficulty in distinguishing a servant-girl from a lady,' she retorted, and Jason Dacre gave a chuckle.

'You have a manner about you that I've not often seen in a maid, but if you're not what you seem, why are you here tending me? No lady would closet herself alone with a strange man for fear her reputation would suffer. You obviously have no fear for yours.'

'Oh—you are insufferable! Your ward is right; you are a monster,' Melisande declared, heaving him with all her might up on the bed and letting him go. He almost slid off again, for his legs were still on the floor. Quickly she lifted them on to the bedcover and retreated out of reach. The look he gave her mocked the thoughts in her mind and brought a faint flush into her cheeks.

'You judge me on a very short acquaintanceship,' his tone was no longer mocking, but cold and unfriendly, 'and if you think that dreadful brew you call brandy has brought me to this state . . .'

'The bottle was full when I brought it,' Melisande said defensively.

'You little fool! If I didn't feel as if my head was splitting apart, I'd put you over my knee and give you a good spanking.' He lifted himself on one elbow, glaring at her. 'I've been drunk with the best sailors in this land, and believe me it took more than a few glasses of second-rate brandy . . .'

Melisande caught her breath as he gave a groan and slumped back. She stood silent, waiting for him to begin another tirade, but he lay with eyes closed, one arm outflung across the cover towards her. So still . . . He had said that his head was splitting apart. The brandy, of course, but no—he had mentioned a damnable headache before he had ever touched it. Had he hit his head when the coach overturned? If so, why had he not mentioned it before? She had seen no other signs of injury apart from those on his cheek and arm.

And then, as she bent to retrieve the broken pieces of glass from the floor, her eyes fell on the clean towel she had left beside the basin of fresh water so that he might refresh himself in the morning when he awoke. It was muddy. He had used it after she left, and amid the dark stains were others—bright red. Tentatively she touched the hand that hung over the edge of the bed. His skin was burning, and despite the pallor of his features, beads of perspiration were forming on his forehead. Carefully she slid back the sleeve and examined the gash she had cleaned. It was not bleeding, therefore the stained towel meant that he must have sustained another injury.

He muttered something incoherently as she gently turned his head upon the pillow and her long fingers probed the base of his skull. His hair was thick and blond, curling about his ears and the nape of his neck. She froze in dismay as her search proved the worst of her suspicions. Just beneath the hairline she felt a large lump, and bending closer, discovered the hair matted with dried blood. Why had he not mentioned it? Or, in his concern for his ward and the pain caused by his arm, had he not realised the full extent of his injuries until later?

He did not stir while she bathed the wound and pressed a folded piece of wet linen beneath his head to ease the swelling. How she had misjudged him: he had every reason to be angry with her. She left the room for a few minutes only to replenish the bowl with fresh water and fetch clean towels, but when she returned she found his movements restless, his face now covered in perspiration. A fever was upon him. She could not possibly leave him alone, and had no option but to watch him through the hours of darkness and hope that by morning it would have subsided. She thought of waking Lucy, then decided against it. There was little her sister could do to help, and no reason why they should both lose a night's sleep.

Tucking the bedcover securely round him, she retired to a chair and settled herself patiently to sit out the long hours until morning.

CHAPTER TWO

THE WIND WAS dropping, Melisande realised, for the room was suddenly very quiet, the silence broken only by the restless movements of the man on the bed. From time to time she rose from her chair to bathe his forehead with cool water and replace the wet towel beneath his head, but it was clear that his fever was increasing. She felt so helpless! Quietly going to the window, she drew back the curtains a fraction and gazed out. It was still raining, but not so heavily, and the sky was beginning to clear. She was relieved it was over, not only because it meant that her father would be able to return early in the morning—at least she hoped he would do so, for she suspected someone would have to fetch the village doctor for Lord Dacre—but because, in her heart, she hated storms. She hated the vivid lightning that split the sky apart like Wotan's deadly axe, or the rolling, booming thunder that continued up and down the valley for hours without respite. She never sat and looked out of the window on such nights, while Lucy thought it exciting, and Priscilla slept soundly.

When she turned back to the bed, Lord Dacre had thrown off the restricting bedcover, and his robe had fallen open to reveal more of him than was suitable for a young unmarried girl to see: long brown legs with a down of fine blond hair on them; searing the skin on one from knee almost to ankle was a twisting scar. Hastily she pulled the robe together and rearranged the bedcover, but as she tried to tuck it about his shoulders, he fought to push it away with a violence that took her by surprise and it was several minutes before he quietened enough to enable her to do so.

He groaned as she lifted his head, removed the towel, re-wetted it and then returned it, relieved that it was no longer spotted with fresh blood. For a moment her fingers lingered on the thatch of blond hair, in some places bleached almost white by the sun. How had he come by that terrible scar, she wondered, smoothing a curl about one ear. In the battle with the Spanish, when his father had been mortally wounded and he had assumed command of the ship? And sailed it right under the Spanish guns, so Lucy had said. How brave he must be, for the English ships were less tall than the towering Spanish galleons. To attack a vessel twice the size of his own, carrying far more men! Somehow the image of him as a stalwart sea-captain, rallying his men to fight in the heat of battle with flames and fallen rigging all about them, did not tally with that of a courtier, a man of flowery words and loose morals. He had given her the indication that, had he not been feeling so unwell, he might have found her attractive enough to warm his bed. The two pictures in her mind were totally conflicting, and without realising it, her slender brows rose into a questioning arch and the colour of her eyes deepened to challenge the richness of the most exquisite amethyst, as they always did when she was lost in thought.

So handsome a man would never lack a beautiful woman by his side, she thought, allowing her gaze to wander freely over the finely chiselled features, noting the firm line of the jaw, the lean mouth. Jason, Lord Dacre, was more than likely a man about whom many a woman had woven fantasies in her mind, each hoping to ensnare him for her own. Perhaps he was married; she had not thought of that. Or did he intend to remain a confirmed bachelor until his middle years, when the desire for heirs forced him to take a wife for that sole purpose, as many men did? The men in the books she read were handsome, as he was, courteous—she had her doubts about that, remembering his curtness—and protective of their women, as he was with his ward. Amanda might think him a monster, but his concern for her was genuine, Melisande was certain. What had he done to deserve her enmity?

She gave a gasp as his brown fingers fastened over the hand still laid against one cheek, then lifted slowly to entwine themselves in the red tresses that fell over one shoulder and were brushing against his chest.

'An angel with hair of fire! What strange phenomenon is this?' Jason Dacre's eyes were open, but from the strange expression in the chillingly cold grey depths she realised that he did not remember where he was or what had happened. 'Am I in heaven or hell?'

'Neither,' she assured him softly, trying to withdraw, only to discover that he would not relinquish his hold on her hair. In fact, the moment she tried to move, he tightened it, drawing her closer. 'You have had an accident. You are in the house of Lord Edwin de Vere, near Kingsclere. Do you not remember? Your ward Amanda is here, too. She is not hurt, and you have but a slight fever which will pass by morning.' How sure she sounded!

'Who are you? I recall a face, but no name . . .'

His words startled her, momentarily depriving her of an answer. How could he know her face? She did not know him. He was mistaken, of course, confusing her with some woman in his acquaintance, perhaps in London.

'Melisande . . .' she answered without thinking, and instantly regretted it.

'Melisande . . . No angel, but a water-sprite! Do you sit on some solitary rock, combing that magnificent hair, and luring men to their doom with those strange eyes? You could, you know. Many a man could be lured to the depths in pursuit of you!'

'You do not know what you are saying,' Melisande stammered, cheeks flaming. In pursuit of Priscilla perhaps, but never of her—she was no beauty. And yet he had made it sound as though she was, and how her heart had somersaulted at the words. He did not know what he was saying, so she must not take him seriously. He had probably said the same thing to many women far more attractive, and accessible, than her.

'I know what I see, and what I see I like. Hair like the flames of hell and eyes with the lustre of a brilliant jewel. Why do you blush, Melisande?' His free hand touched her flaming cheek, swept back the cloud of loose hair from her face and slid behind her head to grip the nape of her neck. 'Have you no lover to praise the gifts with which you have been endowed?'

Lover! Melisande choked back an indignant retort, staring down at him with eyes that flashed a warning of growing anger. His eyes glazed again, and he shook his head as if trying to clear it, wincing as the movement brought him pain. Immediately she seized the opportunity to draw away from him, but the slightest movement tightened the hold on her hair and she found herself drawn closer to the sun-bronzed features, helpless to resist.

She had been kissed once before by a man, at the last ball she and her sisters had attended. It was so long ago that she could not remember where it had been, but the incident in the garden was still vivid in her mind. She had accompanied the young man, a perfect gentleman up to that moment and her partner in the dancing for most of the evening, into the garden to take the air. The moment they were out of sight of the house, hidden from view by tall poplars and thick bushes, he had seized her in his arms, declaring he was enamoured of her and had begun pressing his mouth upon hers. Apart from the shock of the sudden change in his manner, she found the touch of his hot lips against hers, against the bare skin of her shoulders, totally nauseous, but he ignored her pleas that he release her, and was angry when she began to struggle to free herself, striking out at his face with clenched fists.

Had it not been for the intervention of another man, who was walking in the garden with a strikingly attractive woman at his side, she might well have been overcome by her ardent companion. As it was, he was seized by the scruff of his neck and propelled bodily into the house. She heard later that he had left immediately. It had all happened so quickly that she had never known who had come to her rescue, for she wanted to thank him, and she had told no one, especially her father, what had taken place, knowing the great fuss he would have made. She had confided in her mother, and no one else.

She had always believed a first kiss would lift her to the heights of heaven, that she would hear the sound of golden bells pealing, proclaiming that love had found her. It had been nothing like that: she had hated it . . . And now this man who held her sought to subject her to the same loathsome experience.

But it was not! She could feel the heat from him engulfing her as she was pressed against his chest. He was so strong, despite the fever! The lips that fastened over hers were fiercely possessive yet did not seek to dominate her, despite the expertise imparted to the long-drawn-out kiss. She tried to keep her own tightly closed, denying him an answer, but it was as though he were draining her of all will. Her senses cried out to be released from the embrace, but at the same time clamoured for the moment to last for ever. Her traitorous lips parted, growing soft and pliant beneath his own, and she heard a soft sigh escape him. At the same time, his hold on her relaxed, and she pulled back, dishevelled, trembling, shocked at the ease with which he had brought her to surrender. Tears welled into her eyes, but they were tears of frustration as well as anger. How could she have enjoyed it so? In the morning it was unlikely that he would remember it!

'At last the woman . . .' Jason Dacre began, and then his voice trailed away into silence and he was still once more.

The woman who . . . ? Melisande thought in irritation. Had he, in his fever-ridden mind, believed her to be someone else? To substitute her for another was even more humiliating than for him merely to have stolen a kiss from a servant-girl. Which, from the way he spoke, she believed he did quite often.

The last remaining hours of darkness dragged slowly

by. Most of the time she sat listening to Lord Dacre rail with feverish venom at someone called Richard. There was no love lost between the two men, and whoever the other was, he must have committed some terrible act to provoke the blood-curdling adjectives that issued from the sick man's lips. Melisande had never heard the like of them before! Once or twice his ward's name also could be heard. Is there a connection between the two? she wondered. She felt rather like a eavesdropper outside a closed door as she unwillingly shared this burden, which weighed so heavily on him that it preoccupied his mind.

The first grey streaks of dawn filtered through a chink in the curtains, which she pulled back, and to her relief found that the sky was quickly clearing of all signs of a storm. As they had no servants apart from the cook, she would have to walk to the village and find men to attend to Lord Dacre's coach and bring it to the house, although she doubted if he would be capable of leaving his bed for at least another day. She would bring the doctor back with her. It would be most embarrassing to have him and his ward as guests for any length of time, for they would soon discover the poverty in which she and her family lived. Melisande's fierce pride would not allow that to happen. Edwin de Vere had suffered enough, and would be deeply offended to be snubbed by someone who had enjoyed the hospitality—poor thought it was—of his house.

The cook would not be stirring before six, Melisande surmised, as she stretched cramped limbs and smothered a long yawn. She ached all over, and was so tired. Her eyes burned from lack of sleep, and she pulled a face at herself in the mirror as she discovered how pale she was. Little wonder, after being up all night!

'No! Dammit, no!' Jason Dacre thundered, and tight fists crashed down upon the bed with such violence that she ran to restrain him, grasping his shoulders with all her might to press him back upon the pillows.

'Do be still,' she pleaded, but he continued to thrash

and fight against her hold for many minutes, completely draining her strength, before he collapsed, his wild eyes closing again. For an instant he had looked like a madman, and had possessed the strength of one, glaring at her with hatred in his eyes as she bent over him. His mind was deeply troubled, and her heart went out to him, wishing she could in some way ease the black thoughts that plagued him so that he might rest peacefully and grow strong again.

She began to move away, but the moment she did so, a hand went out as if he was seeking her presence and gaining some comfort from the knowledge that she was close beside him. She allowed him to catch her slim hand in his and hold it fast. If she could quieten him and he fell asleep, she would be able to leave him for a moment to rouse Lucy, for she herself could not stay awake much longer. But his grip did not slacken, and the slightest movement caused the lean fingers to tighten.

Thank goodness there was no one to come upon them in such a compromising situation, Melisande thought, struggling against the urge to close her eyes. How heavy her lids were. She forced them open, and concentrated on the growing light outside the windows. In a while she would go down and heat the stockpot, which was always in the corner of the fire these dismal days, and take a little broth to warm her before she went to the village. With luck, she could be back with the doctor before her father and Priscilla returned, and then she could sleep . . .

She was not aware of that last time when she could no longer focus her attention on the window or of her eyes closing, her head drooping. Once, during the two hours in which she slept, Jason Dacre became conscious and quite lucid again, and with incredulity creeping into his eyes, found her head upon his chest, her red hair spread across one arm. Had she seen the gleam that came into those grey depths, the smile that deepened the corners of his mouth, Melisande might have been more than a trifle perturbed, for the way he was looking at her . . .

As it was, she slept on in blissful ignorance, and he, with his arm about her shoulders, also slipped into a normal, peaceful sleep.

And that was how Priscilla came upon them not long afterwards . . .

Melisande came bolt upright in alarm to find a veritable she-dragon standing over her, hurling abuse in a most unladylike fashion. Still fogged with sleep, she could only look up at her eldest sister, not understanding the tirade being directed at her.

'You shameless hussy! So this is what you get up to when Father and I are away!' Priscilla shouted, blue eyes blazing as she looked from Melisande's puzzled face to that of the man who lay in the bed. She recognised him immediately. The moment she had decided that her only hope in life would be as wife to some very rich and influential man, she had drawn up a list of prospective husbands, and heading the list had been Jason, Lord Dacre. She had attended only one ball at his home, Whispering Wood, but it had been sufficient to tell her that this was a man who could give her everything she would ever want. The only trouble was that he was totally oblivious of her smiles and her flattery, and barely spoke to her that night. If they encountered each other, as they did from time to time, in Kingsclere or one of the neighbouring villages, he was polite, but she suspected that he did not even remember her name. And now he was here, beneath Father's roof . . . and Melisande, the insignificant, younger sister with that terrible flaming hair, had been found asleep in his arms! She had planned it, of course. She, who pretended she never wanted to marry, had deliberately tricked them all. How long had they known each other? Could they be lovers? Priscilla was not shocked at such an idea, for she had considered the possibility that, if she could not find the husband of her choice, a rich lover would suit just as well. Chosen with care, preferably a single man, for she did not want to be forever troubled by the problems of a wife and family somewhere in the background, he could still afford her the life she sought.

Jason Dacre—and Melisande! If this was revealed, he could be forced to marry her . . . Melisande, married first, and to the most eligible bachelor in the whole of the county? Never!

'Get up!' Priscilla hissed. 'How dare you sit there, like . . . like . . .' She saw the darkening of Melisande's eyes, the rich hue of blue and violet that made her own seem insignificant in comparison. Her sister was beautiful (but she would never admit it) and she possessed qualities that she herself had long since abandoned in her quest for wealth—had she ever been endowed with them in the first place: compassion and gentleness, an ability to reach other people. The villagers adored Melisande, speculated about Lucy, pitied Edwin de Vere, and habitually treated herself and her haughty manner with silent contempt, speaking to her only when necessary. One more reason to vent her frustration and spite on the pale-faced sister whose innocent countenance infuriated her!

'Like what?' Melisande came slowly to her feet, realising that the scene which had met her sister's eyes when she entered the room had not shocked her but had irritated her beyond reason, and she knew the reason why. 'The visit to Lord Haslett did not go well?' she enquired with icy sweetness. 'Have you decided not to accept his son's suit after all, Priscilla?'

Her sister gave a strangled cry as into her mind came the vision of the man who sought to court her. Rich, yes; of good family, most certainly; but little more than a simpering idiot who held her hand like a little boy and picked flowers for her. They were the same age, but he had not yet grown to manhood and she doubted if he ever would. The prospect of being married to that creature had made her feel ill—not even the money and position which would go with him alleviated the distaste he aroused in her. But, if she did not accept him, who else was there? Who would marry her without a dowry? Drawing back her hand, she slapped Melisande across both cheeks. The sounds hung in the air like those of a whiplash.

'If you do that again, Mistress de Vere, you will prompt me to climb out of this bed and put you across my knee!' The soft tones brought Melisande wheeling round with a gasp of horror, the pain in her cheeks forgotten as she discovered that Jason Dacre was not only conscious, but apparently in full command of his faculties again. He had been listening to them! His lips tightened as he saw the imprint of Priscilla's fingers standing out against the paleness of her cheeks, and as he pulled himself upright as if about to carry out his threat, shame and embarrassment swept over her. Springing from the bed, she ran from the room without another word.

It was inevitable that her father must at some time invade the peace of Lucy's room, where she took refuge from the storm she knew was raging about her. Priscilla would make the most of her discovery, elaborating on it until he must believe that the worst had happened. Even if he accepted Melisande's word that both she and Lord Dacre were innocent of any wrongdoing, she would still be in disgrace for remaining alone with him throughout the night. She washed, and changed into a clean gown, and awaited his arrival.

Lucy brought her a bowl of broth and the news that she was to go to the village for help and a doctor. Amanda Cummings was as rude this morning as she had been the night before, she said with a grimace, adding that Lord Dacre had requested to see their father without delay.

'Father must accept his word as a gentleman,' Lucy assured her, giving her a comforting hug. 'Priscilla is green with jealousy! Now if *she* had been found in his arms . . .'

'I was not,' Melisande protested, still unaware of the arm that had been about her shoulders. 'I fell asleep, that's all.'

'You would have thought you were a fallen woman, to hear her talking with Father! Didn't you know Lord

Dacre headed her list of prospective husbands—even since we went to Whispering Wood?'

'Did we? I don't recall it. It must have been before Mother died.'

'It was the very last ball we attended. She became ill a few weeks later, and you missed so many while you were nursing her. You must remember, Sandy. It was there that silly John Rowles took you into the garden. You can't have forgotten . . . You were so angry! I don't think I've ever seen you so furious before.'

'How could I forget that? But Whispering Wood . . .' His house! She had forgotten. He had said that her face was familiar, but still she could not remember even being introduced to him. She had been only thirteen, so what impression could she possibly have made on him at that age? He had known that she was not a servant, and had been playing a cruel game with her. She hated him! His arrogance and deceit—and, above all, her own vulnerability. When he had kissed her, she had felt as if she belonged in his arms. What a naïve little fool he must think her!

It was almost mid-day before Edwin de Vere appeared. Melisande rose to face him, steeling herself for the tongue-lashing she knew was due, but, to her surprise, although his expression was extremely stern, his voice was quite gentle, and slowly her apprehension dwindled.

'We must talk, Melisande. Sit down, child.' He motioned her back to her chair and stood before her, hands locked behind his back, his usual stance when he was about to reprimand one of his daughters. He was not tall, and years of good living, fine food and wines had considerably widened his girth, but to Melisande he was still handsome, with a hidden strength behind the placid features that had carried them over many a hurdle. He had been a tower of strength when their mother died, but when at last his resilience had deserted him, as was inevitable, for he had loved his wife dearly, it had been Melisande who had come forward to comfort him, to sit with him and read him poetry, to soothe his frustrated thoughts and give him peace. He had never forgotten the wisdom she had possessed even at the tender age of fourteen, and he knew anger would avail him naught at this moment. Fate had played a strange trick on them, he thought, as he gazed into her pale face and saw the uncertainty mirrored in those strangely coloured eyes. So like her mother, who had known so long ago . . . He shook his head to rid himself of the words lingering so vividly in his memory. One day he might be able to tell her, but now was not the time. 'You do realise how foolish you have been?'

'Yes, Father. But all I did was to offer him the same hospitality that Mother would have done. That you would have done, had you been here . . .'

'Had I been here, what has happened would not have happened,' he told her sternly.

'Nothing happened,' she protested, and her indignation told him that she spoke the truth. 'Mistress Cummings was unconscious when he brought her here. We put her to bed in Priscilla's room, the best we could offer, and then I gave Lord Dacre mine. It was my intention to stay in Lucy's room, but . . .' Her father's eyes were upon her, and her words faltered. She had done nothing wrong, yet his expression was puzzling. While she had expected anger, retribution, he had said so little and was content to allow her to continue at her own pace. 'I was about to retire when I heard a noise. He had fallen. I . . . Forgive me, but I gave him your bottle of brandy. He was hurt, more so than I realised at the time when I bathed his wounds.'

'Alone?' His eyebrows rose, and she flushed, remembering those intimate moments spent alone with Jason Dacre before he had lapsed once more into a state of semi-consciousness. Would she ever forget them? 'Why did you not enlist Lucy's aid?'

'Because . . .' Words failed her. Because her sister had just walked from the village, was wet and cold and tired, was what she should have said, but how could she?

That would bring down Father's wrath on Lucy also for creeping out of the house during his absence to meet her young man. 'She was not at all well, Father.' That was some way towards the truth. 'I thought she might be going down with a chill; you know how suceptible she is to them in this unpredictable weather. Mistress Cummings appeared to be quite recovered from her faint, and so I told Lucy to go to bed. There was nothing she could do. Lord Dacre was near insensible. I managed to . . . to get him into bed, and thought it best to stay with him throughout the night. If I had awakened Mistress Annie, what could she have done?'

'Prepared one of her possets, as she has done for him this morning,' Edwin de Vere suggested drily.

'Believe me, the idea did not appeal to him. The *brandy* was his idea. He was not the most polite gentleman I have met, I assure you, and I thought it best to give him what he wanted, and then leave him. I did not know at that time of the injury he had sustained to his head. For most of the night he was feverish, quite incoherent.' When he had taken her in his arms and kissed her, had he been so? Did he remember the incident? Worse, did Father know of it? She suspected he did not, or he would not be so lenient with her now. 'I—I must have fallen asleep. I don't remember when; a little after dawn, I think.'

'Priscilla tells me she found you across his chest with his arms about you.'

'No! I mean, that cannot be! I don't know. I fell asleep . . . You do me a great injustice, Father, if you believe . . .'

'I do not. But you will not attend this man again. Do I make myself clear? Until he leaves, you will stay out of his way. I hope that will be some time tomorrow. His coach is being repaired today, so there will be no reason for him to delay the journey to Basing,' Edwin said matter-of-factly, and Melisande breathed a silent sigh of relief. Until she remembered . . .

'But he thinks . . . Oh, dear! He took it for granted

that I was a servant-girl. I never had a chance to tell him otherwise. He might expect . . .'

'Mistress Annie will do all for him that is necessary, and no doubt Priscilla will be most anxious to make him feel welcome.'

So already Priscilla was moving her attentions from Lord Haslett's son to her first hope, Jason, Lord Dacre. He could not fail to be captivated by her beauty and her charm, Melisande decided, alone once more with her thoughts, for when she chose, her sister could indeed be the most beguiling creature. Only when she was frustrated did the mask begin to slip.

The doctor came and went, and Lucy brought her the news that Lord Dacre and his ward would be well enough to leave the following morning. The former should have remained in bed for at least another full day, but his lordship had firmly decreed that he was well enough to return home. His surroundings were not as comfortable or as pleasing to the eye as his own home, Melisande decided, searching her memory for something that would conjure to mind Whispering Wood, but nothing came to her except the unpleasantness in the garden with her over-amorous companion. No recollection of the house or the interior had remained.

Lucy was as surprised as Melisande, that she had not been severely chastised, especially after the assassination of her character by their elder sister. Priscilla was busy preening herself for the appearance of their guests at the evening meal, Lucy said, mincing about the bedchamber in a perfect copy of their sister's walk, tossing her head in a way she had to show off her shining black hair, the smooth line of her throat. By the end of the evening, she would have the handsome Lord Dacre eating out of her hand.

Melisande gave a headache as the excuse not to go downstairs that evening and took up a light meal for herself before the guests appeared in the dining-room. She did not want to encounter Jason Dacre again, to be subjected to the scrutiny of those grey eyes, so disturbing in the way they watched her, or to the mockery in the deep soft voice as he reminded her of the deception she had practised. It had not been her fault! Besides, he would forget her name and the shabbiness of the house that had sheltered him the moment he returned to his own grand estate and his servants and fine horses.

When Lucy came to bed, she was full of how Priscilla had enraptured their guests—well, Jason Dacre at least—with the excellence of her playing on the virginals and the sweetness of her voice. As usual, her mimicry convulsed Melisande, so accurate was it, as in a way it helped to lighten her slight despondency. She could give no reason for the way she felt, and decided that she had allowed too many sleepless nights, and Lord Dacre's disquietening presence in the house, to add to the discord in her mind. Where was the tranquillity she had always enjoyed in times of stress? Now, when she closed her eyes and tried to think of pleasant things, of far-off places she might never see but which would always be in her mind to bring her joy and contentment, all she could envisage was a clean-shaven countenance with dark sardomic devil's eyes and a haunting voice that followed her into a restless slumber . . . 'Melisande . . . No angel, but a water-sprite! Do you sit on some solitary rock, combing that magnificent hair, and luring men to their doom with those strange eyes? Many a man could be lured to the depths in pursuit of you!' He *must* have been making fun of her.

Magnificent hair! She thought it was too red by far; no man could ever think it beautiful. As to her eyes, Priscilla never stopped reminding her how odd they were, neither blue nor violet, What man would look twice at a girl with such eyes? Yet he had made his words sound so convincing! She was silly to have allowed herself to be drawn by them. She had no idea what he had said to her father, and was grateful that she had been extricated from extreme embarrassment. But had she?

Why had he deemed it necessary to speak with Father so urgently? He had known who she was, of that she was sure; perhaps not at first, but certainly during those last few hours when he had dared to kiss her . . . She turned her thoughts away from that moment lest she become more distracted. Was he seeking to apologise for his unseemly behaviour in order to ease her own position, or to secure his own? Had his arm really been about her shoulders? Priscilla insisted that it had been so, and Lucy actually believed it! Had he held her while she slept? Heaven forbid! What must he think of her? He was afraid of her father's reaction, she reasoned, afraid Edwin de Vere might demand that the right thing be done. Marriage? She and Lord Dacre? It was unthinkable! Thank goodness Father had believed her story; had accepted that she had acted with the best intentions in her heart. She climbed into bed, worn out in mind and body, and slept late into the morning, awakening surprisingly enough to sunlight flooding the bedchamber. The golden glow at once revived her flagging spirits, and she quickly rose and dressed and went out to see what further damage the last storm had wrought on her precious herb and flower gardens.

It was chaos! The stream, when it had overflowed for at least the third time in a month, had completely flooded the lower end of the garden, and she stood stricken with frustration to see seedling plants and heaps of mud and silt where new rows of herbs had once been. It would take a week of hard work to replant everything, and then there was no guarantee that the weather would improve.

Although it did look today as though it might, she thought as she looked up into the cloudless blue sky. She moved to the arbour where faded roses, still heavy with raindrops, hung upon drooping stems, and sat down on the wooden seat beneath them. How pleasant to feel warm and comfortable instead of damp and cold. She stretched lazily, lifting her face to the bright sunlight, drawing its heat to her.

The figure that watched her from a little way off stood silent and thoughtful as she relaxed against the wooden seat, oblivious of any onlooker. The cloud of hair about her shoulders had been brushed until it shone with hues of burnished gold and tongues of fire. Her skin was so pale, like alabaster. The eyes, of which he had not yet been able to determine the colour, were hidden from him as she arched her neck, allowing the sun to fall upon her face.

'Is this the rock from which Melisande the nymph beckons her unsuspecting victims?'

Melisande sprang to her feet at the soft tones which came from the bushes to one side of her, and at the sight of Jason Dacre's tall frame stepping into her vision she froze, her mouth dry, her tongue locked in her mouth. She could find no words. Once again he invaded the privacy of her thoughts!

'From all I have heard of you, sir, it could never be said that you are an "unsuspecting victim".' She had heard nothing about him, but her suspicions that he was well known among the ladies at court seemed to be confirmed, for he laughed, and white teeth gleamed against the darkness of his handsome features.

'Even the wariest of men can be caught in a woman's dangerous web,' came the mocking reply. 'How did you come by such a name?'

'From my mother. She was French.' The words were uttered before she realised she had betrayed herself . . . but then he had known, somehow, who she was.

'Ah, yes, I recall the story now. The fairy in medieval French romance who was turned into a water-sprite, half woman, half fish. She took human form when she married a rich French nobleman, but each Saturday she resumed her mermaid appearance, and on that day he was never allowed to see her. But curiosity . . .' Jason Dacre lifted broad shoulders with a smile as he added, 'The poor man's infatuation cost him his lady-love and her her human form. The ways of love are strange.'

'To those who do not understand—or believe,' Melisande stated adamantly. 'Or who view the world through the eyes of cynicism.'

'As I do? Perhaps you are right; but then I have seen so much more of the world than you, Mistress Melisande de Vere. Why did you tell me you were a servant?'

'I did not! You assumed . . . as you assumed many things last night,' she reminded him, and he inclined his head slightly in her direction, acknowledging the meaning behind her words.

'If my behaviour distressed you, I apologise; but you cannot blame me when, awakening from a most disturbed slumber, I find an angel bending over me and want to kiss her? It is the first time it has happened to me in my life, and I could not allow the opportunity to slip through my fingers, could I?'

'We shall say no more about it,' Melisande said, averting her gaze from the laughter on his face. He was mocking her again! 'A stolen kiss means nothing.' She was thinking of that time in the gardens at Whispering Wood and the distaste she had felt. It had not been like that when Jason Dacre had kissed her. How she wished it had! He was not for her.

'Like the last time?' The question caused her to blench, and his brows drew together into a deep frown. 'You were very angry that evening, with good reason. Young Rowles acted like a love-sick fool. Not that I can entirely blame him, for you did look most enchanting, like a fairy princess in your gown of green velvet, and your hair with its fiery glints. I swear that, when you walked into the room, there was not one man, no matter his age, who did not turn to stare at you and no doubt allow his imagination to run wild.' He chuckled as the colour began slowly to return to Melisande's cheeks while she pondered his words. *He* had noticed her! Or was he simply being kind, and sympathetic after his manner of the night before, hoping she would not elaborate on what had happened between them and so cause him great embarrassment? 'You are still as slender and graceful, like a young gazelle,' Jason Dacre mused, his eyes darkening as they swept her from head to toe in candid perusal. 'Your mother was wise to keep you by her side. I am surprised you managed to elude her watchfulness even for a short while. Like Melisande's amorous husband, Rowles's curiosity proved too much for him.'

'You!' Melisande gasped, a hand going to her mouth in horror. It could not be! 'It was you who—who rescued me . . .'

'And sent the young man out of my front door with his tail between his legs. Surely you knew? But no! My brother was giving the ball and, if I recall, we were never properly introduced. Last night must have seemed a rude introduction to you after five years.'

'I never . . . I mean . . . I did not remember.' Of all people!

'I wondered what kind of young woman you would grow into. I'm glad to discover you are as beautiful as your mother was and have inherited her great compassion, even though I do recall provoking you to some anger last night.'

'The fever came upon you quickly.'

'Not the brandy?' he interrupted, a fair eyebrow rising, and Melisande felt the colour in her cheeks grow.

'No, not that,' she admitted reluctantly.

Lord Dacre stepped closer to the arbour, his eyes growing thoughtful as he stared at her in silence for a moment and further heightened the discomfort she was experiencing. Why was he lingering here with her? Surely he had not sought her out intentionally? Why should he? His clothes had been pressed, she noted, exactly as she had instructed Lucy to do. The velvet doublet of dark burgundy with its slashed sleeves of yellow silk showed no signs of the dirt and mud that had covered it the night before. His hose were clean, too, and the knee-length leather boots shone where they had been freshly polished.

As she studied him, she realised he was also studying her with an interest that was perturbing and made her acutely conscious of her faded gown, which she had tried to revive by adding fresh lace and dividing the skirt so that a frilled under-petticoat showed through. She was skilled with a needle, and enjoyed the things she did to make her wardrobe more interesting. Rarely did she go further than Kingsclere these days, and so fashion was of little importance to her. Yet now, when Jason Dacre looked at her, she wished the ground would open and swallow her up, so dull and uninteresting did his gaze make her feel. No wonder he had thought her a servant; she looked like one! Only Priscilla ever looked the lady. Neither, surely, could compare with the women he knew!

'I have spoken with your father, and assured him that his daughter's honour has not been violated. Your sisters, I gather, thought otherwise. He has accepted that I was not in a situation to have risen to such an occasion, and that you, had I attempted to do so, would have probably smashed the brandy bottle over my head for my impudence.'

And, in doing so, have extricated him from future embarrassment, thought Melisande, her lips tightening. How noble! She was grateful, of course, but why did he have to make it sound so . . . so! The man had an overweening conceit! Did he expect every woman he met to try to ensnare him? If he was the last person on earth, she would not marry him!

'I am grateful, sir, although there was little need to come to my defence. If that is in fact what you were doing,' Melisande returned coldly. 'Father knows me well enough—and trusts me,' she added as her frosty tone brought a tightening of his lips. 'You may leave here satisfied in your mind that I have already disregarded what passed between us. It would not have happened had you not been taken with the fever.'

'I am glad I offended neither your sense of propriety nor your pride, Mistress Melisande.' For an instant there was a gleam in those grey depths that she found infinitely disquieting. 'As you say, it would not have happened had I not been out of my head.'

'What would not have happened, Melisande?' Priscilla asked sweetly, stepping out from behind the arbour. 'Oh, Lord Dacre, forgive me. I did not realise you were here with my sister. Father sent me to look for you. Your carriage has just arrived, and your ward is most anxious to leave.'

Of course she realised who was with me, Melisande said to herself as her sister turned brilliant blue eyes in her direction and the vehemence in them betrayed that she had overheard much more than she admitted. Her sister wore her best gown in honour of their special guest, she noticed, and her hair was piled high on the crown of her head and adorned with the pearls that their mother had left them. They should have been given to Melisande, for she had been promised them, but Priscilla had made such a scene when the contents of the jewel-box were about to be divided that she had relented and given them to her. She had taken instead a small emerald set in silver on a long silver chain: her mother's favourite out of the many pieces she had possessed and worn. So many had been sold over the years, but Melisande had clung as determinedly to the emerald as Priscilla had to her pearls.

'I shall come at once,' Jason Dacre said smilingly, and Priscilla beamed, accepting that one moment of acknowledgment as a beginning to her well-laid plans. He had noticed her at supper the previous evening, and been most complimentary to her music and her voice. He was an easy-going man who liked to be flattered, she decided, and she was good at that. She contained her chagrin as he turned to Melisande. 'I shall not forget your most kind attentions to myself and to Amanda, Mistress Melisande. My thanks seem little enough . . .'

'They are more than sufficient, sir. My sister will escort you to your coach. Pray excuse me,' She turned and left them, relieved to be alone again. If Priscilla had overheard anything she considered damning, then let her make of it what she would! So long as Father believed her innocent of any wrongdoing, nothing else mattered.

In the days that followed the departure of Lord Dacre

and his ward, the routine of the house returned once more to normal, to long days of dull housework, and with the coming of a little sun, Melisande undertook the replanting of the herb garden, praying as she toiled that more rain would not once again wreck her work. In the evenings she would sit and read beneath the rose arbour, inhaling the fragrance of fresh pink blooms until the light faded. But it was not always as peaceful as it had been in the past, for more than once she found herself looking up as if she might find the tall figure of Jason Dacre watching her. What was there about the man to bring him so often to her mind throughout the day? She did not even like him! He was too sure of himself—and of others!

On the day the messenger came to the house, she was cleaning one of the upstairs rooms. It was such a pleasure to be able to open the windows and allow warmth and sunlight in; clean fresh air to dispel the mustiness that always lingered after rain. Lucy found her, with her hair secured beneath a piece of linen cloth, sleeves rolled back above her elbows, polishing the oak floorboards with great vigour.

'Sandy! We are invited to Whispering Wood,' she cried, and Melisande sat back on her heels in disbelief. Whispering Wood! 'Father has just received a letter from Lord Dacre delivered by his own messenger. Oh, you should have seen Mistress Annie's face when the man appeared in his grey and gold livery! He had ridden through the village to get here, and can you just imagine what they will be saying?'

'I dare not imagine it,' Melisande returned. 'What—what did the letter say? Quickly, before I die of curiosity!'

Why should he invite them to his home? It was a gesture, nothing more, out of pity, perhaps, for he must know of their circumstances. She would not go. She had nothing to wear, and she could not stand being stared at all night by his friends, and pitied!

'We are invited to spend two or three days at the home of Lord Dacre. He wishes to discuss some business matter with Father, so he says, and feels sure Father would not be averse to staying a few days and bringing his most charming daughters with him as company for his ward. That one doesn't need anyone! I doubt if she has a single friend! If she has, they tolerate her only because she has a rich guardian.'

'I feel rather sorry for her,' Melisande said, climbing to her feet as she heard Edwin de Vere's voice outside in the corridor. 'She seems rather lonely, and she has some grudge against Lord Dacre . . . But it is none of our business. We cannot go, of course.'

'Of course we shall go!' Priscilla sailed into the room and came to an abrupt halt as she confronted her youngest sister. 'Melisande, do you always have to look no better than a servant?'

'Leave your sister alone. She alone makes this house worth living in!' Edwin chided as he entered after her, and Melisande's eyes widened in surprise. He was not a man given to compliments, especially if it meant relegating Priscilla to the background. 'Priscilla is correct, and we shall go to Whispering Wood. I have already accepted the most generous invitation.'

'Melisande cannot go, Father. It would be too embarrassing, for her . . . for us,' Priscilla protested.

'She is right. I would feel too . . . awkward, Father.' Melisande suspected that Priscilla had said nothing to him of what she had overheard, but if she herself insisted on going, she might speak up, and the questions and suspicions would arise again. She had dismissed Jason Dacre from her mind, completely. At least she tried to tell herself that that was so, but he had the infuriating habit of returning to her as she snuggled in her bed and tried to sleep. She could still feel the strength of his arms about her, and the softness of his voice. 'At last the woman . . .' What had those strange words meant? She was beginning to think they would haunt her for the rest of her life.

'I cannot agree to that, child. Lord Dacre has insisted that all three of you come with me. In particular he mentions you. He wrote that it would greatly distress him if he and his ward could not pay their respects to the one who aided them in their hour of need. You must attend, Melisande.'

'This is unforgivable,' Priscilla gasped, fury showing in her face as Melisande shrugged slim shoulders, accepting the inevitable, 'after what she did. Father, I heard them talking. The things he said to her!'

'You have an evil mind,' Lucy snapped. 'You are jealous that Lord Dacre has noticed Melisande instead of you.'

'I am the eldest . . .'

'Priscilla, believe me, if Lord Dacre is what you want, I shall do nothing to interfere with your plans. He means nothing to me. I do not even like the man,' Melisande proclaimed, and some of the aggravation faded from her sister's expression. 'He is yours—if you can catch him. I do not think he will be as easy as you imagine. He is not a fool.'

'He means nothing to you, yet you sound an expert on what he likes or dislikes,' Priscilla sneered, and their father held up a warning hand.

'Enough! Prepare yourselves for the visits, for there is much to be done. I want to be proud of my daughters—all three of them,' he added, and Melisande that realised his eyes were on her as he spoke. What did he expect from her? With Priscilla and Lucy at her side, she would be an insignificant shadow in comparison; and glad of it. She did not want to be in the forefront. Sighing, she returned to her work. The visit was still three days away, and she wished it could be over as soon as possible. She did not want to be reminded of those days when parties had been a normal way of life for them all—it would only make them discontented with the life they now led. It was not perfect and, at times, with the shortage of money, it became very difficult, but she had accepted it and was happy with it and with the ageing house. She wanted nothing more from life; why should she? Hers was an idyllic existence . . .

CHAPTER THREE

THE CARRIAGE TAKING the three girls and Edwin de Vere passed through the village of Basing late on Friday afternoon and climbed a slight incline, after it left the main track, towards an imposing house that was clearly visible. Melisande sat beside Lucy on one side, their father and Priscilla facing them. The interior of the carriage Lord Dacre had sent to collect them was lined in red velvet, with gold tasselled curtains at the windows, and compartments beneath the unbelievably comfortable seats in which to store necessities for a long journey, such as food, weapons for protection on lonely roads and blankets to be used in cold weather.

Lucy nudged Melisande and winked in the direction of their elder sister. Priscilla had leaned forward in her seat once more as she had been doing for most of the journey so that her face was framed in the window for everyone to see and wonder who was riding in such a grand carriage with its liveried footmen and coat-of-arms on each door, for only the very wealthy possessed their own travelling carriages.

Melisande flashed her a warning look as she caught their father's eyes on her. For the first time in three days Priscilla was not speculating as to why they had all been invited to Whispering Wood. It could not merely be because of Melisande's help to the two stranded people, she had decided, voicing her thoughts aloud whenever Lucy was near enough to overhear. Lord Dacre had noticed *her*, of course, and this was his way of letting her know. He could not have invited her to his home unchaperoned; that would only have provoked gossip. Not that her sister would have minded, Melisande mused, turning her attention to the house looming closer to them at the end of a long narrow cart-track. She had seized on Lord Dacre as the escape from marriage to Lord Haslett's son. Perhaps, if she found the right man to marry, the unfavourable side of her character might never have cause to surface again.

Edwin de Vere was adamant that Melisande accompany them to Whispering Wood, despite her reluctance. She had made the excuse of having nothing to wear, but he had waved aside her words and ordered all three girls upstairs. She could barely contain her surprise when he opened the door of the room that had been their mother's. No one used it these days, but unlike many of the other rooms, no longer in use that had been stripped of unwanted furniture and pictures, it remained the same. Over the years, many of her clothes had been given first to Priscilla and then handed down to the others, but a few gowns still hung in the closet, and Melisande's heart ached as their father threw open the door, and she gazed for a long moment at the array of velvets and silks, the leather shoes adorned with silver buckles, the fine cloaks bordered with rich fur. She had thought them all disposed of long ago.

'Father, look! Will that not be perfect for me to wear?' Priscilla exclaimed excitedly, pulling out a dress of deep lilac brocade lavishly embroidered with gold thread to form tiny rosebuds and trailing leaves. The underskirt and the slashed sleeves revealed an abundance of pure white Brussels lace. The contrast was stunning. The ruff, a combination of lace and ribbons, all threaded with the most delicate gold needlework, rose from each side of the low-cut bodice into three tiers at the back of the neck.

'No,' said Edwin, and Priscilla turned in amazement to stare at him, as did Lucy and Melisande. It was rare for him to deny his favourite anything. 'Melisande shall have that one.'

'Why?' Full lips pouted in anger and vexation. 'The colour will suit *me*. Why should *she* have it?'

'Because that is what I wish. It was your mother's favourite gown.'

'And she doted on Melisande.' Priscilla threw her younger sister a frosty stare. 'If I do not have the best, how can I be expected to find myself a suitable husband? Who will look at me twice in the old things I possess?'

'You shall have the blue silk. It will go well with your eyes, and Lucy will look perfect in the yellow velvet.'

Melisande stared at the lilac brocade and suddenly caught her breath, but both sisters were too busy examining their own gowns to notice her consternation. She remembered well that it had been her mother's favourite gown, and she had worn it on the night of the ball at Whispering Wood. It had been the very last time her poor mother had looked so radiant and alive. A few short weeks later, she took to her bed with some mysterious ailment that sapped her strength and reduced her to skin and bone, a shadow. She could take no solid foods, and for almost two months had survived on broth alone. And then, one morning, as Melisande sat holding her hand and describing how beautiful the countryside was outside the bedroom window, she turned her face away and drew her last breath.

Melisande had never been able to fill the empty space in her heart. No one person would ever be so special to her again. She loved her father dearly, but they did not share the same intimate moments. How she wished it could be so. There were times when she found him watching her, and she knew her likeness to the one he had treasured and lost was causing him great pain. Why had he chosen this dress for her and not for Priscilla?

'Father, I—I do not think . . .' she began, but a look silenced her.

Priscilla wheeled round to glare into her embarrassed cheeks. 'Wear it. I don't care! He will not look twice at you! Why should he, with hair that colour? And why do you always wear it loose—it is most unbecoming. I hope you will take more care with your appearance before we dine with Lord Dacre this evening,' she snapped.

'The jealous cat,' Lucy whispered, as Melisande gathered up her gown and turned to leave. This room had too many unhappy memories for her to linger. 'She is terrified that you have caught Lord Dacre's eye. Would that not be wonderful?'

'It would not! I don't want to marry him.'

'But he's so rich, Sandy. Think of the wonderful life you would have as his wife.'

'Then you marry him. He might take you to France. If I cannot marry a man who loves me for myself, I shall never marry, no matter what Father says,' Melisande declared vehemently, and hurried from the room. It was unthinkable that Jason Dacre might consider her as a prospective bride. In comparison to Priscilla, she was an awkward country girl. The visit would be a disaster for her, she suspected, but hopefully not for her eldest sister. If Priscilla did manage to charm Jason Dacre, that might go some way to satisfying their father in his determined efforts to see them all married. But what would he do all alone? He needed her to take care of him.

The carriage turned again, and as it did so, fields and open land disappeared from view. They passed along a tree-lined drive and came to a halt before a half-timbered manor house that brought a sigh from Priscilla's lips. Already she was seeing herself as mistress here, Melisande thought, alighting behind her sisters. It was beautiful, and the well-laid-out garden and green lawns immediately before it were a blaze of colour, despite the bad weather of the past months. She experienced a twinge of envy as she recalled the drabness of her own garden.

Flanking them on all sides were more trees, poplar and beech, and tall, heavy-branched Spanish chestnuts, and many she could not name. The breeze sighing through them was almost like music. To one side of the house were outbuildings and storehouses and a stable, outside which a young boy was meticulously grooming a black horse, whistling to himself. The mouth-watering smell of cooking wafted to her nostrils as they approached the large wooden door, and somewhere at the back of the house, could be heard a smith's hammer ringing out on his anvil.

A small stone bridge crossed the swiftly-flowing stream which appeared from the trees of to their left, ran past the house and disappeared in a meandering S-bend into the thick beeches to one side of the drive. Melisande paused for a moment as they approached the front door to gaze down into the water, marvelling how clear it was with the sun rippling over the surface. She had no recollection of Whispering Wood, for it had been dark on the night they had arrived to attend the ball, and now she was fascinated by all she saw.

But, unlike Priscilla who turned everything she saw into money and grew more excited at the prospect of one day living in this extremely prosperous looking house, Melisande looked at her surroundings in an entirely different manner. The wind in the trees, the water as it gurgled over its stony bed, the whistling of the groom, even the sound of the hammer, made up the sweetest music she had heard for a long time, and she found a strange peace descending on her. Perhaps the few days spent here would not be as unpleasant as she had feared. Priscilla would spend all the time she could with Lord Dacre, and so she herself might have the opportunity to enjoy alone the peace and beauty she had come upon.

'Melisande,' Lucy hissed urgently. 'Father is waiting for you.'

Everyone else had disappeared inside the house, and she quickly hurried after them. The hall was very light, unlike their own house with its small windows and overhanging upper storey, and the large, carved stairway that rose before her, terminating in a long picture-gallery with its plaster ceiling which completely encircled where she stood, took her breath away.

'I am Thomas, sir. Lord Dacre's steward.' A thin-faced older man bowed low before them and a pair of dark brown eyes studied their faces, although there was no flicker of expression on the dignified features to betray a single thought. 'His lordship has not yet finished dressing. He asks that when you have refreshed yourself after your journey, you will join him in the library for a few moments, Lord de Vere. There is a matter of some urgency that he wishes to discuss with you.'

'Yes, of course. I shall be delighted,' Edwin replied, and caught the flash of triumph that crossed Priscilla's face. He had not expected Lord Dacre to be quite so impatient. Nothing had even been hinted at before he had left about being interested in seeking a wife. He frowned slightly, imagining the fury he would be subjected to if this was, after all, the man's way of repaying a kind gesture. Nothing more! A few days of comfort and luxury at his country house before the matter was dismissed from his mind, the debt paid in full.

'She is going to be impossible during our whole stay, I know it,' Lucy groaned as they followed after Thomas. Behind them, four young men in dark grey and gold livery carried their luggage, such as it was. Melisande had inwardly squirmed as the well-worn trunks were carried into the house, for the sight of them must surely betray the fact that the only real asset they possessed was the proud name of de Vere. 'Look at her! She fancies herself as the lady of the house already.'

Priscilla had paused to admire one of the paintings on the walls of the gallery and enquire who it was.

'Lord Dacre's father,' she was told in a respectful tone. 'Lord Martin. A great seaman. You have no doubt heard of him.'

'Of course.' She had not, but she would not admit it.

Lucy smothered a giggle, and even Melisande found herself smiling as Priscilla lengthened the short walk to their rooms with her constant questions.

'She's trying to impress the wrong man,' she whispered wickedly. 'Shall we tell her to save her charm for Lord Dacre? Although I cannot understand why such a man should find *her* interesting—especially without a dowry.'

'With his wealth, perhaps he considers that unimportant so long as his wife has other qualities, and I am sure he knows all about our poor financial position. If he is indeed interested in Priscilla, he will have made it his business to find out all about us.'

'If he had, we would not be here,' Lucy interrupted. 'I hope he finds her totally repulsive the second time they meet. With her out of the way, Father will begin looking for someone for me. Oh, Sandy!'—the amusement faded from her face—'You don't think he would suggest to Lord Haslett that I—*I* could marry that idiot son? I shall run away . . .'

'No, you will not,' Melisande returned firmly, although she had no doubt her sister was serious. She would have to be most careful how she approached their father, but approach him she must before Lucy did something very foolish and reckless. 'If Priscilla marries Lord Dacre—and it is still very much supposition—we must both impress Father with our usefulness about the house. Why, you could take over the cooking from poor Mistress Annie. She's really getting too old to cook for a family any more, and she ruins half the food she does prepare. He would welcome the change, I am sure. What would he do if we left home? Who would care for him? We must persuade him to think more of himself before Priscilla leaves us.'

'We could make life very comfortable for him, and with Lord Dacre as a son-in-law, money would no longer be a problem,' Lucy exclaimed. 'Sandy, you are clever!'

'If she marries him,' Melisande returned thoughtfully. But if they were not here for Lord Dacre to speak to their father about Priscilla, what was the reason? There could be no other!

Edwin de Vere was given a room at the far end of the gallery, and the girls had a separate room each on the opposite side. As the door closed behind the departing servant who had brought in her small trunk, Melisande stared slowly around her in awe. A four-poster bed dominated the room, hung with velvet curtains of deep violet and tied back with yellow silk cords. It was even bigger than the giant bed in Lucy's room, and the mattress was made of real feathers, she discovered as she sank on to it and almost disappeared into the middle of the violet and gold embroidered counterpane. The bolster and pillows were of feather, too! And the sheets of linen! She would feel like a princess sleeping here tonight.

On the opposite wall hung a large mirror set in a beaten copper frame, and beneath it was a small table with glass jars set upon an embroidered white lacework mat. When she examined them, she discovered that they contained all the kinds of fripperies a woman would use at her toilet, including several aromatic salves to rub into the skin. One was a sweet fragrance reminiscent of roses and honeysuckle, the other a heady, sensuous aroma that reminded her of musk. Someone had gone to great trouble to make the room comfortable.

A marble-topped table held a pitcher filled with fresh water, and a bowl, with clean towels placed carefully beside it. The closet was enormous. Her small variety of clothes would be lost in it, she mused, as she unfastened the leather strap about the trunk and proceeded to lift out the dresses she had brought with her. Despite the short journey, the lilac brocade was quite creased and some of the lace did not hang properly. She was wondering how she should go about asking to have it pressed when there was a knock on the door, and a young girl in a spotless white apron over her grey dress bobbed politely.

'I'm Rose, my lady. I shall take care of you while you are here.'

'But that really won't be necessary . . .' Melisande began, for she always did everything for herself, and then, seeing the surprise on the girl's face, realised that all Lord Dacre's guests would obviously have someone to attend to their needs. She had forgotten what it was like to be waited on. 'Lord Dacre is most considerate. Perhaps you could find someone to press this for me. I shall most likely need it tomorrow.'

'For the ball? Oh, yes, my lady, it will be done well before then. Shall I put these away for you?' Rose took the remainder of Melisande's belongings and disposed of them with a warm smile, unaware of the stunned look on her new mistress's face.

A ball! It was true, then. They had been summoned to Whispering Wood so that Lord Dacre could propose marriage to Priscilla. She should have been pleased for her sister, for here was a man who could give her everything she longed to have: money, position, a fine home, and servants at her beck and call. The kind of life they had once all enjoyed.

Instead, as she watched the maid putting away shoes and undergarments, she felt nothing except a dull ache deep inside. Priscilla's dreams had come true at last. Melisande knew she should accept that her own never would. Why could she not be more like her elder sister and instead of filling her head with fanciful—and totally impracticable—notions, begin to look at the world through realistic eyes? If she married well, would that not also ease her father's responsibilities, the heavy burden he had carried for the past five years of trying to maintain them all?

If only she could, but was horrified at the very thought of living the rest of her days tied to a man she might not even like! Priscilla had a strength of character she did not possess and never would. She was doing the right thing —for her. It was not right for Melisande or for Lucy. Was love dead in the world that not one man had ever looked at them and wanted them for themselves?

'Is there anything more I can do?' Rose repeated again as she stood before Melisande, and she shook her head with an apologetic little laugh.

'I was lost in thought, forgive me. No, nothing. Has my father gone downstairs yet, do you know?'

'I don't think so. Shall I go and find out?'

'No—no, it doesn't matter.'

It would do no good to be impatient, Melisande told

herself, as she moved to the window and seated herself on the bench beneath the leaded panes. Their father would bring them the news all in good time. Why, oh why, could she not be happy for her sister?

'Melisande, no angel but a water-sprite.' How many times had those words haunted her thoughts, the amusement in the deep voice no longer angering her? 'You are still as slender and graceful, like a young gazelle. I am glad to discover you are as beautiful as your mother.'

She tossed her head to dispel the memory of those flowery adjectives which had helped to lessen the pain often caused by Priscilla's caustic comments . . . and as a strand of hair caressed her cheek, she caught it between her fingers and thrust it back over her shoulder. No doubt he would say the same thing to Priscilla when he began to court her. How beautiful *her* hair was, comparing it perhaps to the sheen of a raven's wing. She felt sure he would never be lost for words.

The sound of voices raised in anger outside in the corridor claimed her attention. Then the slamming of a door, and they began again in the room adjoining hers. Lord Dacre's tones were immediately recognisable, vibrating with a fury even she could feel on the other side of the wall, as he lashed his companion with descriptive adjectives that made her cheeks grow quite warm. There was laughter from the other man, and a comment to the effect that there were three of them, and all fair game. She felt like an eavesdropper, but they were conversing so loudly that she could not help but hear.

'I swear, if you approach any of those three young women, I shall take you apart with my bare hands, Richard!' Jason Dacre threatened.

Richard! The name he had muttered in his delirium and spoken then, as now, with the same vehemence behind it. And to whom were they referring? Surely it could not be Melisande and her sisters! But it was too much of a coincidence that there just happened to be three of them!

'The black-haired one took my eye,' the man called

Richard said with a deep-throated chuckle. Priscilla! 'Although the other with that red hair . . . I suppose it is real, or have village girls taken to dyeing their hair to keep fashion with the Queen?' He meant her, Melisande realised, infuriated by the insult. Dyed, indeed! And the implication that he regarded her as nothing more than a village girl was an even deeper humiliation.

'You go to far, brother! My patience is at an end . . .' Lord Dacre's voice was lowered suddenly as if he had become aware of his surroundings and of the presence of someone beyond the communicating door, and Melisande could catch nothing further.

Brothers—who disliked each other intensely! At first sight, she had thought Whispering Wood a happy place from the disposition of the cheerful and helpful servants, for it was nearly always possible to judge the manner of the master by his household. Now she sensed an underlying uneasiness—a rivalry, perhaps, between the two brothers? Or something more disturbing? The attitude of his lordship's ward Amanda she still found strange, and why had the girl not been present to meet them? Was their presence somehow an irritation to her? They were, after all, not of her circle of friends, and they would have little in common with someone so spoilt and rude.

In a more thoughtful frame of mind, Melisande went to her sister Lucy's room to await a summons from their father.

It was an hour before Edwin de Vere sent for his daughters. Sixty long minutes during which Melisande tried to concentrate on the book of poems she had brought with her, most of the time in vain, for she was only too aware of the morose way Lucy stared out of the window, her head in her hands, and of Priscilla pacing the room with growing impatience. Very little conversation passed between them. It had all been said.

A servant showed them into the comfortable sitting-room that adjoined their father's bedchamber, and retired from their presence. A long table in the middle of the room had been prepared with food for them all. Silver gleamed in the glow of the dozen candles lining the centre of the oak table, each item bearing the initials 'J.D.' in an elaborate engraved script. The plates were a mixture of pewter and fine bone china, the glasses, the most exquisite crystal Melisande had ever seen. The many facets gleamed and reflected a multitude of colours in the flickering candle-light. Their father gestured to them to be seated.

'Are we to serve ourselves?' Priscilla asked, noting the absence of servants.

'The matter I have to discuss with you is not for other ears, no matter how discreet they may be,' she was told. 'Melisande, perhaps you would pour wine for us all before I begin?'

'Yes, Father.'

Edwin waited until she had complied with his wishes before eyeing each of them in turn for a long moment in silence. Then, a broad smile widened across his face. Melisande thought she had not seen him look so pleased in many a month. Lucy tentatively sipped her wine, silently praying. Priscilla examined the glass she held, turning it this way and that. She would have many such things about her when she was mistress here. She would surround herself with beautiful things . . . things she had been deprived of since their bad turn of fortune. Melisande sat looking at her father, aware of how his eyes dwelt the longest on her, with an expression of such tenderness in them that she was quite moved.

'Father, we shall all be dead from curiosity if you do not put us out of our misery,' she said with a soft laugh.

'I was savouring this very special moment, my children. My hopes, my dreams for you—all of you—are about to come true.'

'All of us?' Priscilla almost choked over her wine.

'Yes. Not just one daughter shall soon be married, but all three,' Edwin returned, and Lucy's hand smothered the cry of alarm that sprang to her lips. Her wide eyes fastened on Melisande beseechingly. Do something, they pleaded.

But what could she do? Their father spoke as though the whole matter had been concluded in the short space of time he had been closeted downstairs with Lord Dacre. But such matters took an eternity—there were so many details! 'Are we allowed to know to whom we shall soon be wed, Father?' she asked, her face quite pale at the news, for it distressed her no less than Lucy.

'Lord Dacre intends to select a bride for himself from among my daughters. For the other two, he will furnish the most generous dowries and suitors from among the best families from here to London. Think of it, my dearest ones! Dowries for you all—husbands who will provide for you as I was once able to. Think of it!'

'Which of us has he himself chosen?' Priscilla's voice was sharp with anxiety. It had to be her . . . She was the eldest!

'He has not taken me into his confidence as to that—if indeed he has made up his mind.' Edwin ignored the chagrin rising in the lovely face. 'It matters not whom he marries, for the other two of you will also be provided for. It is a most generous offer.'

'Why?' Melisande wanted to know. 'Why should he do so much for our family?'

'My dear girl, he is indebted to us for the help we gave him. He wishes to repay us. I, too, was taken aback by the lengths he has gone to, but we must not question his will to do this—he has obviously given it great thought. No man takes a woman to wife without a dowry unless he is certain she is the right one for him.'

'But to give dowries also to the other two daughters! Oh, Father, because we are poor, we do not have to take this kind of charity! Have we no pride?' cried Melisande.

'Sandy is right, Father.' Lucy joined in the protest, only to have Priscilla round on them, her gaze like daggers.

'Are you quite mad—both of you? You are being offered good marriage, perhaps to men of distinction.

Certainly they will be from the best families, and wealthy, perhaps even titled. How can you prefer the life you have now in that ugly mausoleum we call a house to the ones we are being offered?'

It was clear by her words that Priscilla still considered herself to be the choice of Jason Dacre. Melisande did not care that in her selfish way she considered herself above her sisters, but she was incensed at her dislike of the house they had lived in since birth. It was a regal old place with many happy memories, which she would not allow to be blighted by her sister's cruel words.

'Because the house is alive with memories, its walls reverberate with love and, in the dark of the night, those abandoned rooms are once more full of laughter and gaiety. Have you forgotten how it once was?'

'That was long ago,' Priscilla snapped, helping herself to some of the sliced chicken breasts with her fingertips. 'It is a draughty, miserable dilapidated ruin which we shall never have the money to restore. Besides, who would want to, when there are so many fine new houses about?'

'Perhaps, when you are married to Lord Dacre, it would be a nice thought to ask Father if that is what he would like,' Melisande retorted, her ire rising still more. 'He and Mother lived there all their married lives, and she loved the place as much as he does. As I do.'

'If I had the money, I would give Father enough to do anything he wanted,' Lucy declared, coming to her sister's assistance again, and Edwin smiled in their direction, his expression quite moved. He had not been as close to his two youngest daughters as he would have liked over the years, and was deeply touched by the affection they still bore him. So genuine in their feelings, neither had a malicious bone in her body. He inwardly sighed, wishing that Priscilla had inherited more of her mother's graciousness.

'Then do so, when you are married,' Priscilla snapped. 'Although I was not aware that Christopher Avery possessed any money. If he does, why has his mother to take in washing in the village?'

Lucy gave a cry at the words, and huddled back in her chair as her father's eyes turned on her with condemnation. Gone was the smile, the tenderness, of a moment ago.

'You have gone against my wishes and seen this young man again? After I gave you specific instructions never to communicate with him for any reason?' he demanded angrily.

'Yes, I have seen him, and I shall continue to do so!' Lucy completely forgot her intention to charm her father into accepting the liaison. The gleam in Priscilla's eyes mocked her, spurred her on to reckless words, words that she would not be able to retract after the heat of the moment had passed. 'He has no money, that is true, but is that a crime? Neither have we! He is not looking for some rich bride, either! He is a fine young man; his father was one of Francis Drake's sailors, killed in the fight against the Spanish Armada. Ask Lord Dacre, if you do not believe me! He is apprenticed to the Pilot of his ship, *Moonwynd*. One day he will have one of his own.'

'To spirit you away to some far-off land where you will live in poverty, but blissfully happy, unable to feed the children you raise,' Priscilla taunted. 'Perhaps you should take Melisande with you—she's a dreamer too . . .'

'Sometimes the most fanciful dreams have a way of coming true,' Edwin said in an odd tone. 'Enough! This conversation is at an end. There will be no more discussion on what you have been told. Tomorrow evening Lord Dacre is holding a ball here at Whispering Wood, and he has told me that he will announce the name of his future bride then. I suggest we all enjoy the fine fare that has been provided for us, after which the three of you should retire so that you will appear at your best for the occasion. It is in your best interests, after all. And that includes you, Lucy. You will attend with your sisters, and I will hear no more nonsense about this young man.

Obey me in this, and I shall overlook your rudeness and your disobedience. Go against me, and—and you will have no say whatever in the selection of a husband.'

'No matter whom you choose for me, I shall never marry him!' Lucy jumped from her chair so violently that it crashed on to the floor. 'Never!'

She ran from the room, flinging wide the door and not bothering to close it after her. Melisande also rose, distressed by the sight of the tears streaming over her sister's cheeks, and deeply concerned that she might take it into her head to do something foolish.

'No,' Edwin said firmly. 'Close the door and sit down, Melisande. She must accept her future without your help. Eat some food, child. We must not allow this to spoil this very special occasion.'

Obediently Melisande returned to her seat, but her appetite had vanished. Neither the succulent chicken Priscilla was consuming with great enthusiasm, the asparagus nor even the jellied veal could tempt her. Lord Dacre's generosity had sealed not only Lucy's fate, but her own. For one sister it had brought excitement and the prospect of a life of luxury; for the other two, gloom and despondency. She had no doubt their father would scrutinise the prospective suitors carefully, but she still felt as though she were up at auction to the highest bidder. Without a dowry, no man would look twice at her, but with one—and an ample one at that from the way their father had spoken—she would be acceptable. For the rest of her life she would always wonder if the man chosen for her had been interested only in the money she had brought him. Jason Dacre's offer had deprived her of any chance of marrying for love!

Melisande slept very little that night, and rose early. A small brass-faced clock encased in green marble displayed the hour as a little before seven. She had washed and dressed before realising that Rose would probably arrive later, expecting to undertake these tasks herself.

Oh, well, she thought, she had saved the girl a little work; besides, she was not in the mood for conversation. Priscilla would sleep late, she reasoned, wishing to look her very best for the ball tonight. Lucy would sulk in her room as she always did when she was miserable. Melisande felt so helpless. Her position was as vexing as her sister's, yet throughout the night she had given little thought to herself, only to Lucy.

What if she carried out her threat and ran away? Where could she go? A young girl, alone and penniless, would be prey to all kinds of dangers. Lord Dacre had no idea what he had done. The brush she held was suddenly still against the back of her hair. Why should she not confide in him: tell him that Lucy had a sweetheart? Perhaps, with the dowry, he might be able to persuade Father that Christopher Avery was not such an unlikely candidate after all. He had to be an intelligent young man to have thoughts of becoming a Pilot, for it was an exacting task and of the greatest importance on board ship. The Captain commanded, but the Pilot charted the way, made the all important ruttiers—the charts and notes—to guide her through uncharted waters and, more important still, home again. A young man with prospects! That was how he should be presented to Father!

The thunder of hooves drew her to the window, and she was just in time to see Jason Dacre, astride the magnificent black stallion she had watched being groomed the previous afternoon, soaring over the low wall that bordered the back of the house. Horse and rider were one, a breathtaking sight, and her heart missed a beat as she acknowledged his expertise as a horseman. Her mother had loved to ride and hunt, and Melisande had been taught at an early age. It was a pleasure they had shared for many years. Priscilla hated, as she put it, to be 'perched on the back of the ugly beasts', although the horses they had once owned, when sold to replenish some of their father's losses, had fetched the highest prices.

Now was no time to dwell on the past, and Melisande frowned at her reflection in the mirror. Lack of sleep had left her pale and dull eyed. She needed to walk in the garden and breathe the fresh air, and be alone to decide how best to approach Lord Dacre. She must be subtle and not too forward in her manner, or he might take offence at what she proposed, yet why should he? Once he had announced Priscilla to be his choice of wife, he had no interest in whom the other two girls married.

The house was very quiet. She hesitated for a moment outside Lucy's room, wondering if she should go in and speak to her, but as yet she had little comfort to offer. Perhaps later she would have encouraging news. She took her time wandering along the gallery, pausing from time to time to look out of the window at the perfectly-laid-out garden which could be seen from the tall windows or to examine one of the portraits hanging on the walls. Many of Jason Dacre's ancestors looked as dour and unfriendly as her own, but some, especially the women, were very beautiful, with high bone structure and bright, vivacious eyes. Only one did she think looked anything like the master of Whispering Wood, and she recalled that this portrait was the one Thomas had told Priscilla was Martin, Lord Dacre, his father. The features were the same. Dark, somehow arrogant, despite the slight smile curving about a lean mouth. And the eyes! It was as if *he* was staring down at her, subjecting her to the same open gaze that his son had done.

As she turned away, Melisande discovered a small staircase winding down into the gloom. Believing it to be a back way which would lead her out of the house unseen, she began to descend. At the bottom was an open door, the hubbub of voices, and sounds of great activity. As the smell of freshly-baked bread wafted to her, she realised she had stumbled by mistake on the kitchens, but before she could turn and retrace her steps, the door was flung wide by a young girl with flour-smudges on the rosy glow of her cheeks. At the sight of

Melisande standing in the shadows, she bobbed a curtsy and immediately stepped back, opening the door more fully for her to pass through.

Melisande froze with embarrassment as a dozen pairs of eyes turned in her direction. The cooks stopped stirring the enormous cauldrons suspended over the enormous fire. The wrought-iron basket spit beneath them ceased to be turned as a kitchen-maid gawked at her with open mouth. Women preparing pastries on a long pine table in the centre of the room glanced up and then exchanged puzzled looks before continuing with their work.

But Melisande saw none of this attention. Her eyes were fastened on the figure reclining in a chair against a far wall, one booted foot swinging idly from the arm of the solid high-backed chair. On his lap was a platter of cold meats and a slice of crusty bread lavishly spread with golden butter and, in one hand, a tankard. Their eyes met and locked. Then a smile replaced the look of utter astonishment that had momentarily crossed his face, and Jason Dacre came to his feet with a sweeping bow worthy of an encounter with the Queen herself.

'Mistress Melisande, I did not think you would be an early riser. Come and join me. The fare is simple, but if it is not to your liking, I can promise that you will not be disappointed tonight. As you see, there will be something to suit every palate.'

A chair was brought and placed beside his. The last thing Melisande wanted was to sit with him, but she had no choice under the circumstances.

'I do not wish to disturb anyone . . . I must have lost my way,' she said lamely, watching him finish the last slice of meat with relish and swallow the contents of the tankard. His clothes, like his surprisingly casual manner, were not what she would have expected a man of his rank and station to wear. Gone were the fine velvets and knitted hose, and in their place light-coloured hide breeches and knee-length boots, and a white linen shirt that accentuated the sunbronzed skin. He seemed perfectly at home in the atmosphere of the kitchens, she thought, tentatively seating herself. The fresh bread did look rather tempting. As a child, there had been nothing more enjoyable than a piece carved from a new loaf, with home-made butter and perhaps honey.

'We share the same weakness,' Jason murmured, and carefully splitting the chunk of bread in two, he offered her the platter. Aware of many eyes on her, Melisande hesitated, then with sudden daring, took one half. It tasted delicious. 'I have the best cooks in Hampshire, as they will prove to you tonight. I am sure they will be able to tempt you with something far more exotic.'

'I am sure they will, although I fear we shall all be too—excited—to eat very much,' she returned, fixing him with a pointed stare. 'After all, it is not every day a girl finds herself paraded before the cream of nobility so that her value as a prospective wife and mother may be assessed.'

Her scornful words brought a frown to the handsome features opposite. The platter and tankard were put aside and immediately removed by a hovering servant.

Jason rose, and said quietly but firmly, 'If you intend to take me to task over a gesture that was well meant, I suggest you do so out of earshot of my servants. Shall we walk in the garden? It is a pleasant morning, and the air may dispel the obvious apprehension you feel about my suggestion.'

'Your suggestion?' Melisande looked up at him the moment they were outside the house, her eyes narrowing against the brightness of the sunshine. 'My father has seized upon it as an answer to his prayers.'

'He has the natural wish of a father to see his daughters well married and happy,' Jason Dacre returned, an edge to his voice that told her he was not accustomed to being spoken to with such bluntness. 'There is nothing wrong in that. Am I not correct in believing it is also the wish of your eldest sister?'

'Of Priscilla, perhaps. It is not that of my sister Lucy,

nor of me. Oh, this is beautiful,' Melisande exclaimed suddenly, for as they had turned round the side of the house, following the stream, they came upon a water-wheel, and set in the trees overhanging it, one or more dovecotes where white fantailed doves cooed softly to them as they approached.

'I am pleased you find it so.' For a moment those grey eyes softened as they saw the pleasure on her face, but she was unaware of it. 'But it seems you are displeased with my good intentions. I meant well, as repayment for the kindness you showed to me and to my ward Amanda. I have not forgotten the long hours you sat beside me without thought of your own discomfort.'

Nor had she! But it was not the lack of sleep which remained uppermost in her mind, or Priscilla's nasty thoughts when she found Melisande in such a compromising situation, but the feel of Jason Dacre's arms about her, the fierce urgency of his kiss which had stirred her so. Did he remember it? She prayed not; it would have been too embarrassing.

'It was nothing, sir. I wish you would put it from your mind. No one has ever been turned away from our door when he was in need, nor will he be,' she told him quietly.

They came to the privet hedges, neatly cut and rounded, that surrounded the garden she could see from the window of her bedchamber. They passed through a wrought-iron entrance which curved about their heads, laced with sweet-smelling honeysuckle, and into the garden, as meticulously maintained, she discovered, as everything else she had seen. Tall laburnums graced the centre, swaying in the breeze, and beneath them were oak seats. Paths interlaced the flowerbeds, and set beside the contrast of colours were closely cut lawns.

'Will you sit awhile?' Jason motioned to a seat. Should she? If Priscilla or her father were to leave their rooms and find her missing—worse still, alone with Lord Dacre—they might jump to more conclusions! 'You are in no more danger alone with me now than you were the last time we were together,' he added, veiled laughter in his tone.

He seated himself beside her, some way away, she was relieved to find, and stretched long legs out before him, surveying her from beneath his fair lashes as he asked candidly, 'Are you not eager to have a husband and a family? A home of your own?'

His bluntness quite took away Melisande's breath. Such intimate questions were not asked on such a short acquaintance!

'In time, of course, I shall marry. And I will be a good wife. I can cook and sew . . .'

'You could have servants to do both for you, if you follow your father's wise advice. And a carriage with fine horses to carry you about the countryside. Is that not the kind of life every young woman dreams of from the time she leaves the cradle?'

'You are describing Priscilla, not me. She is more suited to that kind of life.'

'And you prefer a dream world.' The soft voice was mocking, and yet not so, as if somehow he understood how important her dreams were to her. 'Sometimes it is better to accept reality and whatever this life has to offer.'

For someone such as he, who had everything, that kind of decision would not be difficult to make. Why was she so aware of the long limbs stretched out beside her, the casualness of his manner? Did he, as his brother did, regard her as no more than a girl from the village, and therefore of little importance? Why, then, had he gone to so much trouble to invite her family to Whispering Wood, to secure the future of all three girls? Such gratitude went far beyond the bounds of what she had done for him. It had been so little!

'Are you going to marry Priscilla?' She turned and looked squarely into the brown features, and forced herself not to look away when the grey eyes registered instant mirth. Did he consider the situation amusing? She did not!

'Do you think I should?' Was he asking for her true opinion or merely being polite? She could read nothing in his expression. The lazy smile that played across his face betrayed nothing of the thoughts which filled his mind. A very active mind, she had decided from their first meeting. A shrewd brain, and a man accustomed to having his own way no matter what it cost him, and, with his great wealth, money would be of no importance. She felt the pleasantness of their meeting begin to fade as she considered the prospects before her. *He* was supplying her dowry. Therefore she was being offered to the highest bidder, the man best able to support the family in times of need. Her father was done with poverty; had he not declared so time and time again since the change in their circumstances? If it was in his power to change the way they lived, he would do so, believing it was in the best interests of all—but it was not. Her heart cried out against being married to a stranger who would own her, body and soul.

No, that was not true. No one would own her soul or her heart unless she wished it. Her body, yes, she could do nothing about that, for as a dutiful wife she must submit to the demands of her husband. But that was all he would gain from the bargain!

'Oh, yes,' she answered, and one fair eyebrow rose at her reply. 'Priscilla is an excellent hostess; she also has a pleasant voice, and is most talented in many other ways. She will be a perfect wife for you.'

'I am so glad you approve, Melisande.' His voice was suddenly dry, but the words proclaimed that Priscilla was indeed his choice. 'What about your sister Lucy?'

'Oh, no, she would be most unhappy if she were forced to marry . . . She already has a sweetheart.' Melisande broke off, unsure whether to continue. Lucy had been quite adamant that Christopher Avery did not think of her in the same light as she did him. They were fond of each other, but if Melisande spoke hastily, placed the young man in an unfortunate position . . . She was in a quandary: speak up and help her sister, or remain silent and hope that their father would not push them both into loveless marriages? 'Please do not speak of this to Father; he would be furious. She has already displeased him by meeting her young man against his wishes.'

'And what of yourself?' Jason Dacre asked.

'Me? Who would look a second time at me when Priscilla is about? Dozens of suitors have courted her.'

'Until they discovered she had no dowry, and then, I imagine, the interest waned.'

'That is unfair—and cruel.'

'What are you running away from, Melisande?' How free he was with her name, yet it had never sounded so sweet. 'Lucy has a sweetheart, what have you?'

'I have my books—my home—Father. What more could I want?' Slight colour began to intrude upon her cheeks as Jason leaned towards her, hands loosely folded across his knees.

'Dreams cannot last for ever.'

'Love will,' she declared with conviction, and was aghast when he threw back his head and laughed aloud.

'Love! What does a child like you know of love?'

'In the arms of the right man, I shall discover it,' Melisande insisted, spurred by his scorn to baring her heart as never before.

'And how will you know he—whoever he is—is the right man? How do you know I am not?' Jason mocked, and the eyes which studied her suddenly contained glowing embers of fire, to stir her blood once more. Was he insane to speak to her in this way?

'You, sir, are too bold by far! Are you accustomed to taking what you want?' she flung back, and the tanned face split into a wide grin. She was beginning to feel very uncomfortable in his presence, in a way she had never felt before with a man. He was laughing at her because she was not like other women he knew, painted women of the Queen's court, willing to share their favours with any man for a piece of jewellery or a favour. Did he consider all women to be the same?

'What do you want, Melisande, my dream princess? A prince in shining armour to carry you off on a white horse?'

'And what is wrong with that?' How dared he try to destroy her dreams, that world that had sustained her through so many hardships! 'The man I love will be a prince in my eyes, and will make me feel like a princess.'

'Do you not think it better that he makes you feel like a woman?' came the challenging answer, to which she had no reply. Why was he talking to her thus? Was it his intention to amuse himself with each of the three sisters until his choice was made—yet surely he had decided already.

'I—I do not think I understand you, sir.'

'I think you do—and very well. I have not forgotten the taste of those soft lips or the warmth of your body against mine. The woman in you was struggling to be free then . . . Why do you suppress her? Does she possess fire to match those fiery tresses, is that it? Are you afraid of what you feel, Melisande?'

'Afraid?' she echoed. 'Of course not!' Yet it was a lie. She was, and growing more so every moment those narrowed grey eyes stared at her. She sensed they could see down into her very soul. It was as if he was laying it bare, mocking all she held precious, replacing it with a reality she did not want to accept.

His hand fell upon hers as it lay upon the oaken seat, the long brown fingers caressing her own, white and slender, trembling as the caresses stirred something deep within her. This was not right. He belonged to Priscilla! No, he would never belong to anyone! He was his own master, and would be that of the woman he took as his wife. Would he tame a rebellious nature with force or gentleness, she wondered, lifting wide eyes to the face that was but a few inches from her own.

The laughter in his eyes annoyed her, made her want to slap the mockery from him, but there was something else, too, lingering in those deep grey pools . . . something that took her breath away, delayed the hand raised to brush his own away, halted the stilted comment. She felt as if she was being dragged down into quicksand. She wanted to jump to her feet and leave, for she knew he was going to kiss her again.

Again! That first time would be forever imprinted on her memory. Had she not been plagued by dreams of him bending over her as she lay in her bed, seeking the lips she tried to turn from his, claiming them, and then the body which came alive so traitorously beneath his experienced hands?

'One day . . .' Jason muttered, and then laughed softly as the blue of her eyes deepened until they were as violet as the flowers which grew at his feet in springtime. 'Will I ever know the true colour of those eyes? Perhaps no one ever will—only the man to whom you give yourself completely. Such a lucky man . . .'

She wanted to move away. She knew she should. She tried, but her limbs refused to respond. The arm that had lain on the back of the seat was suddenly round her shoulders. The other about her waist, drawing her close against his chest. Dear heaven, if anyone should come upon them! Melisande thought in panic, oblivious of the two gardeners working diligently a few yards away, or the groom exercising a horse beyond the privet hedging, which was low enough for him to see quite clearly the two figures on the seat.

'I have no fever now, Melisande. My mind is quite lucid,' Jason Dacre said, his lips against her hair. He smelt strongly of horse, yet she did not find the scent repugnant. How she wished she did! How she wished she had the strength to push away the arms encircling her, thrust away the fingers tilting back her chin, resist the mouth descending on hers with the same fierce, possessive ardour. This must not happen! Priscilla would never forgive her. Yet, for a few brief stolen moments, could she not enjoy what her sister would have for the rest of her life? Enjoy? She could not deny it. His kisses made her tingle all over, sent the blood pulsing through her veins. She wanted so much to dislike him, but she could not, not the way he made her feel.

One hand against her back pressed her close against his chest. So strong, so unyielding—a man to be reckoned with. The other, about her waist, slid upwards to cup a firm breast, and the touch was scalding despite the satin that covered her. No man had been so bold with her before, except that idiot John Rowles. Five years ago she had been subjected to the same kind of treatment and it had revolted her, angered her. Why did Jason Dacre not anger her, or revolt her? It seemed an eternity before he eased his mouth from hers and stared down into her flushed cheeks.

'There *is* fire beneath the ice,' he said, and if she had not been so confused by the conflicting emotions he had aroused in her, she might have wondered at the steadiness in the deep voice. 'Fortunate will be the man who brings it to the surface.'

His hands fell away, and at the smile which spread across his face, Melisande leapt to her feet, cheeks flaming.

'I hate you!' She spat the words at him, fists clenched at her sides.

He relaxed on to the seat, with a shake of his head.

'No, you do not! I have unleashed the woman in you, and shattered those precious dreams. Accept reality, Melisande. Think of what it could bring you.'

With you perhaps, but not with another, Melisande thought, and then, horrified by such wantonness, she turned and fled, not pausing until she reached her room. Only the presence of Rose, who had returned the lilac brocade pressed and ready for the ball that evening, prevented her from flinging herself down on the bed and weeping.

He had no right to destroy her so. He was hateful. Until that second kiss she had been able to discard him from her mind—with difficulty, perhaps—but now . . . How could she face him that evening, knowing he would announce his betrothal to Priscilla? He had shamed her! No, she had shamed herself, allowed him to rouse her when she knew he would never be hers! But it had felt so right to be in his arms; so good! And his lips on hers had been all she had ever dreamed a kiss would be from the man to whom she would give herself.

Jason Lord, Dacre, was not that man, and she must accept it. He was to be her sister's husband . .

CHAPTER FOUR

'SANDY, YOU LOOK lovely,' Lucy said in admiration when she came to Melisande's room before the ball. Rose beamed as she examined first the gown and then the wild profusion of red curls piled high on the crown of her head and secured with hidden pins.

'You do not think this makes me look too old?' Melisande asked, touching the curls arranged by the maid's nimble fingers. The figure looking back at her from the mirror was no longer a reserved eighteen-year-old who preferred books to balls, but an elegant, slender young woman in a splendid gown which did full justice to her rounded curves.

'I think Priscilla will have competition.'

'But I don't want that,' Melisande declared fiercely, thinking of one man in particular whom she intended to avoid tonight.

'No more do I,' Lucy sighed, wishing herself miles away, in the company of Christopher. She had no choice now but to run away—but where? She would ask him to help her. Perhaps he had relatives she could stay with far from Kingsclere. She would not return until her father accepted that she would not be fobbed off with the first man who took his fancy. 'I wish this colour did not suit me so well. I wish—I wish I were as ugly as sin, so that no one would look at me.'

'Men have been known to marry just to obtain a girl's dowry,' Melisande reminded her, admiring the way the yellow velvet enhanced her sister's darker colouring. And then both girls were silent for a long moment as they considered the enormity of the statement, and Rose left them, wondering why on earth they should look so crestfallen on such an occasion.

The word had gone out in the servants' quarters that

tonight Lord Dacre would be selecting a bride, and speculation and rumours ran like wildfire through the kitchens and the pantry. The probability of the sister with black hair and blue eyes being the main contender was heightened when his lordship's brother bet his valet a whole silver shilling that she would be the one chosen.

'I suppose we should join Father before he becomes impatient,' Melisande sighed, still reluctant to leave the sanctuary of the room.

Neither he nor Priscilla were in their rooms, however. A servant met them at the bottom of the stairs to say that the two girls were required in the library. They exchanged anxious glances as they were ushered into an oak-panelled room where the aroma of lavender and beeswax lingered on the highly polished furniture. Edwin de Vere and Priscilla sat side by side on a padded seat, and beside them Jason Dacre, his head bent towards the latter as he listened intently to what she was saying.

Melisande caught her breath as she eyed her sister. Never before had she looked so radiant. Their mother's diamonds glittered at her throat and about her wrists, and the gown of blue silk their father had chosen for her was a perfect match for the brilliant sapphire eyes, which glowed as she looked up towards the two newcomers. She knew she was beautiful and desirable, Melisande thought. It was a powerful weapon for someone as ambitious as she.

The two girls curtsied politely before their host and seated themselves in the empty chairs alongside their sister, each fighting against the growing apprehension building inside them. Edwin allowed his gaze to dwell on each of them in turn with admiration.

'You have three admirable daughters,' Lord Dacre said, as if to confirm his thoughts, and he smiled.

'Treasures, all of them; a great comfort to an old man. My only wish now is to see them comfortably settled with husbands.'

Melisande felt a spasm of anxiety at his words. Why

could he not have said 'happily' settled instead of 'comfortably'? She felt Jason Dacre's eyes on her, and knew he had not missed the careful phrasing.

'I see no reason to delay matters any longer, Lord de Vere, as we have already been into the details most vigorously. I shall, however, say again that I shall provide dowries for two of your daughters that will be more than ample to settle them with husbands from good families. Should you require advice on this matter, I shall do all I can to assist you.'

'You are too kind, sir,' Edwin replied, still inwardly shaken upon discovering which of his 'treasures' was to become Lady Dacre, mistress of Whispering Wood. Lord Dacre had indeed been more than kind; he had stunned Edwin with the proposed terms for the marriage contract. His troubles were over! His daughters were about to be wed, and he could live out the remainder of his days in comparative comfort. If only his dearest wife could have lived to see her dreams realised. Even now he could not believe that the predictions she had made five years ago had become reality. She had been taken from him, but every word she had spoken was coming true, and in the years to come that knowledge would bring him great comfort, for he felt sure she would know it too.

All eyes watched Jason Dacre turn towards a small cabinet in one corner: Edwin quietly smiling; Priscilla, flushed with excitement as she anticipated what was to come; Lucy, praying that their father did not take to any young man in particular tonight, and Melisande, already confident as to whom would be picked, unable to help admiring the tall figure in doublet and hose of deep amber. Tonight he was once more a courtier, polite yet somehow withdrawn despite the warmth of his smile, the friendliness of his tone. Gone was the laughter from those grey eyes, the casual manner that had so taken her aback that morning. He was a different man from the one who had sat beside her, kissed her, mocked her. The man who turned to face them, holding a leather box in his hands, commanded respect and obedience—and perhaps even fear in those who might oppose him.

'These jewels belonged to my great-grandmother. They are priceless, and I consider them a worthy gift to my future bride.' Jason advanced towards the padded seat, his smile for no one sister in particular, Melisande thought, sensing some atmosphere she did not understand. For a man about to take a beautiful bride, he did not demonstrate much joy. 'I could not find a perfect match for your eyes . . .' Priscilla sat forward at the words, staring eagerly into his face. 'So I matched the fire beneath the pose of calm indifference.' He inclined his head towards Melisande, snapping back the lid of the case so that she could see the contents. 'It will please me if you will wear them tonight, as my betrothal gift and your acceptance of my offer.'

There was a long silence—a painful silence—during which she felt as though the room were reeling about her. The handsome features with the probing eyes that never once left her face receded and then returned, and Lucy's fingers digging into her bare arm brought her back to reality.

'If this is some joke, it is in bad taste, sir,' she gasped.

'Melisande! Remember to whom you speak,' Edwin reproved, coming to his feet in anger. Did the girl want to wreck everything with her careless tongue? Did she not realise the honour being done to her? To the family?

'I assume you I am perfectly serious, Melisande,' Lord Dacre replied quietly, apparently unconcerned by the sudden pallor of her cheeks or the incredulity in her eyes.

Her! He had chosen her! How could he? Father had known, Melisande realised, but when? Had it been his intention to take her to wife that morning? He had said nothing. How cruel he was; he knew she did not want to marry anyone. She was confused . . . and angry . . . and lost for words as Lucy flung her arms about her neck and hugged her until a frown from their father forced her with great reluctance to contain herself.

'This—this is an insult!' Priscilla came to her feet,

ashen-cheeked, blue eyes blazing with venom. 'I am the eldest. He gave me to believe . . .'

'I think not,' Edwin interrupted, and something in his manner halted the scornful words that leapt to her lips. 'From the moment we arrived, Lord Dacre took me into his confidence. I told you all otherwise, because I—I sought to delay this moment of disappointment for you, my daughter. Do not distress yourself; tonight you will be surrounded by suitors all vying for your hand.'

But none so handsome or so rich as Lord Dacre, Priscilla thought, barely able to contain her chagrin. Melisande!—It was inconceivable that he should prefer her! What did Father care who was chosen? The terms had obviously been more than generous, but why should they have been? That night Melisande had spent alone with him, of course! He had seduced her! He had to marry her; his code of honour demanded it. Father had been very clever, for he had no doubt pressed the match, speculating on the unpleasant gossip which could result if the match did not take place. He had got rid of the most unsaleable daughter first, knowing that both she and Lucy were attractive enough to draw a fair selection of men about them from which to choose husbands afterwards. It was unfair! She had been cheated out of what was rightfully hers! In that moment, she hated her youngest sister as never before.

How she managed to retain her composure, Melisande never knew. Her father hugged her, and said he was sure she would make Lord Dacre a good wife. Jason Dacre assured him that he, too, thought so, which increased her embarrassment. He knew how she felt about a loveless marriage, yet he was forcing her into one. How dared he!

He came to stand before her and brought from the case a necklace of the strangest stones she had ever seen. One, the size of a dove's egg, took pride of place in the midst of the heavy gold chain; on each side were set six matching, smaller, stones. The candlelight caught the strange hues of colour. Deep flames lurked amid the mixtures of greens and blues, which, when the light caught them a different way, were not blue at all, but turquoise, lined with iridescent greens of varying depths.

With a smile he handed the empty case to Lucy, who held it and watched in wonder as he fastened the necklace about her sister's neck.

'They are called opals,' he said, studying Melisande's face for her reaction to his gift, but none was forthcoming. He had felt her tense as his fingers touched her skin, but remembering what had occurred between them earlier, he disregarded what he considered to be a natural shyness at his surprise announcement. He had wanted to tell her that morning, but she had been so adamant that she would not marry except for love. What a child she was, but he wanted her, and in time she would accept him. Perhaps not as the prince of her dream world, but as a man who could and would fulfil her every need.

He took one slender, ringless hand, thinking how he could grace it with gems to do those long fingers justice, and touched them to his lips in a lingering caress that brought the colour surging into her cheeks. She was thinking of the gardens, he knew, and that pleased him, for each time he touched her, he knew he must arouse a little more of the woman who dwelt beneath that calm pose. Twice he had roused her. Once unintentionally, the second time with deliberate intent to evoke a response from both her lips and her body, and he had succeeded so well that he himself had been shaken. Such fire as yet unleashed, but it would be for him alone. So long he had waited!

'And now I think we should join my guests,' Jason said, not relinquishing Melisande's hand even though she tried to pull it from his grasp. 'Do you not agree, Lord de Vere?'

'Indeed I do,' Edwin replied enthusiastically, and Lucy threw Melisande a worried look, only to find her sister totally oblivious of what troubled her. She looked downcast instead of happy. It was not what she wanted, but she would never do better, and Lord Dacre was such a handsome man. How good they looked together! He could not have chosen a better wife.

'Then, if you will escort your two most charming daughters into the ballroom, I shall follow with Melisande. I am most anxious to give out the glad tidings.'

'It will be my pleasure,' Edwin replied, and extended his arms to Priscilla and Lucy with a smile that said: Now we shall look for two more husbands!

Melisande deliberately hung back, and when Jason turned to look at her enquiringly, she raised her hand to the necklace about her throat with a feeble excuse. 'I fear the clasp is loose, sir, and I would not like to lose so precious a gift.'

Jason closed the doors discreetly behind Edwin and his daughters and turned back to her, his eyebrows raised.

'There is nothing wrong with the clasp, and well you know it! What is it you wish to say to me? Please be brief, as we have guests awaiting us.'

'We have guests.' Already he was addressing her as though she had accepted his preposterous proposal. She could not marry him!

'I cannot marry you,' Melisande blurted out. 'It is impossible. You know it is!'

'If that is all you have to say, then we can rejoin your father and sisters without delay.'

He was ignoring her! Did she have no say in the matter? It was her life, and she would not allow him to control it. 'Do you not understand? I will not marry you,' she cried defiantly, and he moved closer to her, eyes narrowed at the emotion in her tone.

'Will not?' he echoed, an undercurrent of displeasure making itself evident.

'Priscilla was right: you have insulted her. She expected . . . I mean . . .'

'I am fully aware of what your sister expected and of the means she was prepared to go to to have her own way,' Jason returned bleakly. 'She made it quite clear the day before I left your house and again here this afternoon. How different can two sisters be?'

'It is her right,' Melisande protested. 'She is the eldest.'

'Surely I am the best judge of whom I wish to marry? If you are wise, you will accept my proposal and save . . . Nay, I shall say no more.'

A cold hand clutched at Melisande's heart. He sounded so menacing—almost threatening. What had been the marriage terms? It was not for her to enquire—such things were left to the parents to decide with the prospective bridegroom—but here, she sensed, something more had taken place.

'These matters should not concern you. However, it seems that I must acquaint you with what your father and I have discussed so that you will see the wisdom of accepting what I have to offer you—and your family.'

'You—you cannot force me to marry you. I find the idea quite . . . distasteful,' she said breathlessly.

'Distasteful or not, you will marry me,' came the chilling answer. 'You have no say in the matter. I am accustomed to having my own way, and I will not allow my plans to be upset by a foolish girl with her head stuffed full of fanciful dreams. Let us not mince words, Melisande. Your father is deeply in debt, and I have alleviated a very painful situation for him. When we marry, all his debts will be paid. He will be allotted a very substantial amount of money, which will allow him to live in comfort for the rest of his days—unless he takes to speculating again,' he added drily. 'Unless you marry me, I shall withdraw not only the money I have agreed he shall have, but the dowries for your sisters.'

'You could not be so heartless!' Melisande gasped.

'I owe them nothing,' Jason snapped, growing irritated that she had chosen to go against him so forcefully. Did she not realise what he was offering her? So much more than just his name, to be mistress of Whispering Wood.

'Owe?' she repeated, her eyes widening. So, after all, he was merely repaying the debt he thought was due. Melisande had never been so humiliated in all her young life.

This should have been a moment to treasure, but instead she was numb with shock and more than a little afraid of the stranger who stood before her, demanding her subjection to his wishes—his will!

'Melisande . . .' As if sensing the disquiet inside her, Jason crossed to her side and his arms had closed about her before she could move. 'Do not condemn me with those lovely eyes. I saw you—I want you—and I shall have you. Is that so terrible? You shall lack nothing, I promise, and your family . . .'

'Only so long as I am an obedient, dutiful wife,' she flung back at him bitterly, and immediately he stepped away and his expression grew cold.

'That is up to you. I want only for you to be happy.'

'Then release me from this shameful bargain!'

'I cannot. I want you too much.' Damning words, which condemned her to a loveless existence with a man of whom she was more than a little afraid now she had seen the other side of him—the ruthless, unyielding character hidden thus far by the friendly smile and easy manner.

'Then, if I must marry you so that Father will have all his future years in comfort, I shall,' she said in a low tone. Jason noticed that she said nothing of her sisters. She expected them to manage on their own, he thought, and he knew that each, in her own way, would do just that. He would speak to Edwin about Lucy—that was the least he could do—and perhaps, when he told Melisande he had done so, she would realise that he was not such an ogre after all. 'But I shall never love you, or forgive you for what you have done to me.'

The final defiant words flung at him caused his mouth to tighten into a thin angry line. Damn the girl, she was an exasperating little thing! He sighed, remembering the years separating them. She was so young: only eighteen and innocent of the world. He had been to many places, mixed with an assortment of people who would never be accepted in the world in which he now moved, but whom at that time he had been proud to call friends. He had had his share of women, including a pretty mistress in London. It was a relief that the affair had ended, he mused, as he scanned Melisande's indignant features. What did he want with another woman when he had this all to himself?

Half child, half woman! One day she would be all woman, fiery, sensuous—his! He must strive for that day, and not become too angry with her petulance now. In time it would pass, and patience was only one of the many things Jason Dacre had learned in his thirty-two years.

'Our guests await us, and I do not intend to keep them waiting any longer,' he said in a tone that belied further argument.

Melisande stared at the arm extended towards her, thought of ignoring it and him—and then thought of her father, of Priscilla without a dowry, of Lucy . . . Without a word, she laid her hand on the amber silk and allowed him to lead her into the ballroom and the guests waiting with avid curiosity, no doubt, to inspect the woman about to become the wife of Jason, Lord Dacre. She felt as though she were being presented at some cattle-auction as she entered the gigantic room and the eyes of over a hundred people turned to stare at her, to strip her bare. Fans fluttered, whispered comments beyond her hearing made her grow embarrassed, and then Jason's hand was covering hers, his voice softly in her ear was whispering words of encouragement, and much as she hated him, she found them comforting.

'Courage, my dream princess! They are only envious of what I have found. Look about you. There is not a woman here to match you, so hold your head high. Did your mother ever cast her eyes upon the ground? You are even more beautiful than she was. Let them see the prize I have taken, and envy me, too.'

The prize he had taken, not wooed and won. For an instant her eyes blazed as they encountered his, and soft laughter rose in his throat.

'Oh, what an interesting life we shall have together, Melisande,' he murmured.

What did he mean? she wondered, inclining her head towards her father as they passed him. Priscilla looked the other way. Lucy beamed at her, yet beneath the obvious joy at her good fortune, Melisande saw sadness, and her heart went out to her, for what could she do? She wanted nothing from Jason Dacre. He could give her what he pleased, but she would ask for naught. Yet Lucy . . . How could she go to him and beg for her sister's happiness? What price would be place on that?

'What have we here? A turn-about?' An elegantly-dressed man stepped out in front of them, and his bold eyes considered Melisande from head to toe. 'The red-head! Jason, you are full of happiness, and you have made me lose my bet!'

'Perhaps it will teach you not to jump to conclusions,' came the dry retort. 'Melisande, allow me to present my brother Richard, who has no scruples and very few morals, so do not be taken in by his smile. He is a complete rogue.'

'As always, my brother paints the blackest picture of me,' Richard Dacre chuckled, raising Melisande's hand to his lips. There was very little likeness between the two men. Richard's skin was not so dark, nor his hair so blond, and he sported a neat moustache and well-trimmed beard. His clothes were of the latest fashion and no less flamboyant than those of the women about him. His Venetians fastened below the knee with gold buttons and were lavishly embroidered, as were his brightly coloured stockings, which matched the rich velvet of the cloak which fell from one shoulder. The fine leather gauntlets tucked into his belt were decorated with gold thread, and fringed. Alongside was a white linen handkerchief edged with lace.

A conceited man, Melisande thought, as with an

elaborate bow he moved away from them and was immediately surrounded by women. Priscilla, who had been following her sister's exquisitely gowned figure and hating her and her good fortune more each minute, turned away, angry tears blurring her vision, and cannoned into Richard Dacre.

The gaze focused on her missed nothing, and a smile touched the sensuous mouth as he watched her fight to control the rage inside her.

'My brother is a blind fool, but his mistake may be my fortune. Dear lady, may I offer you some refreshment, as you appear a trifle distressed?' he murmured, offering his arm, and he knew by the swiftness with which she accepted his offer that the evening would not, after all, be a complete waste of time. He would never have risked facing his brother across his blade by attempting to seduce Melisande, but this one was different . . . and willing, he suspected, if only to regain some of the pride that must surely have been demolished by the news that she had been passed over for her youngest sister.

The anger disappeared from the blue eyes, which became quite moist again as they looked up at him, and liking what they saw, she allowed him to lead her to the long tables against the far wall where an abundance of food awaited them. She accepted with a demure smile the glass of wine he handed her, studying him beneath lowered lids as she sipped it. She had not been aware that Lord Dacre had a brother. She had lost the chance of one rich husband, but the brother . . . Why not? He was quite good looking, and from the way he dressed, was equally as wealthy as Jason.

'I am grateful for your concern, sir,' she murmured, and Richard smiled, allowing the full weight of his charm to bear down on her. When he set out to seduce a woman, the times when he did not succeed were rare. Priscilla began to regain her composure as he continued to study her with frank interest. Melisande would not be the only one to acquire a husband tonight, she vowed.

She would show her sisters and her father! 'But, I can assure you, my tears were of joy for my sister's wonderful good fortune.'

'But of course—why else? Although I find my brother's choice devilish strange. Never did I think he would marry a complete stranger . . . Why, he has had the pick of the crop for many years, and none has attracted him thus far.'

'Perhaps Melisande is not—a complete stranger,' Priscilla murmured, her eyes following her sister's progress about the room. Her cheeks were flushed, but she appeared no longer nervous and was talking quite amiably to the people Lord Dacre introduced to her. Already the genial hostess, the wife at the side of her husband . . . How dare she look so—so at home! This should all have been hers!

'You intrigue me.' Richard offered her some sliced mutton stuffed with garlic, but as its aroma invaded her nostrils, she waved it away with a grimace and selected instead a small venison pasty with the addition of some sugared mustard. 'Pray go on. Has my brother been hiding something from me?'

Priscilla's eyes left her sister and wandered round the room. It was magnificent, ablaze with candle-light, with rushlight tapers in wrought-iron holders to chase away shadows from every corner. The heavy carved furniture gleamed alongside the oak panelling. Silverware was displayed on an enormous dresser that took up almost one complete wall. On another were a Turkish wine-jug with English silver mounts and more cut glassware. In times of need, many families pawned such treasures to keep the family estates solvent. Somehow, she suspected, Lord Dacre had never had reason, nor would have, to sacrifice his belongings in this manner.

She could still share in it all, if she married Richard Dacre! She would live here at Whispering Wood with her sister, and then she could show her how to run a household with skill. Just because Melisande managed their father's house, she thought she knew everything.

She would never be firm enough with the servants here, or be able to entertain with the panache that Priscilla possessed.

'I—I must not,' she replied with downcast eyes, knowing that she had his full attention. 'Although it does not matter, now that they are to be married. You cannot imagine how horrified I was when I thought that perhaps Lord Dacre might choose me. It would have been too—too shameful, after . . .'

She lifted her eyes and realised she had not only his attention, but that of several women behind him, whose fans had begun to flutter more quickly at her words. They were not looking at her, that would have been too rude and obvious, but they had ceased conversation among themselves, and she felt a flicker of triumph. How Melisande had managed to persuade Lord Dacre to marry her she did not know, but she would regret it! She would remember this evening for as long as she lived, not as a time of happiness but as one of exquisite embarrassment. What she was about to relate was true, after all, Priscilla mused. How others chose to interpret it was not her concern.

'I discovered them together, you see.' Her voice was low, but not so low as to deprive the listening ears of what they longed to hear. 'Father and I had been away from the house all night and did not return until morning. I, of course, went directly to Melisande's room to assure myself that she was all right. The storm had been so fierce, and she is afraid of them, you know. She—she was in his arms . . . No! No, I must say no more. He has done the gentlemanly thing, and I am pleased for her. Though I would never have believed it possible of my innocent little sister . . .' Her voice trailed away, and she bent low over the glass in her hand so that he should not see the laughter in her eyes. When she looked up again, the eavesdroppers had moved off, but she saw by the heads bent close together that the speculation had begun.

'I think you have a touch of the devil's daughter in

you,' Richard said, with a chuckle. 'You and I are well matched.'

'I do not understand you, sir.' Priscilla tried to sound indignant, but failed, for his look told her he had understood exactly what she had done, yet he had not condemned her for it. Did he approve? He did not appear angry, only amused. 'I have only told what I saw.'

'And left it to others to elaborate on your words. Before the evening is out, your sister and my brother are going to have very sore ears. I have no more love for him than you have for her. I shall enjoy watching him squirm like a worm on a hook; too many times has he done it to me. May I offer you some more wine, while we wait for the entertainment to begin?'

'I should like to dance,' Priscilla said, as musicians in the gallery began to attract people into the middle of the floor with the lilting sounds of a lute and a fiddle.

'Tonight you shall dance with no man but me,' Richard told her. 'In fact, I shall not allow you to leave my side.'

Priscilla bestowed upon him a warm smile, pretending to ignore the intimate way his hand pressed hers upon his arm. He was making his interest in her very clear, and her wounded pride was restored by seeing the jealous glances cast at her by other women. He had a smooth tongue and was far too sure of himself, she thought as they began to dance, but she could overlook both possibly dangerous traits. He was Lord Dacre's brother, and that was all important. How different he was from other men she knew. Lord Haslett's son was a monster by comparison. This man made her feel important. His bold gaze excited her, and made her wonder what it would be like to be kissed by him. The night was young; she abandoned herself totally to the gaiety of the music. If it could happen for Melisande, it could happen for her!

'Amanda, have you only just come down? Our guests have been asking for you.' Jason halted before his ward, his tone registering a note of displeasure at her deliberate absence from the gathering.

The young girl made her excuses to the woman she was with and fell into step beside him, her expression cool. She inclined her head towards Melisande, and said in a frosty tone, 'Allow me to congratulate you, Mistress de Vere. You have achieved in a very short space of time what your sister has been trying to do for years. My congratulations to you, too, Jason. You have surprised everyone.'

The insult robbed Melisande of words. She had been expecting at least a show of cordiality from the girl, but this!

The man at her side stiffened in anger. For days she had been fighting him. Would this conflict between them never end? Once they had been so close, but her attitude made it impossible for him to tell her the truth about why he felt he had to control her life.

'You will apologise to Melisande at once! You will show my future wife the respect due to her, Amanda, or you will remain in your room until your manners return,' he snapped.

'Forgive me, Mistress de Vere, I have been plagued by a headache all day and I am not myself.' The apology was half hearted, without any genuine remorse attached to it. 'I have offered my congratulations, so perhaps I should also offer you my condolences. Jason will seek to rule your life as he does mine and his brother's. Your sisters have had a lucky escape.'

An expletive exploded under Jason's breath as she wheeled about and disappeared into the crowd in a flurry of pale green silk.

'The little minx! I should have spanked her a long time ago,' he muttered.

'I was hoping we could become friends,' Melisande said, still shocked at Amanda's open hostility. She was beginning to think she was about to become mistress of a house where everyone was at each other's throats.

'Give her time. She is angry with me, and has chosen to take it out of you. I shall speak to her.'

'No. If we are to be friends, then it must be by her choice,' she replied, wondering whether she was imagining that people were staring at her rather oddly. Two women passing looked into her face and then turned away to giggle behind their fans. The men following them eyed her with bolder stares, which drew a frown to Jason's face as he became of aware of the uncalled-for scrutiny.

His gaze raked the room as he sensed an atmosphere he did not understand, and the frown grew as he watched his brother escorting Priscilla through the open windows into the garden. Damn him, he did not know what he was doing! Edwin de Vere had seen them too, he noticed. Richard did not know it, but he was being assessed as a prospective bridegroom. The thought was without humour.

Lucy came threading her way through the guests and smiled rather lamely as Jason. She was a pretty little thing, he thought, but too headstrong, from what Melisande had told him. He would speak to Edwin de Vere about her. So long as she had a good dowry, it mattered not if the man she married was little more than a pauper. For the moment, at least. Over many years he had taken an interest in young Christopher Avery's future. A wife would not hinder his life, although a sailor's wife did not have an easy time. Long periods of waiting, and uncertainty while the man was away, made a woman grow old before her time. But if it was what the two of them wanted . . . And perhaps Melisande would regard him a little less as an unfeeling brute if he were able to bring about happiness for Lucy. He had noted that she cared more for her than for her eldest sister.

That one had as few morals as his brother, though less experience of the world. He did not like to see the two of them together; it boded ill. Richard was unscrupulous enough to take advantage of any woman who took his fancy, no matter whom she belonged to, and Priscilla was free, available, and, Jason suspected, anxious to restore her fragmented vanity. To think he would have picked her! She would have come to his bed at any time he beckoned, and had not hidden her eagerness to do anything to please him and so gain an advantage over her sisters.

But Priscilla and Lucy had never had the slightest chance with him: it had always been Melisande. How could he tell her without making her laugh at him or believe he was lying in an attempt to win her approval of the match? He must wait, he told himself. Wait and be patient, and the final reward when she accepted him would surpass his wildest imagination. But to have her and not to hold her. He ached, even now, to take her out into the garden and bruise those soft lips until she surrendered to him. She would. But he wanted her willingly, not coerced into obedience, accepting him because it was her duty as his wife. But how he wanted her . . .

'May I speak with my sister, sir? You have been monopolising her so that I have not a chance to wish her well,' said Lucy.

'I see some friends I would like to speak to. I shall return in a little while.' Jason saw that she wanted to impart to her sister some girlish secret that had come to her ears. How women loved to chatter! Yet, while sharing the deck of *Moonwynd* with his father, he had been surprised at the idle talk that men indulged in to while away the hours of toil and boredom. Talk of home, of wives and family—of sweethearts—and then, when all was exhausted and the night lengthened, of hopes and dreams, of women they wished to meet and never would. Of women they had met but would never wish their wives to know. Of places and people so distant that it was hard to explain them to others. Perhaps Melisande with her world was not so different, after all, he thought as he left them. Everyone in his or her own way shut out reality and substituted something perhaps more pleasant, perhaps unbelievable; a moment's release from the drudgery, the poverty, the dullness of their everyday existence.

He had everything he could wish for, yet had he not stood behind the wheel of *Moonwynd* and wished himself a thousand miles away with Drake, fighting the Spaniards? Or exploring uncharted regions that the Portuguese had discovered. How he wished he could lay hands on some of their ruttiers! With charts and maps to guide him, he could have discovered further lands. Yet why did he want to, when he had Whispering Wood? It was his life; he was content to live where he had been born and brought up. There was so much he could do here—for the villagers who depended on the estate for their livelihood, and the outlying villages; for himself; for Amanda, who so sorely needed his advice and counsel at this moment, yet refused to accept it.

Damn his brother! Would the man never learn? If he seduced Priscilla de Vere . . . He turned towards the door, but a man caught his arm, offering his congratulations and a glass of wine . . .

'Sandy . . .' Lucy drew Melisande to a quiet corner, glancing about her as though afraid that someone was listening. 'She . . . Oh, I shall never forgive her . . .'

'What is it? Forgive whom? Amanda? Was she rude to you, too? She is upset and angry with Lord Dacre; he told me so himself,' said Melisande. 'She will accept us in time.'

'Amanda? No, she has been most friendly towards me,' Lucy returned. 'She is such a lonely girl, but I did not realise it before. Yet, when she talks . . . She has been to court, of course, and has seen much more of the world . . .'

'Then whom are you talking about?' Melisande interrupted.

'Priscilla. She! How can I tell you! Someone came up to me, not knowing who I was, and asked me if I knew the scandalous secret. "What secret?" I asked, and then she said . . . Oh, Sandy! Priscilla told someone, I don't know who, that you and Lord Dacre . . . had been found in each other's arms—in bed.'

'That is a lie!' Melisande blenched, appalled at her elder sister's viciousness. 'She knows it is. I fell asleep . . . that's all. Nothing happened between us. They cannot believe . . .'

'But they do! Don't you understand that they love the idea of your being seduced by the most eligible man in the county! Nothing could have pleased them more. For him to have chosen you because he loves you would have bored them.'

'Love! No, never that!' Melisande declared in a fierce whisper. He wanted her, but that was not love. He had known she would never become his mistress—as some women might have done had he said the same thing to them—and so he was going to marry her. But to go to such lengths . . . and to hold the threat of withdrawing money from her father and her sisters' dowries if she did not! 'Let them gossip! Why should I care.' She did, and it cut her like a knife that women were staring at her, assessing her worth in bed, and the men were doing it also, but more boldly—so boldly, in fact, that she felt herself grow hot beneath the searching eyes. 'I am innocent of their suspicions. Lucy, I have asked Lord Dacre to speak to Father about . . . Well, I hope he will be able to persuade him that, with a dowry, you could select a man of your own choice. Christopher, for instance.'

'Oh, Sandy, if only he would agree!'

'Is it really what you want?' Melisande took her by the shoulders and searched her face with worried eyes. 'Marriage is such a huge step. Do not take it unless you are sure he is right for you.'

'I am as sure of him as I am that Lord Dacre is the man for you,' Lucy assured her with a hug. 'Oh, Sandy, if you could stand back and see how you look together! Never have I seen a man look at a woman as he looks at you. Such possessiveness in those eyes . . . and the way he has kept you by his side tonight. I am so happy for you—I really am!'

Possessive. Yes, that was what Jason Dacre was,

Melisande thought. She was something he wanted. Something he had acquired by means that were repugnant to her. Somehow, she managed to smile for her sister. Lucy's happiness was almost secure. That was a small consolation, but it lifted a little of the heaviness from her heart. Someone would gain from this night. She watched Lord Dacre go over to her father, and the two of them left the room. In a little while they would know what was to happen.

'Find yourself a young man to dance with, Lucy,' she said. 'Enjoy yourself. Perhaps, in a little while, you may be a wife and mother with no time for such things.'

For a moment there was a certain hesitation in Lucy's smile, a reluctance to turn away and seek a partner. Because she wanted to dance only with Christopher, Melisande wondered, or because the idea of being a wife and mother was not what she really wanted? If she did not love him . . .

When Edwin returned alone some time later, Melisande watched Lucy hurry to him, her face alight with anticipation. However, a moment later, she turned and ran from the room in a state of great agitation, and Melisande's heart sank, for it meant that Lord Dacre had not succeeded in persuading him to consider young Christopher. She waited for him to join her and tell her the worst.

'You should not have asked Lord Dacre to interfere, Melisande. You know well enough how I feel about that young man,' Edwin said, fixing her with a stern look. 'He is too young—and penniless—and she does not know her own mind. She tried to tell me she is in love with him, but I cannot accept that. Do you believe it?'

'I don't know, Father. Perhaps she is. Mother married you when she was seventeen, didn't she? And you were very happy. Lucy is not and will not be happy if you force her into marriage with a stranger, no matter how well he can support her.'

'Is that how you feel about marriage to Lord Dacre? Are you happy? I have been watching you, and you do not have the look of a radiant bride-to-be.'

'I—I think I am rather overwhelmed by everything,' Melisande lied, knowing she could never tell him how Jason Dacre had blackmailed her into accepting him.

'My dear child, this is only the beginning. When we return home, you must begin thinking about your trousseau. You are to have the best of everything, and all bills are to be sent directly to Lord Dacre, at his own insistence. What do you think of that?'

Melisande did not think much of it at all, but what could she say? At every turn, Jason Dacre reminded her that he was buying her. How she wished she could refuse the offer, but in doing so she would have to say why, and that was impossible. Not only her father, but Lucy and Priscilla would suffer.

'By the way, where is Priscilla? I don't see her,' said Edwin, searching the sea of faces.

'I thought she was dancing with Richard Dacre. Earlier, she was.

'I begin to worry about that girl. She has set her sights too high.'

'But she is with Lord Dacre's brother, Father. She could not be in better hands,' Melisande said quickly, not wanting him to grow concerned at her sister's absence. What was she thinking of to go off alone with him?

'Nevertheless, I think I should go and find her.'

'Why don't you go and make your peace with Lucy? Please?' she entreated. 'I shall find Priscilla.'

Not giving him a chance to refuse, she picked up her skirts and made her way to the open french windows. A refreshing breeze fanned her face as she stepped out on the wide stone steps leading down to the garden. There were many couples enjoying the pleasant night, but she could see no sign of Priscilla or Richard Dacre. They were neither lingering by the stream nor walking in the garden where she herself had been with Jason. She felt a flush rise in her cheeks as she passed the wooden bench where he had kissed her. In the arms of the right man she would find love, she had declared vehemently, and she could still hear the ring of his laughter: What does a child like you know of love? When he had taken her in his arms and subjected her to the expertise of his kisses, she had discovered the answer. Nothing! And nothing of men!

Do you not think it better to feel like a woman? Is that what he had made her feel like? If so, she had secretly enjoyed it and wanted more. Had he not used such devious tactics to make her agree to the marriage, she might have been able to confide in him. She was rapidly being caught up in an intricate web of emotion, and could not break free. She could never forgive him for having paid handsomely to acquire what he wanted, but she did not feel flattered, only ashamed.

She did not know whether to return to the house without Priscilla or to continue on into the trees ahead. Surely they would not have gone so far from the house? The sound of laughter reached her ears, and she froze, instantly recognising her sister's high-pitched giggle. Then the murmur of voices, those of a man and a woman. Not content with ruining Melisande's reputation, Priscilla seemed determined to do the same for her own!

And then she saw them, entwined in each other's arms on a grassy verge beneath the huge Spanish chestnuts. In brilliant moonlight that clearly illuminated the two figures, there was no mistaking the brightly coloured cloak worn by Richard Dacre when she had been introduced to him, and which now lay beneath her sister's head. Melisande caught her breath at her sister's state of undress . . . Her bodice and chemise were open . . . Her hair dishevelled. She turned away blindly, stumbling back the way she had come. A pair of arms came out of nowhere to bring her flight to an abrupt end and to crush her against a masculine chest, but the scream that rose in her throat was never uttered as she found herself looking up into Jason's Dacre's smiling features.

'Are you looking for me, Melisande?' Had she not

been so distressed, she would have risen instantly to the mockery in his voice, and when she did not, but turned her head away from him so that he would not see the tears blurring her vision, he slipped a finger beneath her chin and forced back her head. He needed only one look into the wide eyes to know that Melisande had found her sister. 'Where are they?'

'Yonder, in the trees.' Something told her it would be useless to lie to him. Had he, too, come looking for them? 'Oh, please, do nothing hasty. If this should reach Father . . .'

'Your sister should have thought of that before she acted so rashly! Stay here.'

A moment after he had left her and disappeared into the trees, she heard a half-choked cry and then the sound of a blow, followed by Jason's threatening tones.

'This time, you will not escape the consequences of your actions. You will marry the girl.' Against her will she found herself edging closer to see what was happening.

'I'll be damned if I will!' Richard Dacre's voice was slurred as if he was drunk, or hurt. He came into her vision nursing one side of a bruised jaw, while Priscilla, her face a mask of horror, struggled to adjust her gown. His brother towered over them both, fists clenched at his sides, but Melisande was surprised to see no anger on his dark features. Yet she could feel it radiating from him, see it in the gleam of the narrowed grey eyes, hear it in the soft, menacing voice as he delivered a terrible ultimatum.

'You will be dead if you don't! Now get to your feet, and let us do what has to be done before we are discovered here.' Jason looked up as if sensing Melisande's presence, and said in the same unruffled tone, 'Come and help your sister to make herself look less like a fishwife and more like the lady she is supposed to be.' It was a command; no refusal was expected, and instinctively she moved forward to obey.

'Already you have her as meek as a lamb,' Richard

sneered, as she tried to restore some order to Priscilla's hair. 'You've always preferred women with fire and long claws! Perhaps what I've heard is true—that there is more to her than one can see at first glance.'

Jason's clenched fist flashed out without warning and felled him to the ground again with a stunning blow, as he tried to climb to his feet. Priscilla buried her face in her hands with a cry which brought his attention to her.

'You shall reap what you have sown, Mistress de Vere. If you were not Melisande's sister, I would not waste a moment more of my time with you.' He was without mercy, and Melisande wondered what kind of monster she was about to marry. Had he no regard for the lives that were being ruined this night: her own, Lucy's, and now Priscilla's? How dared he insinuate that the blame was all hers? 'She knew what she was about,' he added coldly, as she opened her mouth to protest. 'I know it, and so do you. Would you rather your father called him out?'

'Father is no duellist,' she protested. 'He is a peaceful man.'

'Then I should have to take his place.'

'You would kill your own brother?' she gasped, appalled.

'No one deserves to die more, believe me,' came the stern answer. 'Will you do as I tell you, and prevent further problems?'

Mutely, Melisande nodded.

'You are a brute!' Priscilla sobbed. She was upset not so much at being discovered, as at the realisation that her father could be told of her scandalous behaviour. She had not intended to go so far. Richard had been so courteous, so attentive, dulling her fears when he led her out into the garden. They had lingered well within sight of the house for a while, and she had not objected when he kissed her, or when he suggested that they withdraw so that they could not be seen. He was only thinking of her good name, after all, and there were quite a few people about. Even when he had begun to kiss her with an ardour she had not expected and his fingers had probed inside her bodice she had not grown too alarmed. If she allowed him a few moments of pleasure, would he not want to see her again—and again until she could be sure that marriage was in his mind?

Somewhere between that moment and the time Jason had come upon them he had completely overcome all her inhibitions with the expertise of a man who had known many women . . . and, what was worse, as he had loosened her bodice and begun to kiss her breasts, all she could think about was that he would have to marry her now. Yet she knew, as she looked at him, that he never would. He would have taken her, and laughed at her demands that he give her his name, as was her due.

'If you had taken more time to get to know my brother,' Jason replied with a tight smile, 'you would have discovered that he meets and discards at least two women like you each month.'

Women like her! The insinuation made Priscilla's cheeks burn, but she gave no answer. She had none. Richard Dacre would marry her, and she would be the true mistress of Whispering Wood. It was what she had wanted.

'Take your sister to the blue salon, Melisande. It is the room next to the library. Wait there until we come, and send for your father, as my brother will have something to say to him.'

'If you think I'm going to spend the rest of my life with that little trollop . . .' Richard began, and as Jason moved closer, he threw up his arms to ward off another blow which never came.

'You will give her your name. As to spending the rest of your life with her, that is up to you. Go back to your mistress, if you like. It is of no importance to me, as long as Priscilla is your legal wife. There will be no faking this one.'

'You can't force me to the altar as you are doing with your bride,' his brother sneered.

'Then, if a little persuasion is needed to make you see

the error of your ways, I suggest we retire to the stables and settle it there. A taste of a horsewhip may just bring you to your senses.'

Melisande caught Priscilla by the arm and hurried her back towards the house. Was he serious? And what had he meant by the words: 'there will be no faking this one.' How did one fake a marriage?

'Do I look all right?' Priscilla hesitated as they were about to enter the door, patting her curls, which were still not quite as neat as they should have been, but who would think anything was amiss when the two girls entered together? 'Don't look so smug, Melisande. At least I have what I want!'

'I don't feel smug,' Melisande replied stiffly, brushing away a broken twig that had caught up in the underskirts of her sister's gown. 'I feel only shame. You are far more suited to be the wife of Lord Dacre, do you know that? You are both heartless, callous people. You think only of yourselves, and take from the world without consideration for anyone else. No matter whom you hurt in the process, as long as you have your way, that is all that matters. I shall not tell Father what has happened, if that is what is worrying you. I love him too much to show him what his adorable favourite daughter is really like. Let him have his illusions. You know the truth, and will have to live with it. I don't think it will bother you very much.'

Her head held high, she brushed past her sister and entered the ballroom.

CHAPTER FIVE

THE BLUE SALON was a comfortable sitting-room next door to the library, with colourful tapestries adorning the pastel walls. It was a peaceful room, Melisande thought, as she surveyed her surroundings, but how long would it remain so? She could not believe that Jason Dacre, even by force, could make his brother agree to marry Priscilla. The man had clearly given everyone the impression that he considered her merely a casual encounter and worth no more consideration than any other woman he knew.

Priscilla sat staring out of the window into the darkened garden. Several times she turned to glance with an impatient frown towards the door. She did not look at all remorseful for the trouble she was about to cause, and Melisande began to wonder if she had ever really known her elder sister. She no longer envied the determined nature that had set her on this disastrous course. Although not happy with her own future, she would not have changed places with Priscilla for a chestful of jewels.

Thomas, the steward, came and went, leaving a tray containing a platter of sweetmeats and sugared biscuits, together with two glasses of wine for the sisters and, on a separate table, a decanter of brandy and one of rich red wine. Melisande watched a smile touch her sister's lips as he departed.

'He has done it,' she breathed. 'I knew he would. After all, I am not unattractive. We are well matched. Besides, Lord Dacre would not want his brother's conduct to sully his fine name any more than he wished the rumours about you and him to get out of hand.'

'What are you insinuating?' Melisande asked,

growing pale. It did rather seem as if there was to be a celebration.

'My dear little innocent sister, you don't think he is marrying you because you are a raving beauty, do you?' Priscilla flung back derisively. 'I wonder if he offered Father money to keep quiet about your little escapade on that night you were alone? I rather think he did, but Father has set his hopes higher. He would have wanted more.'

'That is what he said about you, and you have proved him right, have you not?' Melisande returned, her voice growing cold. Was there to be no end to the humiliation she was to endure this night? She had been bought by a man who stated that he wanted her—not loved her! Was she now to believe that his first consideration had not been his desire for her—and that in itself had been bad enough—but merely the retention of the honour of his name?

'At least I know the kind of man I am to marry—and I know what I want. You do not, and as for Jason Dacre . . .'

'I do not wish to discuss him,' Melisande retorted, and Priscilla laughed as she reached for a glass of wine.

'Poor Melisande! He will soon wreak havoc with your silly dreams. You will not be able to hold him for a moment. He has a mistress in London, you know. His brother told me so. And he is a frequent visitor to court, quite close to the Queen's friends. That is why he cannot afford any scandal. After the Queen's favourite, The Earl of Essex, secretly married the widow of Philip Sidney and got her with child, and then Raleigh was thrown into the Tower for seducing Bess Throckmorton, the Queen's maid-of-honour, everyone is taking great care to be on their best behaviour lest they offend the royal personage.'

'You are very well informed on court matters.'

'Richard thought that, as your sister, I should know why his brother is marrying in such great haste. The Queen would not take kindly to another scandal. Lord

Dacre's courage during the Armada battle greatly impressed her. Why should he risk everything he has? A quick marriage will solve his problem, and no one will think ill of him.'

'I do not believe you. Lord Dacre has—not that it is any of your business—but he has admitted a great interest in me for many years,' Melisande declared, remembering the passion in his kisses.

'Then why did he not sue for your hand earlier? Of course he will tell you anything that he thinks will keep you docile. He doesn't want a troublesome wife on his hands, but one he can leave behind when he goes to London. He may take his mistress about with him there, but not you. He wants a meek creature he can bed and then leave to bear his children while he goes back to the life he enjoys. Richard thinks he might even join Sir Francis Drake on his next expedition, and *he* leaves England in a month or two. Does that sound the action of a devoted husband? You always were a plausible little thing. Perhaps your dreams and fantasies will keep you happy while he is away at sea or with his mistress. Believe me, you will have little else.'

'Will you?' Melisande flashed back, cheeks flaming at the insinuations. She did not want to consider them, let alone believe they could be true. Could he have been so dishonest? When she had been in his arms, enjoying his stolen kisses, she had briefly allowed herself to be swayed by his colourful rhetoric. Never before had she been told she was beautiful, let alone desirable. He had made her feel so—and also wanted as never before. Was he a plausible rogue—no more than that—an adept liar, bent on deceiving her so that she would not, as Priscilla intimated, bring shame upon his name by elaborating on what had passed between them that night?

But nothing had happened! No one had known they were together except Lucy, who knew her sister well, and knew she would not lower herself to climb into the bed of the first man who attracted her. And her father, too, believed her to be innocent. Only Priscilla insisted that something had taken place. Was it out of jealousy —because she had wanted Jason Dacre for herself? And he had chosen Melisande!

But why had he chosen her? If only she knew! What use was there in trying to make excuses for his behaviour. It was as Priscilla had said. He was afraid of a scandal which might end his life at court and sully his name! He did not care for Melisande at all. She should have realised the truth by the way he was willing to give a dowry to each of her sisters. No man did that without very good reason and Jason Dacre had the best of reasons. To pacify her father.

The image of Jason standing over his brother flashed through her mind, and those menacing words: 'You will marry the girl . . .' 'I'll be damned if I will!' 'You will be dead if you don't!' There was no escaping it—those words betrayed the kind of man that lurked beneath the casual smile and genial banter: an unscrupulous man—a man without a heart. This was whom she was to marry and spend the rest of her life with!

The door opened again, and this time it was their father who entered with Lord Dacre beside him, an arm about his shoulders. They were smiling, and had obviously become—at least to her father—good friends on the most amicable terms. She knew she would never have the courage to tell him of the other side of his companion's character. Behind them came Richard Dacre, and a frown creased her brows as she watched him close the door and take up a position close behind Priscilla's chair. Apart from a slight redness about his jaw, he bore no signs of any mistreatment, yet he did not seem able to stand fully erect, and his shoulders stooped slightly as he moved, as though in pain or discomfort, from one foot to the other. Had there been a fight? Had Jason Dacre taken a horsewhip to him as he had threatened? She inwardly shuddered. To what lengths would the man go to so that he had his own way?

'This is turning out to be a night of surprises for us all,' Jason remarked, acknowledging the sisters with a nod of his head as he crossed to the table and poured a liberal amount of brandy into three glasses. Edwin's smile deepened as the aroma of nectar reached his nostrils and he sipped appreciatively. Impassively Richard took the glass offered and put it to one side. 'My brother has something to say to you, which I hope you will receive favourably.'

Priscilla lifted her head and gazed on the man behind her, and immediately looked away again, a little frightened by his burning gaze. He looked as if he hated her!

'Lord de Vere . . .' Richard began, and then broke off, a pained expression crossing his features.

'Are you unwell, sir?' Edwin asked.

'A trifle. Nothing serious, I assure you.'

'My brother is a keen huntsman. Unfortunately this morning his horse threw him, and he has sustained some considerable bruising. However, I am sure the presence of Mistress Priscilla has taken his mind off the pain—however distracting it is,' Jason said amusedly. Again his voice was pleasant and friendly, but she thought she was not the only one to suspect a veiled threat underlying his words, when Richard threw him a murderous look, fortunately missed by her father.

Turning away, Jason caught the uncertainty lingering in the depths of her blue eyes, which began to darken as she withstood his scrutiny. Still smiling, he handed her the second glass of wine from the tray.

'Allow me to handle this in my own way, or your sister may very well find herself in a very awkward situation.' The whispered comment did not go beyond her ears.

'And how much will this cost you?' she asked acidly in the same low voice, wanting to hurt him.

Nothing changed in his face, but his eyes pierced her like slivers of ice. 'Not as much as you, my sweet. Not as much as you,' he murmured, relaxing at her side.

'Lord de Vere . . .' Richard began again. He would not have dared to address Edwin by his first name. He disliked the little upstart of a man with his excessive debts and a taste for living he could not afford, ignoring any comparison with himself, and refusing to acknowledge that his own dealings with friends and acquaintances at times came little short of swindling when desperation drove him to replenish his empty coffers by any means at his disposal. 'I request the hand of your daughter Priscilla in marriage.'

'Did you know of this?' Edwin asked, looking at his eldest daughter, and Priscilla fluttered her fan on a pretext of nervousness, wondering how best to flatter him so that he agreed to the request. It could have been delivered with more warmth and sincerity, she thought, aware of Richard's sharp intake of breath as he moved restlessly. Her curiosity was roused as she saw that the hand resting against his velvet doublet trembled from time to time. What had taken place in the stables? The thought that persuasion had been used to make Richard Dacre agree to marry her was humiliating. Did he not know of her many attributes? Could he not see the poise and grace about her that would make other men envy him?

'The moment my brother set eyes on Mistress Priscilla, he declared he would consider no other woman as his wife,' Jason said before she could think of an appropriate answer. 'But, naturally, until he had spoken to you, he could say nothing. I rather suspect we have a love-match here.' Melisande stifled a gasp at the impudent words. Love-match! Nothing could be further from the truth, and he knew it. Whom was he protecting now? Not his brother—and not Father—but himself, again. She would never cease to be amazed at his deviousness and at the way he could lie so blatantly, looking for all the world as if this second marriage pleased him. 'Whispering Wood is well known for the effect it sometimes has on people. Richard has luck on his side. He has not had to wait five years, has he, Edwin?'

He gave a smile, causing Melisande to wonder what exactly had passed between her father and Jason Dacre when they had discussed her marriage contract. Father had certainly not been the same all day—as though he were guarding some precious secret known only to the two of them. What could they share that would make him look so content? She had been a mere child five years ago, not yet fourteen. It was inconceivable that Jason Dacre had glanced even twice at her that night.

'We—we shall have to discuss more personal details,' Edwin said, clearing his throat. Two daughters off his hands in one night! If only Lucy was more co-operative, all his troubles would be over.

'My brother is of independent means and quite capable of supporting your daughter in the manner she is accustomed to.' Jason again took the initiative. Melisande caught a slight dryness in his tone as he mentioned Priscilla's mode of living. He was hinting to her that Richard—for all his faults, whatever they were—was better than remaining at home, watching more chances slip through her fingers until men grew tired of calling. Richard's mouth was a tight angry line, she saw, as if his brother's words had held a deeper, more significant, meaning for him alone. 'However, as this is now a family affair, as well as the dowry I shall provide I am prepared to set aside an additional £2,000 per year for them.'

Priscilla could not believe her ears—all that money as well as a dowry? She would be able to have new clothes and jewels to adorn her white skin and a carriage of her own, monogrammed, naturally. Richard's reluctance to accept her was no longer important. Once she had his name and lovely things to wear, there would be many men willing, if he were not, to pay attention to her. Yet why should he ignore her once his pique had disappeared? He had not ignored her in the garden!

'Well, Priscilla?' Edwin looked at her from beneath short, bushy brows, wishing he could see inside her mind. Something was not right here, but he could not lay his finger on it. Lord Dacre looked pleased with the prospect of his brother marrying, and his daughter, he felt sure, would have made her objections heard if she had had any. Melisande looked strange—almost uncomfortable. He was imagining things. This was a wonderful and most satisfying evening for all concerned. 'Does this young man's proposal appeal to you? Where is your tongue, girl?'

'I am greatly honoured, Father, so much so that words fail me.' Priscilla turned large blue eyes on Richard's stony face and was regarded with a softening of the features, but it was more a grimace than a smile. 'With my father's kind permission, sir, I accept. I shall strive to be a good wife, and I am so pleased that I shall be able to remain close to my dear sister.'

'Close?' Jason's fair brows rose. 'You will not be living here. My brother has a place in London, in a most fashionable district,' he told her coolly. She absorbed the shock without betraying herself. Only the slight narrowing of her eyes told him that she would never forgive him for depriving her of a home at Whispering Wood. 'His manner of life is more suited to London. You will never be dull with Richard.'

Exasperating most of the time, Jason mused, never knowing when a new face would attract Richard's attention—but never dull! And then she would have his gambling habits to contend with. Before the year was out, he suspected that Richard would have lost or squandered all the money that came to him upon his marriage. But it was not his concern. Perhaps his brother would change, though he doubted it—and he no longer cared so long as he never set foot in Whispering Wood again. Nothing and no one must be allowed to disturb the fragile relationship he shared with Melisande.

He became aware of surprise flashing through Melisande's eyes at the sight of his hand resting lightly on one knee. The knuckles were grazed and raw and he quickly folded his arms, concealing it from her. He had left no mark on his brother, save for the faint bruise that was barely perceptible on his chin, knowing that Edwin must suspect nothing amiss. He had used his fists in a cold fury, unleashing months of anger and frustration upon his brother's body until he had lain on the ground begging for mercy. Even then, Jason had found it difficult to restrain the urge to continue the beating.

'You will marry her,' he had said between clenched teeth, and Richard had nodded, knowing that the murderous fury he had aroused would not abate unless he did so. He had gone too far. Damn Jason! Damn Amanda who had been the cause of it all in the beginning! Damn Priscilla de Vere, with her doe eyes and wanton body! He would finish what he had started out in the garden, and afterwards she could go to the devil, for all he cared.

What on earth was he going to tell his mistress, he wondered, alarmed at the thought of the ageing woman, who had kept him totally for the past two years, who might suddenly deprive him of money and the easy life to which he was accustomed when news of this reached her. Like most women when they grew old, she was jealous of every woman prettier than her—and that was almost every one he looked at—but her wealth kept him happy and he, in turn, flattered and lied until he was blue in the face. It was worth it, and Richard was not going to allow a scheming little minx like Priscilla de Vere to ruin his perfect existence! Perhaps things were not as bad as he thought. She was not unattractive, and, as his wife, would have no say in his affairs. If he chose to abandon her for the arms of another, what could she do? Certainly not run home to her father, who wanted to be rid of her. Not to her sister Melisande either; Jason would see to that. She would have nowhere to go and no one to turn to. He was as free as he had always been.

The sudden smile that masked his brother's features made Jason momentarily uneasy. What scheme did he have now? Or was he thinking of the extra income that would provide him with more luxuries? He would have to fight Priscilla for it, he thought humourlessly. She had extravagant tastes, which excelled his, and she was not a woman to take No for an answer. He rose to his feet, wishing the farce ended, and raised his glass. 'May I propose a toast? Happiness and long life to all in this room.'

Edwin beamed at him and then at Melisande. What a fine-looking couple they made! Any doubts he had at first had of Jason Dacre's motives for choosing Melisande had long ago been dispelled by the friendly manner and generous nature of this man. The toast was drunk with enthusiasm by Edwin and Priscilla. Richard's lips crooked into a sardonic grin as he raised his glass in Jason's direction before consuming the contents. An acknowledgement that he had been beaten by a better man? Melisande wondered, as she sipped her wine. How grand the toast had been, but she did not for one moment believe he meant a word of it. Jason's eyes met hers, and she quickly looked away, disturbed by the smouldering gaze.

As she rose to follow the others back into the ballroom, Jason stepped in front of her and, closing the door, stood with his back against it. 'Well? Have my arrangements met with your approval this time?' he asked, and she shrugged slim shoulders.

'What do you want me to say? You have saved my sister from an embarrassing situation—but did you do it for her, or for yourself?' The words were out before she had thought, and he folded his arms across the broad chest as he regarded her.

'Am I to understand that you somehow think all this was for my benefit? How so, Melisande?'

'To protect yourself and your name from scandal. No one in the Queen's favour can risk that, can they?' she returned coolly. Whatever happened, she must not allow him to ruffle her, or she would lose the battle of wills. And she must not let him touch her or kiss her, lest he roused her again and she forgot the deception he had practised on her and on everyone else.

'My dear child, how little you know of me! But that will change after we are married, and soon you will realise what a foolish statement that was,' said Jason, suppressing the anger that still lingered inside him, which threatened to rise again at her thoughtless words. Did she really believe he would allow anyone, even the

Queen of England, to rule his life? He was his own master, like his father before him, and no one gave him orders!

'I do not think I shall ever know you,' Melisande said, stepping back. 'You would never allow it; you never tell me your thoughts . . .' She broke off, as he laughed and followed her to the window, where he pressed her gently down upon the cushioned seat.

'Now tell me why you think such a preposterous thing.'

Melisande ignored the overpoweringly masculine frame that lowered itself beside her and the smiling features so close to hers that she could feel his warm breath on her cheek. She dared not look into those gleaming eyes.

'You should not always allow others to know what is in your mind, Melisande. If you do, you become vulnerable, and sometimes—very often, in fact—that can bring pain and unhappiness. You must learn to wear one face for the outside world and another for those you care about,' Jason murmured softly.

'Is that what you do?' What was he suggesting, that she became like him? 'Which face have I seen so far?'

'Would you recognise the true me? I doubt it,' he replied.

He took the hand nearest to him and raised it to his lips. As he did so, Melisande saw the raw knuckles once again, and her expression grew guarded.

'I am not sure that I like what I have seen so far. I do not like the way you use people, sir.'

'Oh, dear! So formal! I have displeased you.' His amusement grew. 'Here was I believing I had averted a near disaster and how pleased you would be that your father had been spared the unpleasant truth, and now you sound as though it is of no consequence.' The soft voice held an undercurrent of reproach, which brought a flush of colour into her cheeks. Whatever his reasons, he had spared her father, and she was grateful for that. 'Let us say I accept that Priscilla was—overcome—by my brother's worldliness and charm. However, I do not think your father would accept that.'

'You—you are not suggesting that Priscilla planned this, are you?' Melisande gasped, trying to snatch her hand away, but he held it fast. 'You will be accusing me next of trying to entrap you! Everyone else here tonight believes that is so.'

'Yes, I did hear some ugly talk, thanks to your sister. Women can be such vindictive creatures, even to their own. However, we are the only two people that matter —no one else—and we know the truth, don't we? Life for your sister could have become most uncomfortable had the rumours begun about her, and if there is a child . . .'

'A child!' Melisande's eyes showed her disbelief. 'You cannot believe . . . I mean . . . She would never . . .'

'Are you so naïve? Many women have passed through my brother's life, and some may not have been willing to fall blindly into his arms—at first—but a determined man can bring many persuasive forces to bear on the most reticent creature. Your sister was no challenge to him.'

Melisande swallowed hard, wanting to fling the words back in his face although she knew she could not, for they contained more than a grain of truth. 'Amanda was right. You do like to control the lives of others. Hers, your brother's, mine—and now Priscilla's. It is a game with you.'

'A game,' Jason echoed quietly. 'I play no game with you, Melisande. The dreamer in you rebels at accepting me; the woman I have aroused is curious as to the kind of man whose bed she will share. Perhaps I should show you which is the stronger,' Jason murmured, bending closer so that his lips brushed the nape of her neck. She flinched from him, but a steel band about her waist drew her back against his chest. Instinctively she threw up her hands to push him back, only to find them imprisoned as she was drawn more tightly to him. Wicked, devilish lights flickered in the grey pools which devoured her frightened face. She was frightened, there was no denying it. She remembered only too vividly the easy way he had brought her to surrender out in the garden. It must not happen again!

'Look at me,' Jason commanded. She could not. Each moment she was growing more afraid of him and the power he seemed able to exercise over her. He drained her of all will to resist! 'Look at me,' he repeated. Still she did not lift her head, and with a curse, while still holding her immobile within the circle of one arm, he cupped her chin with his free hand and forced back her head. 'That's better. It's always preferable to stare the devil full in the face, especially if you intend to defy him! Little idiot! Come down from the clouds and accept reality. Is it so terrible for me to want you with your feet on the ground and by my side?'

The laughter was suddenly gone from his voice and sunburnt features, and she grew weak as his face drew closer. She tried to struggle against the arm that imprisoned her so closely, but her limbs refused to respond. As he slowly lowered his mouth to hers, she clamped her lips tightly together, resisting him in the only way left to her. Yet even that failed. The moment he realised her intent, she expected force to provoke an answer from her, but Jason had no intention of doing anything that would make her run from him in fear, and imparted into that long-drawn-out, passionate, heart-stopping, numbing kiss, many, many years of knowledge—and Melisande knew that she was lost!

His lips against hers were tender and sweet, yet they scorched her own with fire, parting them, savouring them, dulling her senses like some heady wine.

'I—I am not Priscilla,' she managed to gasp when breath returned.

'No, thank God, you are not!'

Jason altered his hold on her so that she was lying across his chest, her head over one arm. He had no intention of letting her go, she realised half in panic, half in expectancy of another kiss. Pale shadows flickered in the grey depths as his fingers gently stroked her jaw, her cheek, caressed the pink lobe of one ear where a stray curl had fallen loose and brushed his fingers. She could hardly breathe, and she knew it had nothing to do with the tightness of her corset! *He* was doing this to her! This restriction in her throat—her breathing—in the way her dislike of him was receding and now seemed to be totally without foundation.

She quivered as his fingers slid down over the smooth line of her throat, momentarily lingering on the necklace he had placed there and then continued along a bare expanse of shoulder and down to where her breasts rose tantalisingly above the low-cut bodice. Her skin was tingling from every contact, no matter how slight. Every single one was intended to rouse something in her—and it did! Her traitorous body began to relax against his as though it belonged there, and she fought with every fibre of her being, aware of his eyes intent on her face, watching every tiny flicker of emotion that passed across it. She could do nothing against him! She was powerless! She was horrified—ashamed—and yet at the same time aware of a deep excitement welling up from inside her, such as she had never known: a strange ache that needed somehow to be satisfied. But how would that happen?

His mouth sought and found hers again, parting it this time with an insistence that brooked no refusal, and she was unable to deny herself the pleasure he was offering. She had enjoyed the stolen kiss in the garden, never believing that she would ever again experience such ecstasy—but a miracle had happened. She was his! His kisses were hers! He was hers—if only she could bring herself to accept him. He would never allow her to refuse him, she thought, as her hands slid upwards seeking the solidness of his shoulders beneath the velvet doublet, and then rose higher to clasp themselves behind his blond head. But could she ever dismiss from her mind the methods he had employed to make her his wife? The thought rose in her mind to obliterate briefly the sweetness of the moment, and a moan broke from her lips, but died beneath the renewed pressure exerted on them—and all but the fire sweeping through her was forgotten.

Jason felt the change in her, but for a moment he could not draw back as he knew he should. The softness of her body pressing his was as intoxicating as the perfume of her hair or the salve that had been rubbed into her skin. He wanted her! He had always wanted her and no one else, but he had not been prepared for the effect she was having on him. The little innocent . . . Did she not realise what she was doing? He had succeeded with her far beyond what he had intended. It had been his purpose to show her how easily an experienced man could rouse an inexperienced young woman—and that had been achieved. But she also had shown him—albeit unwittingly—something he had not known. She had exposed his own vulnerability!

Melisande never knew the effort it cost him to put her away and casually rise and cross to the decanters on the table. He reached for the brandy; then, acknowledging that he needed a clear head to absorb not only this unexpected shock but to be able to mingle again with his guests, he poured wine for himself and a smaller amount for her.

When he turned back to offer her the glass, she was staring at him with cheeks almost as red as her hair. Never had she been more beautiful or more desirable, Jason thought, as she took the glass in silence and, to his surprise, drank it quickly.

'Retain your dream world, Melisande, if it is so important to you, but make me a part of it, and be sure my bed is never without you.'

'As my husband, I am sure you will ensure that it never is,' she answered, a bitter edge to her tone. He had rendered her defenceless against him, and she knew this was only the first time. She had no armoury left, except perhaps her scorn, and she lashed him with it as she fought to recover her composure. 'You have proved your point, sir. I know nothing of the world, or of men.'

'I shall teach you . . . about me.'

'As you have taught me about myself,' Melisande flung back bitterly. Were all women so weak? She had once thought Priscilla strong, but even she had succumbed to the charms of Richard Dacre—or had she? Did Jason know her sister better than she did?

Rising to her feet, she smoothed her crumpled skirts and raised a self-conscious hand to her hair; then once again she was withdrawn, resenting him and their forthcoming marriage. When he opened the door and offered his arm, she did not refuse, but how she wished she could have slapped that mocking, infuriatingly satisfied smile from his face as he led her back into the other room.

From the moment Melisande returned home, her life began to change. Frequent callers, who had heard of the ball at Whispering Wood and the two projected marriages, besieged the house. Neighbours from Kingsclere and nearby villages who had been frequent visitors until the family money began to dwindle returned to wish the two fortunate sisters well and to take another look at the young woman who had caught the eye—and captured the heart, it seemed—of the most eligible bachelor for miles, and who, within four weeks, would become his wife.

Merchants came with bolts of cloth, sent, they told her, by Lord Dacre for her to choose materials for her wedding gown and trousseau. No sooner had she reluctantly begun to decide than two seamstresses from Whispering Wood, accompanied by two serving-maids and a liveried footman, followed to take measurements and carry the selected materials back to Basing. Suddenly the credit of the de Vere family was no longer in doubt. Merchants and shopkeepers alike vied for the family trade: fresh vegetables, eggs, poultry and the like were delivered—and no account demanded.

Melisande had no doubt that Jason Dacre was behind everything. Was this another way by which he was demonstrating his power over her? Priscilla, at first annoyed that none of the attention was paid to her—the merchants and seamstresses were quite adamant that they had come only to attend to Melisande herself, that her wishes must take priority—found consolation through providing for herself in style, something she had been unable to do for several years. Ribbons, jewellery, new leather shoes arrived at the house in great quantities, and she engaged a local seamstress to begin making her a new wardrobe.

When Melisande questioned her extravagance, she was dismissed with the casual comment that Lord Dacre was taking care of everything—and could well afford it. She dreaded to think of the amount that was accumulating. Even Lucy rose to the occasion and allowed herself to be persuaded to several new dresses. As the days passed, Melisande tried hard to accept what was happening to her, but without success. Nothing seemed real any more.

'Sandy . . . Here you are! Father is calling for you. You have a visitor.' Lucy came into her sister's bedchamber to find her curled up in a chair, her head in her hands. 'Are you unwell?'

'No. A visitor?' Another merchant eager to make a handsome profit, she thought idly. How people changed when money was plentiful! Where had all these so-called friends been when they had been needed? It increased her frustration. 'Who?'

'Why, Lord Dacre! And he has brought you a present! Oh, Sandy, you are lucky.'

'You can be his wife instead of me, if you think that,' Melisande retorted, and her sister drew back, a hurt expression on her face. Instantly she was contrite. 'I am sorry. I must not take out my ire on you.'

'What is it?' Lucy asked, kneeling by the chair. 'Tell me. You know all my secrets.'

'I have none from you, either . . . I do not want to be his wife, that's all. Not in this way.'

'In what way, Sandy? Has he not shown you his great regard by all the things he has done for us, and for

Father? I have not seen him so happy since Mother died. He feels as if his troubles have been solved overnight.'

'As they have,' Melisande replied with a frown. 'He thinks his money can buy anything—even people.'

'Perhaps it is given in love,' Lucy murmured. 'Why do you believe it is so hard for a man to fall in love with you?'

'No man has approached me since we became penniless,' she was reminded, and a smile lit up the plump features.

'*He* has!'

And everything she now had and would have in the future would be paid for by Jason Dacre. That thought did not dispel Melisande's despondent mood. With a sigh, she rose and accompanied her sister downstairs. She and she alone must bear the burden of knowing the truth: that so long as she obeyed Lord Dacre in all things and remained a true and obedient wife, her father, and presumably her whole family, would want for nothing. It was not pleasant.

'Melisande, my dear, you are looking so pale these days. You have not caught a chill, have you?' Edwin looked quite concerned at his daughter's pale cheeks and lustreless eyes. She should have been radiant, brimming over with enthusiasm about the wedding. What a grand affair it would be! Held in the chapel at Whispering Wood, it was to be attended by over two hundred guests from as far afield as London, Southampton and even Plymouth. His thoughts were of his dead wife and her prophecy as he drew Melisande to him and kissed a wan cheek. She trembled slightly, and that was not like her. Excitement, he supposed, drawing back and turning to the man who had risen when she entered the room.

'I shall leave the two of you alone, as I am sure you have much to discuss,' he said, and ushered Lucy out of the room before him.

Melisande felt her whole body stiffen as Jason came to stand before her the moment the door had closed behind them. Slowly she raised her head, determined not to be intimidated by the forceful nature of this man, but the moment their eyes met and locked, the challenge was there once again—and she knew she would lose.

'You look as if you are about to attend a funeral, not a wedding,' Jason said, perturbed by her lack of colour.

'Perhaps that is how I feel.' She regretted the words instantly, for his arms reached out and clasped her. 'No,' she protested. 'My father . . .'

'I am but greeting my bride-to-be,' he chuckled softly, and kissed her with ardour. She hung suspended in his embrace like a rag doll. 'Do you need to be reminded of what I am offering, Melisande? Or is it perhaps that you are growing to enjoy my kisses and are too shy to tell me?'

'You must stop this . . .' she protested, referring to the money he was willing to pay out for her family. It was too humiliating. Could he not understand how she felt?

'Stop what? Kissing you? I enjoy it, and you do also, if only you would be honest with yourself.' He kissed her again, and when he drew back was pleased to see a faint blush returning. Four short days, yet it had seemed like weeks: never had he missed a woman so, and he had not even bedded her yet! Nor would he until their wedding day. Much as it pained him and drained his self-control when he was with her like this, he would not anticipate their wedding night. It would be a night of nights, and there would never be another to match it! 'Are you not pleased with all the materials I have had sent to you and the other things you will need for your trousseau? Mistress Agnes was my mother's seamstress, and she was very disappointed at your lack of enthusiasm. Most women love fine clothes and jewels, and jump at the chance of having them.'

'I was thinking of the cost,' Melisande told him.

'To whom? To me? A trifle! You shall have everything you want; I have promised that.'

'To me,' she replied, and the smile upon his face hid

the jolt of her words. Did the little idiot think he was trying to buy her? Heaven forbid!

'Melisande, why are you still fighting me? Will you not accept that my desire to have you as my wife is all-important to me. Your family I now regard as my own, therefore anything I can do to help them, I shall. What a strange little thing you are! Am I so replusive to you? I think not; at least, that is not the impression you gave me the other night.'

'You set out to prove a point, sir, and you succeeded,' Melisande retorted.

'Could you not say "Jason" as nastily as you say "sir" or "Lord Dacre"?' he chuckled, and she knew her anger was having no effect on him. He was impossible! 'Come and see what I have brought you.'

Taking her hand, he led her outside and through the side gate that opened on to the meandering path to the village. Tethered to the wall was his own black stallion, the one she had seen him ride at Whispering Wood, and beside it a smaller mare, whose coat gleamed in the sunlight and was as red as . . .

'Does this gift also displease you?' Jason asked, and he knew it did not by the warmth which came suddenly into her face. 'You did mention that you like to ride. She's not as docile as she looks, but I feel sure you can handle her.'

Melisande stroked the glossy coat, and the mare nuzzled her affectionately. Her own horse again! As she lifted her head and gazed across the fields and cottages to the rolling distant hills, it was not difficult for Jason to guess her train of thought.

'The downs are but a short distance away. Ride with me, Melisande.'

She could not refuse. To be free of the house and all its noisy activities for a while! To feel the wind in her hair, the sense of freedom she had missed these past hectic days. Yet dared she? Was she not playing into his hands by accepting his gift, proclaiming that it pleased her?

'Thank you, sir. I will ride with you, if you will give me

a moment to find something suitable to wear.'

'I am prepared to give you ten whole minutes, so long as you begin calling me "Jason"!'

'As you wish.' She turned and ran indoors as if her feet had suddenly developed wings, his amused banter no longer bothering her. For a while at least she could be herself again . . . and her misery vanished.

'Did you enjoy your ride with Lord Dacre?' Lucy asked, as they sat together in her room drinking hot chocolate before retiring for the night.

'I did indeed.' Melisande's cheeks still bore a healthy glow, and her eyes were brighter than when she had left the house. As though a great weight had been lifted from her mind, her sister thought. 'I had forgotten how good it felt to be on horseback. It has been so long.'

'Lord Dacre seemed most attentive, I thought.'

'Did you?' Melisande turned questioning eyes on her sister. 'And where, may I ask, were you?'

'On London's Hill. Christopher and I watched you for almost an hour.' Lucy giggled, remembering how astonished she had been to see her sister being kissed quite ardently and without protest.

'You crept out of the house to meet that young man again,' Melisande declared, hoping that the reproach in her voice disguised the embarrassment she felt at knowing she had been seen in Jason's arms. 'Father will be very angry.'

'Lord Dacre has spoken to him again—he told me so before I went out. I have promised Father that I shall meet any young man he cares to invite to the house, and in return he has promised not to force me into a choice —I have until after Priscilla's wedding to decide on a husband.'

'And will you?' Melisande asked, not liking the easy way Lucy had accepted the ultimatum.

'Who knows what will happen by the time Priscilla is wed?' came the answer, which added to her concern.

They kissed and said good night, and Melisande went

to her room, but sleep evaded her for many hours. No sooner did she close her eyes than she felt strong arms close about her as they had done that afternoon, and a determined mouth parted hers until her senses reeled and she sank against that broad chest in silent surrender. Her eyes flew open and she sat up, clutching the bed-clothes to her, as if afraid he was standing at the end of the bed, watching her, whispering her name, drawing her to him like a spider watching a helpless fly threshing on its web of destruction.

What nonsense! She was allowing him to unnerve her with such silly notions. Then why was it, when she lay back and closed her eyes again, that it was his face which came out of the darkness to mock her? Why could she feel the heat of his body against hers? Feel the hardness of his lips?

CHAPTER SIX

WAS THIS REALLY happening, Melisande thought, catching her breath as more gifts were deposited on the long table before her. Already it was well covered with presents of every size and description. Some were simple offerings from the villagers and people who worked on the estate, such as fresh fruit and flowers, a saddle for her mare and a beautifully carved cradle. The latter had brought a fierce blush to her cheeks as she caught Jason's amused eyes on her. Was that the reason everyone suspected they had wed in such haste? They did not know her—or him! He did not have to go to those extremes to take himself a wife.

And then there were richer, more elegant, gifts for the bride and groom. Cut-glass Venetian goblets, pewter tankards, and plate, colourful tapestries for the walls. Kitchen items, linen, everything a woman could think of to begin a new home. Everyone had been exceedingly generous, she realised. Because they liked her, or because they liked Jason—or perhaps because they wished to impress him? She had not realised what a powerful figure he was in the county and the sway he held in so many matters. Among the guests who came to the masque now in progress after the wedding formalities were the most prominent men and women for miles around: lords and their ladies, even earls! And she was sure she had heard someone mention that somewhere in the crowd was Sir Francis Drake himself! It was implied that he had come to try to persuade Lord Dacre to captain *Moonwynd* personally and accompany him on the voyage he was undertaking into Spanish waters, to attack and capture more treasure ships with which he hoped to fill the coffers of the Queen of England, and in return she would sanction the building of new ships, bigger and better armed men-of-war, to confront the Spanish foe. It was Drake's intention that no English man—or woman—would ever forget the great Armada that had come to destroy their country. Next time, he had vowed, they would not reach the Channel!

Melisande's heartbeats quickened at the thought of her husband sailing into enemy waters. It was a dangerous undertaking. How strange, she mused. She had thought of him as such without hesitation, and they had been wed less than four hours, but she was determined she would never accept him as her lord and master. Not after the way he had forced her into the marriage.

Had anyone other than Jason noticed her quietness? If they had, she hoped they would attribute it to nerves on such a special occasion, for she did not want to embarrass her father by arousing speculation that all was not as it should be. She had indeed been seized with an unwonted nervousness as she lay in a scented bath that morning. Their father had insisted, prompted by Jason, she suspected, that they all spend the night before the wedding at Whispering Wood. Did Jason think she might take flight? How she wished she had the courage to do so. Yet, while part of her wanted to flee the man who would claim her as his wife that night, and the bargain she had made for her father and sisters, there lingered in her a desire to know more of this strange man, so forceful and ruthless in his determination to have her. She should have been flattered.

He had been most generous with gifts of jewellery and the like, which unfortunately only increased her suspicions that he intended to try to buy her affection—or at least her willingness to comply with his every wish. When they were alone, he never lost an opportunity to kiss her, and despite her attempts to remain unaffected by that burning mouth which devasted hers, each time he did so she felt herself losing a little more of her self-control. His manner with her was always pleasant and friendly—sometimes too friendly for a betrothed couple—but there were moments when she noticed a certain hardness in the depths of those grey eyes that watched her constantly, as though he was aware that beneath her air of meekness and docility lay an inner rebellion that one day he would have to curb.

From beneath lowered lashes she stole a look at the man who sat at her side, laughing at the mummers who had come from Newbury to entertain them. He was everything a young girl could ever want—the embodiment of all fanciful dreams. How young he looked, when he smiled and the hard line of his mouth softened and deepened into a boyish grin that could capture any heart. Except hers, she reminded herself fiercely. Yet she could not deny that he was the handsomest man she had ever met, and in his wedding apparel he did come very close to the prince of her dream world. He had drawn the eyes of every woman present with the magnificence of it. His doublet and trunk hose were of white velvet, slashed with inserts of white silk. The half cloak carelessly draped over one shoulder was lined with pale grey silk and threaded with gold. The sword hanging low at one side rested in a jewelled scabbard, as did the long dagger with its jewel-encrusted hilt. The blond hair had been meticulously trimmed, but still a few fair curls still rested at the nape of his neck just above the wide lace collar, which was the latest style from London and fast replacing for many gentlemen the high, often uncomfortable, ruff.

Jason turned and looked at her, and Melisande realised he had been fully aware of her scrutiny. The smile playing on his lips was mocking her interest, and in return he slowly considered his bride.

Melisande's wedding gown was of pale ivory satin and lace, the high ruff which had been cleverly shaped to follow the line of the very low neckline that left bare much of her shoulders and the rise of her full breasts. This was the very latest thing at court, she had been told by Mistress Agnes, the dressmaker from Whispering Wood, who had insisted that all Melisande's trousseau must be of the latest designs and materials as now befitted her station. She had been completely in the woman's hands and, in the end, had secretly enjoyed the attention lavished on her and the knowledge that her wardrobe could now rival that of any great lady at court. Was she growing like Priscilla—her head turned by such material things? Yet it was so nice to feel silk against her skin again. How she wished her mother had lived to see this day.

She noticed that his gaze lingered for more than a brief while on her bare shoulders and the necklace of opals about her throat, before dropping to force bright colour into her cheeks. The mass of red hair was piled on to the crown of her head, with just a few curls hanging loose above the pearl-studded ruff. Rose had brushed it until it shone, and had confessed, when Melisande had questioned her adeptness and competence at such a young age, that her mother had been maid to the late Lady Dacre and had taught her all she knew.

Without a word, Jason reached out to take her hand and touch it to his lips. Her fingers were ringless, he noted, apart from one simple little emerald ring, and the gold-engraved band he had placed there earlier. 'Why are you not wearing something that I sent you?' he asked quietly, remembering the huge cabochon ruby among the others he had given her.

'I did not want people to think I was marrying you for your money only,' Melisande replied in a low whisper. 'I am well content with what I have. This belonged to my mother.'

'As the jewels I sent you belonged to mine. Please wear them, Melisande.' It sounded like a request, but she saw from the darkening of his eyes that it was more, and gave a faint nod. Immediately he smiled again, and wicked lights flickered amid the charcoal embers. 'Even without them, there is not a woman here to match you! I do not think you realise how beautiful and desirable you are. When I take you to London and present you at court, I shall be damned lucky not to fight a duel over you every other week! I warn you, I am a very jealous man, and I shall not take kindly to others ogling you.'

'At court!' Melisande whispered in sudden awe. *She* was to be presented at court! Almost immediately the exciting prospect was curtailed, spoiled by his words. 'If you are so afraid of other men looking at me, do not take me. What do I care?'

'You shall have no less than your sister, but, unlike her, I suspect you will not enjoy the glitter and falseness that prevails at court. You will see beneath the flattering smiles, and hear something more in the soft, welcoming voices,' Jason said, watching her face.

'You credit me with an intelligence I do not possess. You have forced me to accept reality—and I shall continue to do so.'

'I have not destroyed your dream world,' he reproved, bending closer so that no one else could overhear their conversation. 'Time has done that—and the woman in you that wishes to be done with foolish, girlish, fancies. Let me free the woman, Melisande. Let her satisfy my needs as I know only she can do!'

She could lose herself in the depths of those grey pools, Melisande thought, dragged down into their dark, unknown depths, floundering, helpless . . . Yet was it not what she wanted? When he spoke to her so boldly, she almost believed he meant every word. Satisfy his needs? And what she did not, his mistress in London would. She had not forgotten the other woman in his life, although he had never mentioned her and she had not dared to broach the subject. He knew she had no interest in the court, so what was his true reason for taking her to London? So that he could again meet his mistress? But why go to the trouble of taking along his wife, when he could so easily leave her at Whispering Wood? He confused her at every turn . . .

He wanted the best of both worlds, like most men. A wife to grace his fine home and bear his children—and another woman to share his bed—and his heart, perhaps. Melisande had not thought very much about that side of her marriage . . . Secretly, she was terrified of the thought of having a baby. Although her parents had been very much in love, she had never forgotten the insidious malady that had sapped her mother's strength until that final time when both she and the baby boy she had been carrying died within a few hours of each other. Six long months of carrying new life inside her, nurturing it with love and care, only to bring forth a child that could not breathe properly. Melisande had listened to her mother praying to God for its life, even if it meant sacrificing her own, but her prayers had gone unanswered. The fragile little thing had died, and so had she. Three daughters, strong and healthy, but six children either dead before their term or within hours or their birth. Life had not dealt kindly with her mother.

Would she herself bear a healthy child, Melisande wondered, withdrawing her hand and returning it to her lap. She could not longer withstand Jason's searching eyes, and lowered her own. She had no reason to suppose she would not—but how that memory of her mother haunted her!

Jason saw something near to fear flickering in her eyes, and was concerned. Be patient, he told himself. She is yours now. Be patient and reap the reward of being so, for when she became his totally, he knew his restraint would have been worth while. She was still a child in so many ways, although to look at her on her wedding day, few would realise it. She portrayed the picture of a full-bodied, exciting woman, unaware of her beauty, unsure of the capabilities he felt dwelt inside her. She needed to be given confidence, to be drawn out of the safe little world in which she had lived for so long. He would protect her now! He hoped she would accept that soon.

Thomas, the steward, bent to whisper in his ear, and he nodded, but held up a hand to detain the man as he turned to Melisande. 'There is much food left over; far more than the company here can eat tonight,' he murmured. 'What do you wish done with it? Shall it be returned to the kitchens?'

For a moment she was startled by the question, and then she accepted that, as mistress of the house, she was now in charge of such mundane decisions: from this moment on they would be an everyday part of her married life. She was not surprised that there was food to spare. The wedding breakfast could have fed three times the number of guests. Everyone had launched with great relish into the sliced mutton cooked on an outside spit and basted with its own juices and wine. Side-dishes of rabbit, pigeons and pheasant had been attacked with equal vigour. There were hundreds of pastries, and fresh fruit from the estate gardens, covered with cream. Rye bread, baked that morning, with golden butter. Drink in abundance: beer, and an assortment of wines. More than a few of those present had already eaten and drunk too much, and had disappeared from the proceedings to recover.

If she was to be a frugal wife, Melisande knew the food should be returned to the kitchens and put to good use for further meals. Many people would remain for several days at Whispering Wood, needing to be fed, and she had no doubt that the cook was a past mistress at making over the odds and ends. And then, through the open door of the hall where they were sitting, she saw the villagers and estate workers still gathered watching the dancing, and heard the merriment going on inside the house. As she then surveyed the full table before her, the simple gifts laid with love amid the others, she made a bold decision and prayed it was the right one. Thomas was still at her husband's side, impassive as always, yet she sensed that he was waiting with some interest for her answer . . . waiting to see how the new mistress would conduct herself.

'We must ensure that our guests have sufficient, of course, but I have already seen the energy and enthusiasm expounded in your kitchens and I am sure that cook will rise to any occasion. I shall leave Thomas to see to this, and the remainder of the food shall be distributed to the villagers. Their gifts have given me great pleasure, and I would like them also to enjoy this day.'

Was that approval she saw on Thomas's face? When he had moved away, Jason leaned close to her again, a warm glow in his eyes.

'Beneath the ice, is there a warm heart? Am I less than one of my own villagers that I am not allowed to benefit from it, too?' he mocked gently. It was customary after such a grand occasion that the surplus was sent to the poor and needy, and to his workers. He could have ordered it without consulting her, but he had wanted to involve her from the very beginning with everything that went on at Whispering Wood . . . and she had not disappointed him with her answer. How would Priscilla have reacted? he wondered, as she blushed and quickly looked away. Similarly—but as a magnanimous gesture that she hoped would bring her popularity and respect. Both things had to be earned, as did loyalty. Melisande, with one simple well-meant gesture, had endeared everyone to her. There would not be a man or woman who would not remember this day and thank her for her thoughtfulness, for that was what it was. She did not seek to curry favour. She thought of others, since she herself had experienced the distress of poverty and so understood it. Her pride remained, as it did in the common people. So few understood that. Pride was the backbone of England, be it peasant, merchant, gentleman or lady, or Queen! Pride held England together.

The hall was cleared for dancing, and for the first time in that strange, unreal day Melisande did feel like a princess as Jason led her out on the floor to lead the guests in the first of many lively measures. It had been so long since she had last danced—and with such a handsome man at her side, how could she not enjoy herself! When they rested, he brought her cool wine and stayed at her side, only once or twice leaving her to take another partner. She danced with Richard, and hated the way he held her hand too tightly and the boldness of his eyes. In a few weeks he was to marry her sister, yet he looked at her as if . . .

Melisande was pleased that Amanda, too, seemed to have put aside whatever was troubling her and appeared to be enjoying herself, dancing with any young man who asked her. She noticed Jason's eyes watching her throughout the evening, but he did not object to any of her partners and the three of them chatted quite amicably together. She was young, Melisande decided, and as rebellious at her guardian's strictness as Lucy was of their father's insistence that she marry a man of his choice. She hoped that soon they would become friends, as she had with Lucy.

'My lady . . .' Thomas was at her side when she sat down to regain her breath. The man looked almost apologetic, and she looked up at him in surprise. 'There is a child outside . . . with another gift, but I am not sure . . .'

'A child? Bring her to me,' Melisande said smilingly. More wild flowers: she must have been presented with at least a dozen bunches. How sweetly they smelled, and so many different varieties. She had never forgotten her long excusions into the fields to pick her mother bright red poppies, which she used in a herbal sleeping-potion, or honeysuckle to make the rooms smell fragrant. How she missed her wise counsel and companionship!

Jason turned to watch curiously as a little mite of not more than five was led into the room clutching something black against her worn, patched dress. Her eyes were large and as blue as cornflowers, her smile mischievous, yet appealing and heart-warming.

'She is Rose's daughter,' Thomas informed Melisande, while the child's eyes grew wider as she considered the exquisitely gowned woman who smiled down at her. 'A love-child, my lady. Cared for by her grandmother. They have very little . . .'

And yet the old rogue had deliberately allowed the child to come to the house with a wedding present! Jason thought to himself. His steward was testing the worth of the new mistress of Whispering Wood in more ways than one. Ordinarily, she would never have been allowed past the door . . . and for Thomas to approach his wife on such a triviality was out of the question.

The black object clutched in the tiny hands moved uncomfortably, and mewed. Melisande's eyes shone at the furry thing held out to her, and she gently took the black, bone-thin kitten and placed it on her lap. A kitten! Scrawny, undernourished, as was the child who had brought it, she thought, with pale grey eyes shaped almost like almonds. Without a sound it curled up on her skirts and placed its head beneath one paw.

Melisande drew the little girl to her, and to the surprise of many, placed a kiss upon one pale, thin cheek.

'I do not think I have ever had such a lovely gift! I shall treasure it always . . .'

'Him,' Jason whispered. 'He's a tomcat, and in years to come he will keep you awake galloping across the roofs at night and wailing for someone to keep him company. You don't have to keep him.' But he knew she would, and the knowledge pleased him.

'I shall call him—Merlin!' Melisande declared, and Jason burst into uncontrollable laughter.

'He will be no match for me, my sweet, if that is what you are hoping for! No wizard's sorcery or fairy-tale world shall keep us apart. Thomas, take the animal and have him bathed, and then find something for him to sleep in. Take the child, too, and give her a cake; such a worthy gift is deserving of the best. Send something back to the grandmother, too . . . Take it yourself and see how great their needs are. Perhaps we can help in some other way.'

'That was kind of you,' Melisande said, and the twist to his lips became mocking.

'I acknowledge that I have a responsibility to all these people,' he returned, 'but it is not always possible to do as much as I would like. I have sufficient money to provide for this house and the estate. My parents were each wealthy in their own right, and when I sailed with

Drake, I did not return home empty-handed. But I hope to live to a ripe old age, Melisande, and I shall always have these responsibilities, therefore I must plan well ahead. This estate eats money, as you can imagine. If anything should happen to me, I must be certain that you, my wife, are well provided for. You—and your family,' he added meaningfully. Why did he have to add that and spoil everything, she thought with chagrin. Always she was being reminded of her role in all this! If just once he had allowed her to forget what she had done—what *he* had done—she might have been able to accept her lot. It would be *so* easy . . .

'I am fully aware of the extra responsibilities you have taken on,' she replied in a frosty tone. 'I do not need to be forever reminded.'

'That was not my intention.' Jason frowned, realising that he had again upset the delicate balance between them. 'I simply wanted to warn you against allowing yourself to become too emotionally involved. Rose's daughter is a sweet little thing; her grandmother is in her seventies and, if I remember correctly, a veritable tyrant. She turned Rose out of the house after the child was born and she came to work here with her mother . . . But she retained the baby and has cared for her since that day. Of course she is in need; of course she cannot care for the child as her real mother would.'

'Would it not be feasible to allow Rose to care for her own child, here?' Melisande suggested. 'It need not interfere with her duties. The smith has a son about her age, and there are many other children for her to play with.'

'And deprive the old woman—who, for all her faults, has cared for the child well—of perhaps the last thing she loves in the world. No! I shall not allow you to bring her into this house, and that is final.' There was a sudden harshness in his voice that took her aback. Why was he so opposed to the suggestion? He would rarely see the little thing. A love-child, Thomas had said, born out of wedlock. Was the father a village man, or one who worked at Whispering Wood? Melisande's fingers closed tightly round her lace fan as she encountered the anger deep in those grey eyes. He would not relent, she could see that—and she did not want to think what his reason was for such an unreasonable decision. He had a mistress in London; did he also amuse himself with the servant-girls in the household, as so many gentlemen did, taking their moments of pleasure and abandoning the poor girls afterwards with a piece of silver for what they had lost, the shame they must bear and the unwanted child which would be reared in ignorance of its true parentage! As if that was compensation enough! How could she even think him capable of such a thing! Yet if he did not wish to allow it, he would not, and that would be that.

Slowly Melisande nodded. 'I shall, of course, obey you in this.' In her eyes blazed magnificent fire, challenging the command, angered by it, frustrated by the reason behind it.

If it came to a confrontation between them it would be wild, explosive, total commitment on both sides to what they considered was right, Jason thought—knowing instinctively that he would win. But what an encounter it would be! To see her fully roused, fighting for something she believed in regardless of the consequences. He suspected that was how it would be, for she had little regard for herself, only for others. Their needs, their desires, their dreams—and yet he knew she had dreams of her own . . . How could he awaken them in his favour?

The moment of tension hovering between them was broken as a well-dressed man threaded his way through the dancers to where they sat, and put down on the table a full pitcher of wine and three goblets. Melisande noticed how many eyes followed him and that fans fluttered more quickly. Her guess that this must be the legendary Francis Drake, scourge of the Spanish Main, was confirmed as he stood back, put his hands on his hips and said in a voice that almost drowned out the music,

'You did it! I never thought I'd see the day. I'm damned if I did!'

'I'm damned if I did myself,' Jason laughed, rising to clasp the man in a warm embrace. 'But the knot is tied. Come, meet my bride.'

'Why do you think I am here, lad, but to meet this extraordinary creature that has captured the best sailor —apart from myself—in this country, and to drink the health of you both?'

'Are you sure there is no ulterior motive, such as an attempt to steal some of my men to go with you on your next campaign?' Jason suggested with a raised brow. He made light of the question, knowing exactly why Drake had come.

The weatherbeaten features split into a wide grin as Francis Drake filled the goblets with deep red wine. As he held one out to her, he scrutinised her as though he was still puzzled—or perturbed—by the suddenness of his friend's marriage. He was a handsome man despite his fifty and two years, straight of back with a proud carriage. His sacque coat was of rich burgundy silk with the slashed sleeves picked out in cloth of gold, and breeches to match. His beard was meticulously trimmed, as was the curled moustache that gave him rather a piratical appearance. 'El Draque', the devil incarnate to the Spaniards he sailed against, was a veritable sea-monster who could not be destroyed. Melisande liked him, and decided that beneath the awesome mantle surrounding him was a very humane man. No one with such warm, brown eyes could have done all the terrible things attributed to him over the years.

'Your health, Lady Dacre.' He drank deeply without taking his gaze from her for one second. 'I hope you know that you have deprived me of a needed sailing companion. Men like this I cannot do without.'

'Your loss is my gain, sir,' Melisande returned, acknowledging the toast, but barely sipping her wine. She had drunk far too much already, she thought, remembering how glass after glass of Malmsey and claret had been pressed into her hands by well-wishers. She was tired beyond belief, and the evening had not yet started.

'A heartless creature,' Drake said with a grimace, and Jason refilled his goblet, chuckling as he did so. 'I know you would have sailed with me this time if you had not met this fascinating creature. I can't say I blame you, though!'

'You shall have *Moonwynd* as I promised, and I shall find a trustworthy captain to sail her. My men are always at your disposal, you know that,' Jason assured him.

'We shall be away one short year.' Drake looked at him with a mock frown of annoyance, knowing that this man would not change his mind once it was made up, but determined to let him know how valuable his services would have been. There was a strange rapport between them that it had existed from the first time they had sailed together, when Jason had been little more than a lad, learning from his father the ways of the sea. He had taken to it as Drake had, instinctively, with a manner that brought men to him no matter how difficult the circumstances, kept them at his side and brought them safely home. But, unlike Drake, Jason Dacre could return to dry land and be equally as content on his estate. Two different worlds, and he was able to live in both. Drake envied him that. Not many men were so lucky—or so strong willed. 'The Queen has jointly commissioned John Hawkins and myself to undertake a large-scale raid on the Caribbean. I don't think she trusts me,' he added, indicating to Jason that the partnership was not a happy one. The two men had not sailed together since San Juan de Ulua in 1568, and Hawkins was no longer in his prime, unlike his cousin, and for many years had been plagued by misfortune which had all but broken a once fine spirit.

'Do you sack Panama?' Jason asked, a momentary excitement rising inside him as he considered the prospect that had always been one of Drake's schemes, although not considered a good proposition by the Queen herself. He had always wanted to take Panama and hold it as an English stronghold.

'Alas, no. She still refuses me that, but she is providing six of the finest warships England possesses and investing over £30,000 to make our venture a success. It will be! By God, it will be! Think of it, lad. One year only—she has tied us to that time. We must be back in Plymouth no later than May of next year. Think of those twelve months, the ships we shall take . . . the rewards . . .'

'I am thinking of it,' Jason murmured, turning to look at Melisande, a deep glow in his eyes. 'And of what I could miss during those twelve months. They would be the loneliest of my life, and no rewards could be great enough to compensate me for them.'

'The man is bewitched . . . He has taken leave of his senses!' Drake snorted in disgust. 'Here I am, come all this way . . .' And then he smiled again, the moment of rancour gone. 'Have it your own way. Your ship will come home laden with riches enough for you. By then, I suppose you'll be bouncing a fine strong son on your knees.'

'Riches of a different kind,' Jason answered, realising with a start how wonderful that moment would be. A son born of his union with Melisande . . . Beauty and strength—independence—and wilfulness—so many conflicting characteristics would they bestow on their children. He would enjoy the years ahead, watching his family grow to maturity. He would never attempt to mould them in his image or allow Melisande to do likewise. Life would do all that was necessary. He could offer advice, but never dictate. Good heavens, he thought, here he was thinking like a father already, and he had not yet discovered the charms of his young wife! 'Besides, my brother Richard is to be married next month to a sister of my wife, and we are knee deep in preparations for that, too. I could not leave Whispering Wood just now.'

'Marry! Him!' Drake ejaculated. 'How did you bring that miracle about? I expected that young fool to end his days at the blade of some irate husband.'

'Let us say that, this time, he went too far,' Jason replied, his voice dropping so that it did not carry beyond the two of them.

'Lucky for you that there was no scandal to reach the ears of the Queen! Casual affairs are not her favourite topic since Raleigh seduced her maid-of-honour Bess Throckmorton. Poor man—he didn't deserve the Tower.'

'It's a whim. She has had many in the past when someone injured her pride. It will pass, and he'll soon be free and back at court in her favour. Mark my words.'

Was that the reason behind Jason's desire for Richard to marry in haste, Melisande wondered? To avoid a scandal which could harm his position in the Queen's favour at court? A precarious position, from what she had heard, when a man could be cast into the dreaded Tower for daring to marry the woman he loved!

'My blessings on you both.' Francis Drake drained his goblet and stepped away, waving a hand to someone who stood back out of sight. 'And those of the Queen, who speeded me on my way here with her good wishes also. She expects to receive you and your wife soon at court. She has sent gifts for the bride and groom.'

Melisande caught her breath at the jewel-studded silver-backed mirror and brush that were laid on the table by a servant, together with four exquisite porcelain pots to hold perfume. For Jason, there was a heavy gold ring set with an enormous sapphire.

'And entertainment,' Drake added, raising his hand again. Immediately, the musicians fell silent and the dancers moved to one side of the room. A band of gaily dressed men and women appeared, not ordinary mummers, Melisande saw, and was instantly intrigued. 'May I present to you a humble group of entertainers from London? They are fast becoming in demand there and are much favoured by the Queen herself. Their leader is

Will Shakespeare, the tall man on the right. They will perform something he has written himself.'

'You are leaving?' Jason asked, as Drake turned to go, and the man nodded apologetically. 'Surely you have time to watch the play?'

'I wish to be in Plymouth as soon as possible. I plan to sail, God willing, before the end of August, and there is much to be done. Come and see us off . . . By then, you might have changed your mind.' The words were accompanied by a faint smile that told Jason he knew that would not happen and deeply regretted the absence of a good friend and worthy seaman alongside him on the voyage. 'As for young Will's plays, they are for lovers, not old men like me.'

They clasped hands for a long moment, then Drake turned and left them and Jason returned to his seat. Although he showed no sign of it and had vehemently insisted that he did not wish to sail to the Caribbean, Melisande suspected that his thoughts were far removed from the lively and often funny play that was performed for them, which brought great clapping and enthusiastic cheers from the many guests.

Will Shakespeare at her wedding feast! She could not believe it! And sent by the Queen herself! The honour did not go unnoticed in the crowded room. Particularly by Priscilla, who was beginning to wonder if she might also be extended the same honour. Richard was, after all, Jason's brother, and therefore he should be afforded similar courtesies. He had laughed when she suggested it, but she had not been dismayed, vowing to make her own wedding day even more spectacular than her sister's. What Melisande could do, she would do better. What Melisande had been given, she would receive in greater abundance. The silly little ninny was tongue-tied at the honour paid her, and remained seated, with bright red cheeks because everyone was talking about her. Priscilla had more decorum than that! She would show her how to act—and all those others fawning about her. If they wished to be a part of her close circle of friends, they had better start paying attention to her now, she decided. She would remember, and discard those who did not.

Melisande realised that the time has come for her to leave the celebrations. She had been aware, although she had pretended otherwise, of Jason looking at her with an unspoken question in his eyes. It was well into the early hours of the morning, and it would be at least another hour before she had been extricated from her wedding gown and petticoats, her hair brushed, her skin perfumed and then covered by the pastel silk nightgown and robe that Rose had laid out on the bed ready for her return. An hour before Jason came to claim what he had bought.

'You look tired, Sandy.' Lucy stood before her, her face flushed with wine, her hair awry from dancing. Her eyes twinkled as she looked from one to the other. 'Never before have I seen such reluctance for lovers to be together. You were not like this on London's Hill!'

'Lucy!' Melisande gasped, as Jason smothered a chuckle. He might not care that they had been seen, but she did.

'Do not mistake shyness for reluctance,' he murmured. 'The natural shyness of a young bride, which I suggest, if you possessed just a little of it, would make you more of an appealing prospect rather than the wilful little thing you are.'

'Oh!' Lucy's lips pouted, but she did not really mind his telling her that she was not all that she should be—not when he did it so nicely.

'Go with your sisters,' Jason murmured. The fingers he touched lightly to his mouth were trembling. Turning them over, he planted a gentle kiss upon Melisande's palm. 'I shall not keep you waiting long, my sweet,' he promised.

It was not until Melisande rose to her feet that she found she was to be escorted upstairs not only by Priscilla and Lucy, but also by a surprisingly friendly Amanda and several other women guests. Their clatter fell on deaf ears, their suggestions also. How to be a good wife and mother . . . that if she placed a special herb beneath her pillow on her wedding night she would bear a son within nine months . . . how to deal with an unfaithful husband . . . By the time Lucy had managed to usher them all out, except for herself and Priscilla, Melisande felt near to tears. Advice was not what she wanted, but courage—a great deal of courage to see her through this night and all the nights to come. When Jason touched her, she knew she would forget all that had passed between them and allow him to do what he wished with her. It would not matter at that moment if she had been bought or not . . . Nothing would matter, but in the morning it would. Then she would feel shame and regret again, and hate the weakness of her body that allowed it to succumb to his charm.

When Edwin came to bid his daughter good night and to wish her well, with all the solicitude of the father of her childhood, he found Melisande sitting up in the huge canopied bed in Jason's bedroom where she had been led by her sisters, who were reclining in nearby chairs. Neither of them had any intention of leaving until the very last moment, it seemed. Soon it would be their turn to experience this sublimely happy moment. His youngest daughter was the image of her mother, he thought, as he bent to kiss one rather flushed cheek, noting how she trembled with excitement, as he thought! And how bright her eyes were! She had never looked more beautiful—and desirable. Now he was able to understand better what Jason Dacre had first recognised in her, that he, in his closeness to her, had overlooked. And, he suspected, Melisande had not yet accepted it in herself . . . if she even knew it existed.

His dead wife's wisdom returned once more to his mind, and in a sudden show of emotion that took all three girls by surprise—for over the years he had shown very little affection for anyone apart from Priscilla, and then only with monetary implications in mind—he seized Melisande's hands in his and held them tightly.

'My dear child, tonight your mother's last wish will become reality. If she could be here now to see it . . . But I suspect she is. She would not miss this for the world. So many years have I remembered her words, believing them said in jest, and now they have come true.'

'Father, I don't understand . . .' Melisande began, and was silenced with a loving kiss, which brought her near to tears. She so desperately needed someone to confide in, yet had no one, and here her father was showing her more consideration and affection than for a considerable time. She wanted to tell him her fears, how unhappy she was at the prospect of being Jason Dacre's wife. Yet how could she when he was so happy, so pleased she had been selected from so many more eligible women? How could she tell him that, if she had not married him, Priscilla and Lucy would have no dowries of their own, and he would not have a very considerable income to support him for the rest of his life. She could not, and so she bore her despair inside her, but was barely able to force a smile to her lips. Watching her, Priscilla felt a growing satisfaction at the knowledge that her sister's marriage was not all it appeared to be. She would never forgive Melisande for stealing such a fine prize from her.

'You don't really remember the last time we were at Whispering Wood, do you? Except, of course for that unpleasant episode with that silly young man in the garden.'

'I know now that it was Jason who rescued me from him,' she confessed. *You are still as slender and graceful, like a young gazelle. You did look most enchanting, like a fairy princess in your gown of green velvet and your hair with its fiery glints*. Five years ago he had seen her and remembered her, and—if she was to believe him—had wanted her since that moment! Now she was his! But she must not allow herself to think of his words. They were meaningless.

'Apparently, after Lord Dacre had ejected the young

man rather forcefully from the house, I understand that your mother spent quite a long while talking to him. I never knew what passed between then, but that night, as we were about to retire, she suddenly turned to me, and with a strange smile, declared, "One day Melisande will become Lady Dacre. Mark my words well, it will happen." I confess I thought she had partaken of too much wine. How so? I asked. What has been said to make you believe such a thing could take place? But she gave me no answer to that, only repeated. "One day, your daughter will be mistress of Whispering Wood." And she was right.'

'How romantic,' Lucy whispered from her chair. 'Do you not agree, Priscilla?'

'A coincidence . . . How could it be more. Melisande was a child,' her eldest sister snapped with obvious contempt at the suggestion that an attractive man like Jason Dacre could have found Melisande desirable at that young age. She refused to accept that, even in those past days, her sister's likeable nature and natural charm had reached out to others, apart from her striking looks. It would have been too humiliating!

For her part, Melisande sat in a stunned silence at the revelation. Had there been some agreement between her mother and Jason that he would one day marry her? The idea was preposterous. He had never visited the house in Kingsclere, and to her knowledge had never made any contact with her father or attempted to see her over the past five years. Of course she knew him by sight and had seen him riding many times through the village, but he was little more than a name that had stirred no memory—she had certainly never associated him with the gallant man who had come to her rescue that night.

'I shall leave you now.' Edwin kissed her brow and rose to his feet. 'And I suggest you two ladies do likewise. Your turn will come soon enough. This night belongs to Melisande. Away with you now.'

'Yes, Father,' Lucy murmured meekly, kissed her sister and followed him out of the room. Melisande could hear the sound of voices on the stairs, and as though to try to protect herself from what was to come, she drew the linen sheet higher about her shoulders. Priscilla smiled as she saw the gesture.

'I trust this night will be all you wish, Melisande. After all, you went to so much trouble to acquire the richest man in Hampshire!' Colour surged into Melisande's pale cheeks at the taunt. Priscilla had never ceased to remind her that she had been discovered asleep in Jason's arms.

'Good fortune came my way without my having to use such desperate means as you did to find myself a husband!' She flung the words with an unusual bitterness of tone. They had never been close, and her marriage seemed to be the last straw to part them finally.

'I shall have no trouble in holding my husband after we are wed,' Priscilla declared, smoothing down the skirts of the brilliant red gown she wore and noting with satisfaction, as she eyed her reflection in a mirror, how the colour complemented her black hair and the slightly olive tint of her skin. 'You know, of course, that Jason has a mistress in London? Also one near here, I suspect. More than one child I have seen today has grey eyes . . . Like the one who brought you that wretchedly filthy kitten. Rose's brat, isn't she? It will be a few years before anyone will be able to see a true resemblance to the father,' she added spitefully. 'Sleep well, Melisande. Dream of the day you will bounce healthy children on your lap. You will be alone, naturally. Men are never interested in their wives when they are pregnant, or in their children when they are young and in need of attention. It gives them a reason to sow their wild oats elsewhere. Once your husband has proved his manhood to you, he will be like all the rest, you'll see.'

The parting shot robbed Melisande of speech. As the door closed behind her sister, she fell back on to the pillows, her countenance as ashen as the winter snow.

CHAPTER SEVEN

THE LAUGHTER OUTSIDE the door grew and the comments became more suggestive as the men accompanying Jason to his bedchamber tried to push their way past him to see the bride, awaiting her new husband, for themselves, but he firmly kept them at bay, opening the door only a fraction so that he could slip through and slamming it shut against the grinning faces. He commented that they should all return downstairs and continue their celebrating there, leaving him in peace to enjoy his good fortune. As an afterthought, Jason slid home the huge bolt to ensure that he and Melisande would not be unexpectedly disturbed.

A long sigh escaped him as he turned towards the bed, relieved at long last to be alone with his bride. He had thought at times that he would not be able to escape from the merrymaking until it was light. The pale creature who sat in his bed, clutching the bedsheet against her breasts, momentarily took him aback. He expected reticence, and modesty, but she looked afraid! What had taken place during the short hour since she had left him to make her shrink still further amid the pillows as he slowly advanced? Had his brother said anything to her? He had seen them together during the evening. Or Priscilla, still determined somehow to ruin her sister's day? That one would stoop to the lowest level, he decided. Thank God she would not be residing beneath his roof!

Pretending not to notice Melisande's gaze following his every move, he began to remove his surcoat and then the sword-belt about his waist. He had deliberately dismissed his attendants for the night, not wishing anyone to intrude, only too aware how precarious was every step he now took. She believed he had deliberately bought her with no regard for her own feelings. In a sense that was true, and yet it could not have been further from the truth, but Jason's experience of women told him that she would not listen to him now. It would be better if she grew to accept, no matter how slowly, that what he had done had been done in love! Even now his feelings astounded him, but he had long since given up trying to justify or explain them . . . and now she was his for ever more.

Melisande felt the breath catch in her throat as he turned and looked at her. He had removed his shirt, and once again she faced the bronzed torso that brought vividly to mind the night he had stayed at her father's house—the night, she believed, that had forced him into this decision to marry her. He wanted no scandal to ruin his precious friendship with the Queen. Why, he had even forced his own brother into marriage with Priscilla to avoid unpleasant gossip! No one but she and Jason had seen them together in the garden, and, had he wished, he could have hushed up the whole matter. She was sure that a slight addition to her sister's dowry would have settled the matter.

What a terrible thought! How bitter she had become in such a short time. Where had the dreamer, the girl who could lose herself in the lightheartedness of poetry, gone? The same girl who, a short while ago, had enjoyed Will Shakespeare's brilliantly funny comedy and been so proud when Jason had presented him to her? She was disappearing into the fanciful world of dreams and unreality that had sustained her for many years. In her place was emerging another being—a woman stirred by the sight of the man before her, remembering his kisses and the strength of the arms that had crushed her against that broad, muscled chest. A woman that was frightening, for Melisande knew she had no control over this being who had invaded her body. This one would not be content with poetry or dreams; this woman wanted reality—wanted the man who stood watching her, a slight frown etching the blond brows, her husband now—her lord and master.

Jason crossed to the windows. Drawing back the heavy curtains, he opened one before turning back to her.

'Come here, Melisande. Come and stand beside me,' he said quietly, and instinctively her hand reached for the pale robe at the foot of the bed before realising quite what she was about. Jason's eyes dwelt on the slight figure which approached him, very little of her hidden beneath the flimsy night-attire. It was of the palest blue, like the softness of cornflowers, and highlighted her blue eyes. But the moment she drew close to him he noticed how they deepened once again to that strange violet colour. An indication that she was afraid. Of him? Of tonight? Did she think him some ogre about to pounce on her? Perhaps she did. This marriage was not to her liking, she had made that very clear, yet when he held her in his arms, her mouth crushed beneath his, he knew the power he wielded over her, the demands he could make which would not be refused. He was beginning to think like his brother, Jason thought, taking one of her hands and drawing her closer to the open window.

'Listen . . . What do you hear?' he asked, a smile tugging at the corners of his lean mouth.

She looked at him in surprise. This was not what she had been expecting! 'Why, nothing . . . Only the wind in the trees. There are so many of them,' she stammered.

'There is a legend at Whispering Wood. If a new bride stands by an open window she will hear the name of the man she loves being whispered by the wind in those trees outside.' Jason chuckled. 'Do you not hear my name, Princess? Do the trees not whisper "Jason" . . . "Jason" . . . ?'

'I—no . . .' Melisande pulled her hand free with an angry toss of her head that sent her red hair swirling about her shoulders like tongues of fire. 'You make mock of me!'

'I suppose it was too much to ask—so soon. No, I do not. Ask anyone—servants or villagers—they will tell you as I have. One day, perhaps . . . Are you tired? Will you take a little nightcap with me before we retire?' Jason moved to the decanter on the table and poured wine for them both without waiting for her to answer. Melisande's head already ached from the assortment of drinks that had been pressed upon her that day, but she thought a refusal might anger him and so said nothing, taking the silver goblet from him without a word.

'Poor Melisande! You really do look as though you are about to be devoured by some legendary monster with five heads that preys on innocent virgins! The gentleman in me dictates that I should leave you alone tonight to give you time to accept this new role thrust upon you, but the man who desires you . . . I am sorry, my sweet, but he is stronger. He cannot leave you alone. He has wanted you for too long.'

To what was he referring? To her first visit to Whispering Wood! How could she accept that when he had seen her, an awkward, shy thirteen-year-old, he wanted her as his wife! But to do so . . . Was this not what her dreams were woven of? A handsome man who would sweep her off her feet, clothe her in the finest gowns, adorn her with jewels? Had Jason not already done this? It could have been the answer to all her dreams, her hopes . . . yet, as she stole a glance at him from beneath lowered lids, she saw the smile which played about his mouth as he studied her. He was not the kind of man to be patient when he passionately desired a woman! There was strength and determination behind that lazy smile, a ruthlessness which did not show itself until someone went against his wishes, as she had tried to do. Then the true man was revealed: a man who would use any means at his disposal to have his own way. That was no imagined prince, no ideal man, for her! This man sought to dominate her and, in her heart of hearts, she knew he would succeed—but with her untrustworthy body only. Her heart would always be free to be given, to him she loved. Her spirit was her own, and it would continue to rebel against the insidious bargain she had made.

Jason finished his drink, and then continued to undress. As he divested himself of more clothing, Melisande hurriedly pulled off her robe and climbed back into bed, turning away so that she would not see the splendid, Adonis-like torso that lowered itself on to the feather mattress beside her.

'Will you snuff the candles, Jason?' she asked breathlessly. 'Please.'

'But I want to look at you, Princess. How can I do that in darkness?' came the mocking response that caused her cheeks to burn.

'It—it is not seemly,' she began lamely and was seized in strong arms which turned her completely in the huge bed to face him.

'You are my wife. As your husband, who else should gaze on you but I? What takes place between us, in the privacy of this room, is for us alone to enjoy,' Jason mocked gently, slipping an arm about the slender shoulders provocatively bared so close to his lips. He could not resist bending his head and laying his lips against the satin skin. She smelt of sweet-smelling salve, rose and honeysuckle, and he could lose himself in the deeper, more sensuous, aroma of musk in her hair. Rose had worked well, he mused, to make his bride as appealing as possible. The poor girl did not realise that Melisande needed no perfumes, no jewels, no fine clothes, to endear herself to him. She was Melisande, sweetness and innocence—all a man could want in a woman. And now she was his! Poor thing, she trembled in his embrace. She did fear him . . . or . . . He drew back slightly to gaze down into the flushed face. Him—or herself? Her own feelings, the depth of which he had only lightly touched upon?

'Put your arms about my neck,' he ordered, and felt her instantly recoil. Damn her—was she being deliberately awkward? 'Melisande!' His tone changed, and slowly she obeyed. He kissed her slowly, with great thoroughness, seeking to evoke a response, and knowing from the way her lips refused to part that for some reason she was holding back. Again his suspicions were aroused that something had happened to make her more skittish than the kitten she had been given.

Melisande's body grew rigid as his hands gathered the nightgown and lifted it up over her body. As he drew it above her head, she resisted for one futile moment, then allowed her hands about his neck to loosen, so that it could be dispensed with. She was pressed against a hard, sinewy body that made the blood course faster through her veins. His touch burned her, from breast to thigh, as his hands explored what was now freely accessible. She was pressed back against the pillows with the weight of him upon her, making resistance impossible.

'Melisande . . .' Jason whispered, pressing light kisses on her brow and cheek, following the smooth line of her throat down to the rise of a firm young breast. 'If only you knew . . .' And then, as her eyes flew open, she recognised the same lazy, mocking smile . . . so confident that it made her want to scream. She had no defence whatsoever against him! His lips devoured hers, parting them, sending strange, tingling sensations through the whole of her body. He had managed to rouse her before with his expertise, but this was different. There was a gentleness about him, an unhurriedness which, for all her misgivings, made her want to relax—and respond to the advances which continued to inflame her body. Was this love? No, how could it be; she did not even like the man. Or did she? He attracted her—annoyed her—infuriated her—mocked her—but when he took her in his arms and claimed her mouth, she felt as though it was right! Was this what she had been waiting for?

'Look at me, Melisande,' Jason commanded, and she could not do otherwise. His gaze tore at her soul, laid it bare, recognised the indecision there and yet took no advantage of it. He would leave it to her, she realised, and in doing so, he had won his battle, for she could not fight her pleasure in being held against him, in feeling his mouth on hers, his hands on her body. What had he done to her? 'Tell me to stop, and I shall. But the choice must be yours, my sweet. I am not strong enough to walk away from you.'

He, not strong enough? The breath caught in her throat. Slowly her fingers touched the dark face above her as if to seek an answer from the emotionless features. His eyes told her he wanted her. How they burned, like the grey embers of a dying fire, yet, as she gazed into them, the dark coals awakened, and stirred her also.

'I—I . . .' She did not know how to put her fears into words. 'I am not like your other women.' His fingers tightened so fiercely about her shoulders that she winced in pain. 'I have no knowledge of—of the court. I have never been instructed in how to please a man . . .'

'Instructed! Dear God, woman! Respond to what you feel inside you!' Jason almost shouted, startled by the sudden and totally unexpected confession. She knew of his mistress! Richard, of course, or Priscilla. How they had plagued this child with their grievances and hatred! In time, they would pay! 'What do you feel when I kiss you—like this?' His mouth parted hers with unbridled passion, leaving her gasping for breath. 'Or this!' His lips travelled slowly over her bare skin, trailing hot kisses like red-hot cinders everywhere they touched. 'This is the first night of a new life for us both, Princess. I shall do nothing that offends or displeases you, though I might have a sleepless night if I have to leave you to spend it alone. I shall do nothing—nothing, do you understand? —that is not to your liking.' How his eyes gleamed in the candle-light. As if she would dare to send him away! Her fingers stole up to touch the blond curls at the nape of his neck. Such a man would never be without a woman, yet he wanted her! He had chosen her and gone to great lengths to have her. The woman in her became triumphant. Jason felt the tension melting away from her body, felt her begin to relax beneath him, and knew a mounting wonder at the unexpected miracle that seemed to be happening. He had been prepared to give her days, weeks even, before he made her his wife, if in the end she accepted him totally. Now it appeared as though she was prepared to succumb.

'Have—have you had many women?' It was not the kind of question a young bride usually asked of her husband on their wedding night, and Jason's laughter could not be contained. 'I—I mean, you have sailed with Captain Drake, and there was much talk of the plunder he took from Spanish towns . . . and the—the women freely accessible . . .'

'Are you asking if I joined in the rape and plunder, Princess?' Jason murmured, trying to remember how it had been ten years ago when he had first sailed the Spanish Main. He had been no better and no worse than any other man at that time. He had his own code of morality and had remained true to it. 'I came back rich, with enough money to rebuild and extend a great deal of Whispering Wood, but I swear to you that, never then, or since, have I taken an unwilling woman to my bed. It happened with many of the crews. They were away from home, missing their own women . . . But, believe me, Drake allowed no leniency where there was a cause for complaint. He is a hard man, despite the jovial smile and manner. Do you believe me?'

How could she not, when every fibre of her being cried out to do so. To acknowledge that it was the truth, to relax in his arms and be fulfilled.

'Yes.' The word was a whisper, almost lost on her lips.

'Do you accept me as your husband? Show me.'

Her eyes grew wide at the question. Was he demanding her submission as proof of her word? His hands were resting lightly against the upward curve of her breasts. He did not move. He was making her come to him, she realised, but suddenly it did not matter. She moved slightly to mould her body closer against his. Her hands locked, and drew his face down to hers. Never had she been so bold!

His kiss seemed to last for ever, parting her lips, bruising them with increasing ardour. This is how she had always dreamed it would be! Passion to take away her breath and make her senses reel. Why had she denied him for so long, deprived herself of these wonderful moments?

'What a fine son you will give me, my love,' Jason murmured in her ear. Barely were the words uttered than he felt Melisande's body become rigid. She twisted her face away, her hands thrusting against his chest in an attempt to repel him. 'What is it?' He drew back, utterly astounded by her reaction, and was shocked by the bitterness blazing out of her eyes. 'Have you no wish for a family? I have. A large one.'

'And while I am great with child, you will be elsewhere, with your—mistress. Priscilla was right . . . Men never stay faithful to their wives. They keep them pregnant and then go off as free as the wind to follow more—enjoyable—pursuits.' The words came fast and furious, heedless of the consequences, even when she saw the silver flints beginning to spark in his eyes, the tightening of the mouth that a moment ago had plied her own with such tender, searching kisses.

'I think you have said enough, Melisande,' came the quiet but firm statement. 'The moment I came into the room, I knew something had upset you. I should have known it had something to do with your green-eyed witch of a sister. She's jealous, don't you understand? She has had to make do with second best, and it sits ill on her shoulders. She has a venomous tongue, which you must not allow to touch you.'

Everything he said was true, Melisande admitted silently, but she could not bring herself to relax again, even when he began to caress her gently, trying desperately to regain what they had captured moments before. Why had he to mention a child! She did not want the confines of a family yet . . . not before she had had a chance to explore further this wondrous new world he had opened up.

'Believe me, you will feel differently when you have new life inside you,' Jason said reassuringly.

'That would ensure the Queen's continued favour, would it not?'

'Take care with your words, Melisande!' he warned. 'You are overwrought. It has been a long day—for us both. Let it not end with angry words.'

'Pray, why should I be overwrought?' she flung back. 'I have only been accused of trapping myself a rich husband by crawling into his bed at the dead of night when he was out of his head with fever.'

'No one believed that stupid rumour started by your sister,' Jason retorted, his temper barely restrained by her apparent determination to destroy what had begun to blossom between them.

'Did they not? Why has it come to my ears, then, that Lord Dacre paid a high price for silence?' Melisande's heartbeats quickened unsteadily at the frown which leapt to his face. She had gone too far, she knew it, and longed to retract the harsh words she had flung at him, yet she did not know how.

'No one has heard such nonsense from my lips! Nor from yours—if I am to accept that this marriage is not to your liking.'

'It is not.' Again, reckless words spoken without thought. 'Nor is the role of being merely a breeding stock—to die, like my mother, before her time!'

'Enough!'

'It is not enough! Priscilla should have been the one you chose. She would not care if you neglected her for others, not when she had your name and your money, and the position in society that she craves like some sickness. It means nothing to me . . .'

'But *you* have it,' Jason reminded her coldly. '*You* are my wife. I may not be the prince of your dreams, but I am your husband and, as such, I have certain rights.'

'Take them! Why should you consider my feelings now?' Please, let him take me in his arms, Melisande prayed. Let it be as it was for us a few minutes ago.

'I shall not. Be warned, Melisande, I shall not. If a man had tossed at me the accusations that you have tonight, I would kill him! With you, I shall employ less drastic measures to bring you to your senses, but, believe me, you will accept me, and you will rue this night for a long time to come. Your meek manner hides a stubborn, wilful nature. Nay, I shall not break so strong a spirit, tempted as I am to show you how far you have goaded me; rather, I shall tame it. You shall not deny me what is mine by right before God and the law. I shall touch you when and how I please. But . . .' He paused to watch his words sink in and glimpsed the stirrings of alarm in the depths of those violet pools. 'I shall not make you my wife until the day you crawl into my bed for a second time . . . and beg my forgiveness for your words.'

Melisande gasped at the cruel taunt, and lashed back at him with a tongue she had never known she possessed. 'Hell will surely freeze before that happens!' He would touch her—yet she would not be his wife! What kind of torture did he plan?

'Hell may prove to be a lot hotter than you imagine!' A smile returned to Jason's taut features, but his eyes were those of a frightening stranger. 'One word of warning. If, by so much as a word or a single look, you betray to others that all is not well between us, I shall despatch you to hell with my own two hands! Now, my wife, it is late, and I wish to sleep. But not with you.'

Melisande cried out as he swung away from her, pulling her after him. What did he intend for her now? When she resisted him, she was lifted in his arms, carried through into the adjoining bedroom—her own chamber —and tossed unceremoniously on to the huge bed. As she gasped and feverishly grabbed the sheets to cover her nakedness, he cast a long look at her from the doorway, and the chuckle which rose in his throat mocked her show of modesty.

'Goodnight, my sweet. Sleep well. Have no fear that I shall invade your privacy tonight. But tomorrow . . . Tomorrow, beware. The taming will begin!'

'You monster!' Melisande almost choked over the

words, but they fell on emptiness, for Jason had already gone out, and the door had closed behind him.

Melisande slowly opened her eyes. The lids felt so heavy . . . as though she had been drugged. Too much wine and Malmsey . . . and perhaps crying herself to sleep. It had been almost light, she remembered. She could not have been asleep for more than two or three hours, so what had woken her? Her sleepy gaze roving the pleasantly furnished room came at last to alight on the silent figure in a high-backed chair close to the bed.

'I was beginning to think that cannon-fire would not waken you,' Jason said pleasantly. His eyes rested for a moment on the puffiness of her cheeks and the redness still lingering round her eyes. 'Did you sleep well?'

'Very well. I—I was utterly tired.' He did not sound angry with her, she thought in relief. Perhaps she could mend the rift between them. He had opened the gates of Paradise for her, and she had closed them with her thoughtlessness. 'I—I think, perhaps, that was why I—I was so silly last night. I should not have said the things I did.'

'No,' he agreed, 'you should not. You have every reason to offer an apology.'

'I was not . . . I mean . . .' That was not what she had been intending at all. An explanation, perhaps, of the confusion that had raged inside her—the misgivings that Priscilla had brought to the surface with her spiteful remarks. Had he not provoked her, too? Yet she saw no sign of contriteness on his part. Apology—no! She had nothing to apologise for. 'Perhaps we could begin again . . .' she finished lamely, and one blond brow rose sardonically.

'By all means. You know what is expected of you.' Melisande sat bolt upright in bed, pulling the sheet close against her breasts. Surely he did not mean! He could not! Crawl into his bed, like some tavern wench?

'Please leave. I wish to get up,' she said frostily. He did not move, but sat looking at her in a manner that made her blush until her cheeks were almost as bright as the hair tumbling past her bare shoulders. Then he stretched and rose, turning towards his own room. Her robe and nightgown were in there, still lying across the bed, she saw. If he left the door open, he would see her as she crossed to the closet to find something else. She gave a sigh of relief at a knock on the door, and Rose entered in answer to her quick response to come in.

'Forgive me, my lord . . . my lady . . .' The girl looked confused to find Jason in his wife's room. 'I didn't realise . . .'

'Come in, Rose,' Melisande instructed. 'Please bring my robe from the other room.'

'I can do that, my sweet.' Before the girl could move, Jason had spun on his heel and retrieved the flimsy garments. When he returned, his smile mocked her attempt to make him leave. 'Here we are.'

He stood at the bedside, holding the robe open for her to slip into. He expected her to get out of bed!

'Your modesty is most becoming, Melisande, but you must not be shy with your own husband.' There was an undercurrent in his tone telling her that if she refused, he might pull back the clothes anyway! He was deliberately humiliating her, proving to her that he was master—she could do nothing about it, or she would arouse Rose's suspicions, and if that happened . . . She felt a twinge of apprehension as she recalled Jason's threat. For an instant last night she had glimpsed another man behind the smiling mask—and he frightened her more than a little.

Blushing still more, if that was possible with her cheeks as crimson as a poppy already, she rose and allowed him to slide the robe over her. Briefly his fingers brushed her breast as he pulled it together and tied the ribbons, and instantly she quivered. His eyes locked on her face but betrayed nothing, and then he bent to kiss her full on the lips.

'Your father and sisters will be leaving soon. Don't delay too long at your toilette, or you will miss them,' he murmured, and left her. Not until the door had closed and she heard him calling for his man-servant some moments later did she manage to contain the tremors running through her.

Later, in the kitchens, when the other servants gathered to hear how Lord Dacre and his new bride had looked after their wedding night, Rose described to them how romantically he had helped her on with her robe and the way he had kissed her. As though they had been apart for weeks, she said dreamily, wishing that her experience with the father of her child had been something to be cherished. And how the new mistress had trembled just to be with him, she added. Anyone could see they were madly in love.

In the days following the disastrous wedding night, Merlin the kitten became more of a companion for Melisande than her own husband. Before she awoke, Jason would be gone from the house on an early morning ride. A usual occurrence, she was to discover, which he maintained in all weathers. And so, first thing, she would laze in bed, and Rose would bring her something light to eat. Merlin would crawl, stretching, from the basket where he curled up for most of the night upon a bright red cushion, and climb up beside her, whiskers twitching at the smell of fresh milk, and his small pink tongue darted eagerly towards the butter dripping from thin slices of warm bread. He was a little imp, but Melisande grew to love him, and soon good behaviour earned him small pieces of toast and his own little saucer of milk. After which, he would make himself comfortable beside her pillow and not stir for most of the day.

An easy life for them both, Melisande had decided upon the fourth day. Four days a wife, and she had barely seen Jason. Returning from his ride, he would wash and change, and often be closeted with the estate steward for several hours or accompany him to settle some dispute in the village. She always saw him at the evening meal, when he would take his place at the far end of the long oak table in the dining-room and she would sit facing him, and he would pleasantly enquire after her day. Within a short time she had easily settled into the routine with the servants, who ran the house with efficiency and seemingly little effort, making her feel even more useless. She inspected the kitchens and the dairy daily, discussed fresh menus with the cook in an attempt to engage her active mind in something worth while, but always she had time on her hands. Time she spent alone . . . or with Merlin.

Even Amanda's growing friendship did not help to ease the chagrin and growing humiliation she was experiencing at Jason's treatment of her. The servants thought no less of him for leaving her alone so soon after their wedding. He was master of Whispering Wood, with many responsibilities that came before wife and family. He was an unselfish man who laboured long hours, yet he still returned with his wife always uppermost in his mind. Did he not greet her with much affection, and she, still so shy before the servants when the offered cheek was ignored and she was taken in his arms and soundly kissed.

Everything he did was intended to bring her to heel, Melisande knew. The prolonged hours away from the house, so that when he returned she was dying for want of conversation—her books no longer brought her the satisfaction they once had; the way he would sit at table, smiling at her, questioning her about her day, when he knew how bored and lonely she had been. And when he did condescend to honour her with his presence, it was at the most disconcerting times. Just as she was about to take a bath, to while away an hour in scented water to try to put out of her mind the memory of the next room, the enormous marriage bed with its velvet hangings where he waited for her night after night. Did he really expect her to go to *him*? Or he would come out of his chamber, as Rose was helping her to undress for the night, and send the girl away. Embarrassed, inwardly fuming, yet knowing she could say nothing, Melisande was forced to accept him in Rose's place. Each time he touched her,

her skin tingled with anticipation. The boldness of his gaze excited her as much as she tried to contain it. And then he would kiss her and she would respond, hoping, each time it happened, that he would relent and stay with her and they could recapture the moments briefly shared four days ago. But he never did. As soon as he felt a response from her, a soft sigh or the relaxing of her body against his, he would draw back, and bid her good night and once more she would sleep alone.

Each time it happened she swore she would not allow him to play with her in such a cruel manner again. Before the servants, she must conduct herself as a loving wife at all times, but alone, if he touched her again, what would she do? Burst into tears and beg him to make her his wife—that was what she wanted? What had become of her determination not to submit to the strange emotion he awakened in her? But there had been times—and she knew there would be again—when he would hold her, and she would gaze into those wicked eyes and believe every word he said. She was acting like a love-sick fool! The situation was impossible, but the only way she could resolve it was by complying with his wishes and going to him.

Love! This ache in her could not be love! Dear heaven, she must not fall in love with him, or she would be powerless to refuse him anything! Yet was she not that now? With the passing of each day her resolves were weakening, the woman in her growing stronger, more demanding.

'Melisande, are you not well?' Amanda asked with a frown, and Melisande, startled, looked up from the embroidery in her lap. How long she had been staring at it she did not know. 'I asked what you will be wearing for Priscilla's wedding. It is only two days away. One of your new gowns, perhaps? It is time Jason took you to London and showed you some excitement. Why he did not take you there directly after the wedding is a mystery —he did mention that he might.' She shrugged her shoulders and returned to her needlework. 'No one will ever understand the workings of that man's mind. I thought I knew him once . . . I was even quite—fond—of him, but now I detest him!'

'Why?' Melisande asked. This was the first time Amanda had seemed willing to discuss her relationship with her guardian. It was a strange one, fraught with arguments and stormy scenes, but Melisande had noticed that Jason never once lost his temper with her, or shown any sign of the anger he had displayed to her on their wedding night. He was like an elder brother trying to protect a younger, innocent sister—an attitude that Amanda resented, and let him know it in no uncertain terms.

'I am eighteen, the same age as you, yet you are married and have control of this huge house! He treats me as a child and I hate him for it! I am old enough to know my own mind!' came the defiant retort accompanied by rising anger in the pale hazel eyes.

'I am sure Jason would be happy to find you a suitable husband, Amanda. If he has not yet begun to think of you as a wife and mother, perhaps it is because he wishes you to retain and enjoy your freedom a little longer,' Melisande answered, frowning over her needlework. 'Marriage means being tied to one man for the rest of your life. You will have to obey him in all things whether you like it or not. Enjoy your youth while you can.' Mine has been taken from me, Melisande thought, and I miss it dearly. Jason's presence about the house, the way I sense him near even when he is not, forced me to dispense quickly with my former day-dreaming. How could I lose myself in that pleasant world of my own making when he might come upon me at any time and shatter it with a mocking comment or that quizzical smile? He knows what I am about, and even his silence reproaches me for trying to escape from him.

'Oh, yes, he will find me a husband when it suits him. A man of his choosing.' Amanda's voice was filled with bitterness. 'I am like Lucy—I do not want to have a husband found for me. The man I wanted . . .' Melisande quickly looked up at the wistful note.

'Wanted? Is there someone? Perhaps I could speak to him on your behalf . . . Tactfully, of course,' she suggested.

'There was—someone. No, there is nothing you can do, for he is about to marry someone else. Jason arranged that, too. As much to keep me from him as to avoid a scandal.'

Richard and Priscilla! It had to be . . . She knew of no one else whose wedding was so close at hand. Without warning, Amanda threw aside her needlework and buried her face in her hands, her slim shoulders shaking with sobs.

'I won't go! He can't make me!'

'Go where?' Melisande left her chair to sit down beside her and gently draw her against her breast. 'Hush, don't upset yourself. Tell me what is troubling you, and somehow we shall resolve it.' She must discover how she could fulfil that promise!

'There is nothing you can do. Nothing anyone can do,' Amanda sobbed, clinging to her tightly. It was obvious that the girl had been in torment for many weeks, since long before Melisande came to know her. She stroked the fair hair and tried to soothe her, but it was many minutes before the tears began to subside, and then the words fell from her lips fast and furiously as she could no longer bear her secret alone. 'I was in love—' hastily she corrected herself 'I—thought I was in love with Richard. Jason has always treated me as a sister, and sometimes I felt as if he did not see me as other men did. I am no longer the awkward, shy little thing who came to Whispering Wood seven years ago. I was eleven then, and my father had just been killed in a riding accident. My mother had been dead for many years . . . I hardly remember her. I used to come here so often when I was young that I thought of Jason's mother as my own. You would have liked her. She was gentle, like you, and so wise.'

'Wisdom, unfortunately, is not one of my attributes, or . . .' Melisande broke off. She had been about to say, 'or I would accept what could be a very satisfying and happy marriage.' This was not the time to think of her own troubles, or to unburden herself on Amanda, whom she believed was under too great a strain to accept anyone else's problems. 'What objection did Jason have to your—friendship—with his brother? I know they are not on the best of terms, but I am certain he has always had your interests at heart.'

'That's what he said. How I hate those words! They mean that he doesn't give a fig for my feelings! Jason and I were so close once, and then—as I grew older—it was as if he became jealous of others looking at me. When Richard first began to show an interest in me there was a terrible row. Why? Richard made me feel—wanted. Pretty. A woman. Jason ignored me, yet did not want another man to look at me, or court me! I felt as if he owned me—without wanting me . . . It is difficult to explain . . .'

'I understand. Believe me, I do,' Melisande said quietly, producing a handkerchief to wipe the tears from Amanda's cheeks. Another 'thing' to be acquired in his household. What kind of a man had she married? He collected people, and bound them to him as other men collected priceless ornaments!

'I ran away.' Amanda's voice fell to a whisper. 'I ran away with Richard. He hasn't told you that, has he? I doubt if he has told anyone—or that he followed us to London and dragged me out of the inn where we were staying after the wedding . . . and brought me back here to Whispering Wood. That was the night of the terrible storm—when our coach overturned and he sought shelter at your house.'

'You—and Richard—are married?' Melisande echoed. 'But you cannot be—he is to marry Priscilla in two days!'

'It—it was not a real ceremony.' Tears came again into Amanda's eyes. 'He used me. He did not really love me. All his sweet words and promises were only to get me into his bed . . .' She broke off, bright colour flooding into her cheeks at the delicacy of her confession. 'I came into a great deal of money on my eighteenth birthday, and we eloped to London a week later. I believed he really wanted to marry me. I didn't care about the money; he could have had it all . . . but that's all he wanted. Not me. Jason followed us and was waiting in my room when I left Richard to retire. He bundled me out of a back door and into his coach like a madman. I've never seen him so furious. He hit me!' She raised a trembling hand to one cheek as though the pain of the blow was still with her. Perhaps it was, Melisande thought, pitying her with all her heart. So young and so treacherously dealt with. 'I wanted to die. When he told me that the minister who had performed the service was not even a true man of the cloth, I wanted to die. I was so ashamed . . . The friends who had acted as witnesses had known what Richard was about, and helped him in the terrible act.'

'Why should you hate Jason when he saved you from the consequences of that fateful day?' Melisande could not understand the girl's reasoning.

'Because he shamed me as much as Richard! He had always told me that his brother was a rogue and a wastrel, and I had never believed him. You do not know how persuasive Richard can be when he chooses. He was the first man ever to make me feel like a woman . . .'

'He and Jason are not so different in that respect,' Melisande replied, and Amanda threw her a puzzled look. Poor Amanda, her dreams had been extinguished by a smooth-tongued rogue, and she was forcing Jason to share the responsibility of her mistake. 'The hurt you have suffered may take a great while to heal, but it will, and then you will accept that Jason was only doing what he thought was right for you.'

'How can you say that? Was what he did to you —right? Do you think I don't know that he forced you into marriage with him? I heard Priscilla and Richard talking. Jason paid all your father's debts and gave a dowry to each of you . . . That is not the act of a man who is in love, but that of a man who will have his own way, no matter what it costs him! Although, once, I did believe . . .' Amanda threw her a challenging look. 'Tell me it was a love-match, and I will believe *you*!'

'It was not.' Melisande did not answer for many minutes. The rising wind outside the windows had caught her attention and she lifted her head attentively . . . 'If a new bride stands before an open window she will hear the name of the man she loves being whispered by the wind in the trees outside.' How those words haunted her day and night. Was she in love with Jason? She was beginning to believe it was so, for each day the ache in her grew, the loneliness she was experiencing becoming more unbearable. Would she hear his name only when she had gone to him and proved her love—become his wife? 'But it is different now. I have fallen in love with him, so it matters not what lengths he went to to have me. I am content to be his wife, and I shall make him happy. And the generosity he has shown to my sisters and my father . . . Why can you not believe he sincerely wanted to help them, Amanda? He had no need to spend so lavishly. I am sure he could have devised other means—such as buying up Father's notes from the local merchants in order to persuade him, shall we say, of the wisdom of the match.' She was beginning to persuade herself of the potency of her argument. He need not have been as considerate as he had been. Even now, when he could have asserted his rights over her, he did not.

'I had not considered it in that way,' Amanda confessed.

'And what could he have done in your case, other than whisk you away from London before the whole unpleasant story became known? You would have been so vulnerable, and the shame you think you suffered would have been as nothing compared with life with Richard—with your money in his possession and you little more than an unwanted guest in his house. Oh, my dear, you are so like Lucy.'

'I always believed you were the one with your head in the clouds, dreaming the day away, but you are more in touch with reality than any of us,' Amanda returned with a shaky little laugh. 'I shall try to be nicer to him . . . But I can promise nothing.'

'Try to put what has happened out of your mind. Wake up tomorrow with a determination to re-establish your relationship with Jason as it used to be. Priscilla's wedding is a perfect opportunity. You must show yourself, and prove to him—to Richard and to yourself—that it is in the past.' Impulsively Melisande caught her hands and squeezed them gently. 'You are eighteen, Amanda, and a woman now, with responsibilities to others as well as to yourself. You must accept that.'

'As you have? You have changed since your wedding day, do you know that? I have seen Jason watching you sometimes with such pride in his eyes—and yet with a strange expression I do not understand. Perhaps I never shall know what does on behind his smile.'

No more will I, Melisande thought as they returned to their needlework. But if it was at all possible, she was going to find out.

CHAPTER EIGHT

'I KNOW IT IS late, Father, but I must speak with you a moment.' Melisande closed the door of his bedroom behind her, and advanced towards the figure who, until she entered, had been studying a sheaf of papers. For the past hour she had been trying to catch him alone, but people were milling everywhere in the house and the gardens, waiting for the carriages to return from the church in Kingsclere and convey them next to the wedding ceremony of Priscilla and Richard Dacre, and he had scarcely had a minute to himself.

'Can it not wait, child? It is time you and Lucy were leaving for the church.' Edwin's expression registered great pleasure at the sight of his daughter. How elegant she looked these days: a grand lady, as her mother had been, and married life agreed with her by the glow in her cheeks.

'Priscilla is having a last-minute alteration made to her gown. She will be a little while yet,' Melisande answered, marvelling at the infinite patience of Mistress Agnes. The woman must have made a dozen alterations to her sister's wedding dress in the past week, none of them to the satisfaction of Priscilla, who seemed to be taking great delight in the fact she could be late at the church and would be keeping not only her future husband, but over a hundred guests, waiting with her pettiness. 'I must speak to you about Lucy. She is so miserable, Father. Why do you insist that she finds a husband so soon? She has her own dowry now, and you have no need of money. Why could the two of you not enjoy some time together before you make her leave you? If she thought she was no longer being rushed, she might well select a fine young man herself.'

Edwin considered his youngest daughter. How she

had matured these past weeks. As close as they had once been, she would never have dared to voice her opinion on such matters before. Life with Jason Dacre was bringing out a hidden strength in her character. 'Am I being reproved for wanting the best for all my daughters? Or for seeking to end my own days in better conditions than I have endured these past years?'

'No. Oh, no! I did not mean to imply . . .' Melisande laid her lips gently against one lined cheek. 'Nor to hurt you. But Lucy worries me.'

'Since your betrothal ball at Whispering Wood, that girl has been inundated with prospective suitors and has hardly spent a whole day in the house! Had I not been in possession of some money, I would not have been able to welcome those young men into this house, or to provide for your sister to be properly chaperoned in their company. I have done everything a father should do for a daughter, as I have tried to do for you and Priscilla. You judge me unfairly, Melisande. It is obvious that you know of my—financial agreement—with Lord Dacre?'

Melisande nodded, knowing it was useless to lie. She had given herself away too easily. 'We—we have no secrets from each other. I know you only wanted our lives to be as comfortable and as untroubled as they were when Mother was alive, and I love you dearly for it. I have a fine home and a—a loving husband, and Priscilla in a few hours will have all she desires. We have to think only of Lucy, Father. *You* must think only of her now. Now that our position in society has been restored, can you not be generous and share the love I know you have for her—with her? You will need someone to take care of you.'

'I am not in my grave yet, young woman,' Edwin returned, not minding her bluntness. He would be lonely when his daughters were all gone, and secretly he dreaded the moment he had once dreamed of, but how could he tell her. 'Lucy obeys me and entertains the young men who call on her, but each in turn is dismissed, almost contemptuously. And I know she is still seeing Christopher Avery, though she denies it to my face. She has been seen with him—albeit accompanied by Lord Dacre's ward. I suppose she considers the presence of another female adequate protection against gossip.'

'I did not know that,' Melisande confessed. Only an hour before, while she helped her sister to dress, Lucy had told her that she had not seen Christopher for some considerable time, that he had been offered an opportunity to sail in *Moonwynd* when she accompanied Drake, and so all the young man's spare time was taken up with additional studies. If she had lied to Melisande—the only person she had ever confided in! It shocked her, and she wondered whether Lucy was planning some drastic action to escape an unwanted marriage, making her all the more determined to resolve the situation before it was too late.

'If you accept that I do love her, my child, that is all that matters. I shall pray that she will accept it, too—and soon.'

'Father, listen to me. I have thought of a way . . .' Melisande placed on the table before him the embroidered leather bag she had been clutching, and from it removed a folded velvet cloth. Her heart began to race as she thought once again of the enormity of what she was about to do. If Jason discovered it . . . Would he care? He had enough money to replace what she was giving away, if he wished to. She was sure he would never notice that she did not wear certain items of the jewellery he had bestowed on her, and if he did . . . she would have to face that moment when it came.

'Next month, Lucy will be twenty. Make her an independent young woman in her own right, Father. Sell these and give her the money, and—and pretend it was a legacy from Mother.'

Edwin caught his breath at the shimmering stones which were unwrapped. A diamond bracelet set in a basketwork of gold as delicate as a spider's web, and a matching ring and earrings. And a sapphire brooch, the stone as big as a pigeon's egg.

'Melisande! I cannot! Why there is over a thousand pounds here . . . More! And she would never believe that the money is from your mother, when we have lived for so long as paupers.'

'From you, then. Yes, that would be even better. Independence is all she has ever wanted. Give it to her, and let us see what she does with it. Once she is at liberty to do as she pleases, perhaps she will not want to run away and leave those who love her. If she does, she may do so in style. Could she not perhaps go to France for six months and stay with our relatives there? You have always kept in touch with Mother's brother, have you not? She is like a fledgling bird, Father, needing to try out her wings. Let her do so.'

'And you?' Edwin asked with a smile. 'Do you still fly free in your dream world when you close your eyes, or did I take that from you?'

'Don't be silly!' There were times when his insight took her by surprise. Did he suspect that all was not well between herself and Jason? She had been so careful not to say a word to betray the fact, and knew Jason would not do so. 'I shall always be a romantic dreamer, even though I have everything I want in this world.' But how she wished it still brought her the satisfaction, the contentment, it once had. 'Please take these.'

Edwin's fingers touched the beautifully cut stones in the bracelet, a faraway look stealing across his face.

'Do you know, when I met your mother, I was penniless. I had a title, but nothing else. She was the daughter of a rich Huguenot merchant, and I never thought I stood a chance with her, but she loved me, Melisande. From the first time we saw each other, she loved me—and her parents saw in me something I did not know existed: a good head for business. They accepted me, gave me a chance to prove myself and, when I did, they gave me their daughter. I never looked back . . . not until the day she died, and when that happened, my world was destroyed. That sounds cruel, I know, considering I possessed three lovely daughters, but she was everything to me in a way I cannot describe to you. Only when you love as I did will you be able to understand. That is why I know you give me these jewels without the consent of your husband, and that you do not love him, or you would have mentioned that you brought them with his blessing. But we shall say no more of it just now, or we shall never get to the church.'

Quickly Melisande recovered the items and replaced them in the bag, which her father locked away in a drawer of his desk. He knew, and yet he had said nothing!

'Give me time,' she said quietly, afraid he might mention the conversation to Jason, and recalling the threat which hovered over her head like the sword of Damocles. 'We have been married such a short while. If there is any fault, it is in me, and I shall try to rectify it. I promise.'

Priscilla's wedding day was not the great occasion she had meticulously planned. It began as such, on a bright, sunny day, and she knew, as she stood at the side of Richard Dacre in the small village church in Kingsclere, that she looked radiant. The bodice of her gown of pale turquoise satin and brocade was sewn with hundreds of tiny emeralds. A magnificent emerald necklace adorned her throat, and her creamy shoulders were left bare by the daring low neckline, causing many a male eye to linger on the firm swell of her breasts above the single layer of lace. Her satin slippers were dyed to match her gown and sewn with silver buckles. Even Richard's flamboyant outfit, created for him in London at great expense, seemed dull in comparison, and she revelled at the admiring glances that were continually directed towards her.

However, she was soon to discover the petulant nature of her husband, and that to anger him or detract from him the attention he also craved was the worst mistake she could make. From the moment they returned to the house he began to drink heavily, and when the dancing began, he ignored her or sought another partner. When his eyes turned in her direction, she boldly selected Jason to escort her on to the floor. He had not hesitated, although Melisande glimpsed a flicker of anger on his face as he passed her. It was difficult not to feel a little sorry for Priscilla! Her sister's unfortunate problem vanished from her mind when Jason sought her out and told her they would not be returning to Whispering Wood that night, but remaining at the house.

'As you can see, my brother will be drunk within the hour, and in his present frame of mind, not in the best of humours. I have arranged for the carriage to take him and your sister back to Whispering Wood so that they may spend their wedding night alone. When Richard is in an ugly mood, he is foul-mouthed and inclined to lash out at whoever is close to him. Thomas has dealt with him before, and will see that your sister does not bear the brunt of it.'

'We are to stay here?' Melisande echoed, and the grey eyes watching her gleamed with amusement at the tremor in her voice. 'Surely that is not necessary?'

'Have you no romance left in your soul at all, my sweet? We must leave the newly-weds alone to work out their own problems. Perhaps Priscilla will learn a little tact overnight. If she continues to flirt with every man in the room . . .'

'When her husband of a few hours ignores her deliberately, what do you suggest she does?' she returned angrily. She could not condone her sister's boldness with the men partnering her, knowing that it was to spite Richard for his brutish manner, but she could understand the humiliation she must be experiencing, realising how she was being watched, whispered about. As Melisande had been on her wedding day! Had she, too, drawn that comparison?

'She should remember that she is now a married woman. The days are past when she can flash those blue eyes at every handsome face she chooses. By the way, did I tell you I have offered young Christopher Avery a chance to sail on *Moonwynd*?'

'No, you did not,' Melisande said sharply. 'I have hardly seen you these past three days.'

'That was your choice, my sweet. You gave me to understand that you preferred your own company. If you do not . . .' His smile became wickedly challenging, and two spots of colour rose in her cheeks. 'Perhaps we can rectify that tonight. We have been given your old bedchamber. The last time I slept in that bed you were most attentive to me, as I remember.'

They were to share one room! One bed! It was impossible!

'I shall make other arrangements . . .'

'No, you will not.' Lean fingers with the strength of iron in them fastened over her wrist as, panic-stricken, she turned to leave him. 'We shall do nothing to arouse your father's suspicions that all is not well between us. You can always sleep in a chair, as you did that last time.'

'If you were a gentleman, you would not force this upon me,' she protested, knowing by the brilliant gleam in his eyes that he was enjoying her discomfort.

'A gentleman I most certainly am—and do you also need reminding that I am your husband? Your place is at my side, in bed and out.' Bending his head, he brushed her lips with his own, and the colour in her cheeks deepened as he drew back and she glimpsed her father's smiling face a few feet away from them. 'Come, dance with me—and smile. Enjoy yourself.'

'Why are you sending Christopher Avery away? Because of Lucy?' Had her father known of this? Was that why he had not refused the offer of her jewels? 'You are a cruel man, Jason, to think you can always plan the lives of others.'

The fingers about her own tightened quite painfully, but it was the only indication that her words had touched a raw nerve. Still smiling, he led her on to the floor, wishing he could be a little more like his brother—more ruthless, perhaps more devious in his attempts to get this proud, wilful, hostile woman into his bed where she belonged. How much longer must he wait? Had five years not been long enough?

'As it happens, I offered Avery a choice, unbelievable as it may sound to you. He could go with *Moonwynd*, or stay with his mother and marry Lucy. Had he professed the slightest indication of caring for her, I would have intervened with your father, but he does not love her, Melisande, and well you know it. Nor does she love him. You know that, too, don't you?' His gaze challenged her and she nodded, unable to deny it. 'Well, what have I done wrong?'

'I—I am sorry. I thought you were—manipulating people again.'

'Again!' For an instant the smile vanished, and she saw anger on his face. 'Do not judge me, Melisande, lest I sit in judgment on you. A wife who will not consummate her marriage, yet who takes all that is given to her. How would you like that to be judged? A fair exchange is all I ask from you. Not love, if that is beyond you—but surely some show of honesty, of the character I once glimpsed . . . No, perhaps that is too much to ask. You were an innocent child then, with no knowledge of the world—except that dream world in which you once dwelt. I know the woman in you wants me—wants more from life than you are having at this moment. Why will you not let it happen? Why do you deny the desires in you—deny me the right to fulfil them? I can, you know.' As the music ended, he led her away to a quiet corner of the room. She waited, she thought, for him to turn away to fetch refreshments, and was startled and horrified when he pressed her back against the wall, the weight of his body holding her helpless, totally unable to move.

'Jason, let me go! People are looking at us!'

'Are they? Let them!' Jason's glittering eyes transfixed her, made her legs grow weak as she saw the passion there. How long could she withstand these outrageous assaults! Had he no shame that they were being stared at, commented on! Husbands did not take their wives into secluded corners and—and what? Jason was no ordinary man—certainly no ordinary husband. He would do with her as he pleased, where and when he pleased. He had said so, and had done so many times since their wedding night and, as now, she was helpless to prevent him. As before, when his mouth sought hers, forced apart her stiff lips and tantalised them with burning kisses, she did not want to resist him.

Tonight they would share the same room—the same bed. Was this his way of persuading her to agree to more? How she wanted to! How she wished she had the courage to tell him what was in her heart. Could she trust her heart? Was it love, or just a longing, a need she had never known before? How would she know love? Her father had known it and it had almost destroyed him; was she destined for the same fate? Would she love Jason so passionately, so completely, that her world would end if anything happened to him?

It was frightening! But when Jason kissed her like this . . . his fingers, gently sliding across her bare shoulders were like the touch of a scalding hot iron, burning her delicate skin. His body moulded against hers . . . She could feel the hard muscles of his leg and thigh pressing against hers even through the wide panniers of her skirts.

'Please—oh, please, stop!' She was drowning beneath those kisses, her head reeling, her mind unable to come to grips with reality. Nothing mattered while he held her . . .

'Come to bed, then.' The softly-spoken words against her ear brought her eyes wide open with horror. She had been right! He thought to persuade her to go to him and truly become his wife.

'You—you are insufferable!' She wrenched herself free, and picking up her skirts, fled from the room, not caring what comments her hurried departure caused. Not until she was safe in the sanctuary of her old room did she cease to tremble. When he came, she would pretend to be asleep. She would not be used!

But how she longed to surrender once again to his burning kisses, the devastating touch of his hands as they explored her body! She did belong to him, whether she wished it or not. Why was it so wrong to want him? She *was* his wife, his property. Oh, to relinquish all her foolish thoughts and sink into his arms and have done with this farce that separated them. She could end it . . . But, in doing so and satisfying the longing inside her, she would have to comply with his wishes and offer the olive branch, to submit to total subjugation. If he cared for her at all, as he professed to do and took great pains to convince others, why was he so determined to break her spirit? The answer was always the same. He did not care! His pretty speeches and shows of affection were for onlookers, and meant nothing.

Why was it, after allowing Annie to undress her and climbing into the bed where she had spent so many nights before, that she found it impossible to sleep? Why was she waiting for the sound of his footstep outside the door—for the sight of his tall frame filling the doorway? Why did her heart beat faster when she did hear it—and see him illuminated for a moment in the light of a wall lamp—and when the door had closed behind him, huddle beneath the bedclothes as if he was the devil incarnate? She sensed him looking down at her, but dared not peer out. Then she heard him move away and begin to undress, whistling softly to himself as he did so.

The mattress sank with his weight as he lowered himself into the bed beside her. The candle was snuffed, plunging the room into darkness. Only then did she cautiously ease her head from beneath the sheet. Jason had turned away on his side; he was not going to touch her! Was it relief that swept over her and caused her to tremble, or anger at his indifference? He had deliberately led her to believe he would make her his wife tonight—and now he was ignoring her! Tears welled up, and she quickly brushed them away. She would not allow him to make her cry! She would resist him—and his charm—and his determination to master her. She would never give in to him!

'Never! Never! Never,' she whispered defiantly to the darkness, and too late realised that she had inadvertently spoken aloud.

'You will, my love. You will,' came the mocking, horribly confident murmur from her side. 'And soon!'

Melisande's parting from Lucy the following morning gave her cause for thought on the return journey to Whispering Wood. She could not define what was wrong, yet she sensed it in the way her sister hugged her and held her for several moments—as if they were to be parted for ever. How Melisande wished she could have told her of the wonderful surprise she would receive on her birthday, but she had promised her father to say nothing. Three short weeks, and then Lucy would have all she had ever wished for—her freedom. Melisande hoped she would not hasten away to France, leaving their father alone in the house in Kingsclere. If that happened, she planned to ask Jason if he might come and live with them.

If Lucy had seemed quieter than usual and preoccupied with her own thoughts, Amanda was in high spirits. Melisande had never before seen her look so happy: there was a glow to her cheeks, which made her look quite radiant. More than once she saw Jason watching his ward, a strange gleam in those grey eyes. Had they resolved their differences? They did talk more amicably together, and without Amanda's usual coldness towards her guardian.

Richard and Priscilla were ready to depart by the time Jason's carriage reached Whispering Wood. Their conveyance, loaded with trunks, was standing in the drive. Melisande needed only one look at Priscilla's heavily rouged cheeks, which could not hide the puffiness beneath, to know that her sister's wedding night had been less than she had anticipated.

'Will you not stay and eat with us?' Jason enquired

politely. His brother would soon be out of his home and, with luck, his life for ever, so he could afford to be a little generous.

'I want to be in London before it's dark.' Richard's head ached like the devil, and his tone was far from civil. He ignored Melisande and Amanda and strode past them to the waiting carriage, climbing in without waiting to see if his wife was behind him.

'Priscilla—sister . . .' Melisande went to her, and was about to kiss one rouged cheek when she pulled back, eyes flashing angrily.

'Don't patronise me with your pose of sweet innocence! It makes me sick!' she hissed, and Melisande recoiled from her, horrified.

'That was not my intention at all. As we are about to part, I thought we could at least do so as friends. We have not been as close as sisters should, but . . .' She shrugged her shoulders, acknowledging that they never would. 'I hope you are happy in London. Perhaps Jason and I will come and visit you soon.'

'Delay the pleasure as long as possible!' Priscilla's gaze swept upwards, and then round the beautiful room in which she stood. She would never forgive her sister for having all this. She had nothing! A drunken brute of a husband who had broken down the door in the dead of night and woken her so that he could take his pleasure. There had been no sign of the suave, persuasive man who had made love to her in the garden. This one had given her no thought at all, and when he had finished, he had muttered something about being cheated and staggered back into his own room. She had cried herself to sleep, appalled at the prospect of further encounters with him. But this morning he had calmly told her that she had his name, and that was all she would have. The dowry was his, and the allowance from his brother. She would see nothing of either! Two thousand a year would not pay even his gambling bills, let alone his tailor, or the countless other merchants who supplied his needs.

For an hour she had stared at her reflection in a

mirror, at her swollen cheeks and red eyes. No man had ever done this to her before and none would ever do so again! What Richard would not give her, others would. She was beautiful—sensuous—and once again in control of her life. She would make no more mistakes. London and the court would be full of handsome men —rich men who would pay well for her company, and she had the protection of her husband's name. She would be discreet, but never without an escort, never without money and jewels.

Her eyes returned to Melisande's pale features, and a smile twisted the corners of her mouth as they wandered over her sister's slender form. 'Do you really think he will bring you to London? You, his little country bride? You would be so out of place. You would never know how to conduct yourself in the circles in which he moves. He will leave you here, Melisande; I have already told you that. You will be big and swollen with child—an heir for his precious Whispering Wood—and he will leave you here while he goes to his mistress in London. Shall I find out for you who she is? If she is pretty?' The venom in her voice robbed Melisande of speech. The words were spoken too low to carry to Jason who stood a few feet away, staring out at the carriage which held his brother, but they reached Amanda's ears, and the reaction they provoked was as startling as Priscilla's poisonous remarks.

'No, he will not! He *cares* for her. Do you hear me? He always has, since the first time she came to Whispering Wood. He will not desert her as Richard will you! Nor will he allow her eyes ever to stray in the direction of another man, as yours will! Richard does not care what you do or who you are with, now that he has your dowry and Jason's allowance. Do you think I don't know what he is like? I do, oh, I do! So many have gone before you, and many will come after. He does not have one genuine feeling in his body. He will use you as he did me. As he did poor Rose.'

Priscilla's lips formed the name, but no sound came

from them. Rose! Melisande's maid, whose child's eyes eyes were so like those of . . . Not Jason, but his brother! With a stifled cry, she fled out to the carriage. It moved off immediately, and Melisande was left with a fleeting glimpse of her sister's tortured features at the window.

Her own mind reeled under the shock of Amanda's words. Richard—not Jason—was the father of Rose's child! Not her husband! Jason turned and looked at her curiously as Amanda, bright-cheeked and embarrassed by her outburst, excused herself and hurried upstairs, but Melisande remained, looking wide-eyed into the face of her husband.

'What was that all about?' he enquired with a half smile. She looked as if she had just been struck by a thunderbolt. What the devil had Priscilla been saying?

'You . . . I mean Richard . . .' Melisande faltered, acutely conscious of the way his brows were drawing together in a deep frown. 'I was told . . . I thought . . .' The words suddenly came rushing out to bring glittering embers into the grey depths surveying her. 'Richard is the father of Rose's child.'

'One of many skeletons released from the Dacre family closet,' Jason said humourlessly, then, 'Why, who did you imagine? Dammit, Melisande . . . you didn't think?' Her silence condemned her! Any words of apology would sound futile. How she had wronged him. 'I could hit you for your shallow little mind, do you know that?' he snapped tight-lipped, and stormed into the study, slamming the door behind him and leaving her alone—shaken and remorseful—and wishing he had!

Melisande could not sleep. She tossed and turned in bed, tormented by the memory of Amanda's words. He cares for her! Did he? Why, then, had he not told her? Her eyes flew open as the communicating door was pushed ajar, and Jason was standing there, framed against the light on the table behind him. He was still fully dressed, even though it was after three in the morning.

'Are you asleep, Melisande? Don't worry, I haven't

come to force my unwelcome presence on you. I thought you might be pleased to hear that I am going to London next week, and taking Amanda with me.' Merlin yawned and stretched, annoyed at the light that slanted directly across the spot on the bed where he was lying. Jason did not move from the doorway, as though he had no wish to enter her room. 'I shall sail with *Moonwynd* to Plymouth, and be away a week, perhaps more. If you wish, you may invite your father to stay with you, if you feel the need for company, although I assure you that there is plenty here to keep you occupied.'

Melisande had never heard his voice so uninterested—so devoid of emotion. It was as though he had closed a door between them. In part, Priscilla's malicious words were coming true. He was going away! To London first, where he would no doubt be entertained by his mistress before boarding *Moonwynd*. And taking Amanda with him, whose company she had grown to enjoy over the past weeks. It was deliberate, as everything he did to her these days was deliberate, meant to hurt her—to subdue her!

The door closed behind him, once more plunging the room into darkness. Satisfied that the disturbance was over, Merlin cautiously crept on to the pillow beside her, as he did every night while she slept, and settled down for the night.

Melisande threw back the bedclothes and ran to the door, to fling it open again. Jason, in the act of pouring himself a glass of brandy, turned to see the ashen-faced creature who stood on the threshold of his room, desperately seeking the right words to say. His eyes remained riveted on the red hair that streamed past her shoulders before they slowly descended—with an eyebrow rising sardonically—to her flimsy night-apparel, for she had given no thought, as she leapt from bed, to slippers or a robe.

'Has hell frozen over that you come to me like this?' he asked with a soft laugh.

Melisande ignored the taunt. 'I will not be treated like

an unwanted piece of furniture,' she declared bravely, and over the rim of his goblet, Jason's eyes glittered with silver sparks. How easy it would be to take her in his arms and teach her the enjoyment of being a woman, but he had promised himself he would not give in to her again, or to his own desires—no matter how damned difficult it was; at times, the sight of her tore his heart apart with longing. She must come to him and apologise for the words spoken on their wedding night. Was that the reason for this startling visit now?

'A piece of furniture?' he queried, the intensity of his stare growing until she began to blush. 'No, you are not that. More like a statue: a piece of cold marble that has no heart. Beautiful, but of little use except to admire from afar.' He heard her gasp at the insult. 'As for being unwanted . . . far from it.'

'You—you still want me for your wife?' she stammered, unable to believe her ears. 'Then why are you leaving me alone, deserting me?'

'My dear girl, I am only going to Mousehole. As I shall not be sailing with Drake, I need a captain for *Moonwynd*. I know such a man, and if he agrees to my offer, he will take the ship on to Plymouth and join the fleet gathering there. Deserting you? If you continue to look at me with such appeal in those lovely eyes, I shall begin to believe you will miss me, and that would be a misconception, would it not?' Jason flung back, putting his drink aside, untouched. 'Perhaps I should consider Drake's offer and leave you for a year. When I returned, I might find a wife waiting for me.'

The look of shock on her face took him aback. He thought she might welcome the idea, but she looked quite stunned at the prospect. She was thinking of herself, of course. The boredom of those long days alone—the loneliness . . .

'Why are you taking Amanda to London with you?' Somehow Melisande found her voice, but the question was not the one she meant to ask.

'The child has not enjoyed much social life this year

—you know the reason for that. I understand she has told you about her involvement with my brother. I am glad. I believe it means she has at last acknowledged that what I did was the right thing for her. And perhaps she has gone some small way to forgiving me for the pain I caused her then. If only you . . . 'Jason broke off, and picked up his brandy again. 'She needs to be among more people of her own age to give her back some self-confidence.'

'While you amuse yourself elsewhere.' Melisande's voice trembled as she forced out the hateful words. Again, they were not those uppermost in her mind. If she asked him to take her—would he? Would he show off his country bride to his London friends? How Priscilla's words stung her. By the harshness that came into Jason's face, she knew he had understood her meaning.

'At least I should be made welcome—in her house and in her bed,' he snapped, and she flinched from him, floundering once more on the brink of indecision. It was a lie. He had parted on good terms from the woman who had been his mistress for just eight months, and two weeks later she had transferred her affections to one of his friends. Why could he not tell Melisande that there was only one woman in his life—a red-headed witch who plagued his thoughts night and day? Pride, he thought wryly. He always had possessed too much. And in Melisande he had found a soul-mate. At least they shared something! 'Go to bed before we both say more things we shall regret.'

She turned away, tears blurring her vision. If she allowed him to go, she might lose him forever to his mistress—or to another woman more willing to please him. He would never know that she loved him, she wanted so desperately to be everything he desired of her. Love him! Yes, now she knew it with startling clarity. She *did* love him. She spun about, and he barely contained an oath at the sight of her tearful face.

'Jason . . .'

'Melisande . . .' They both spoke at once and then fell into an awkward silence, staring at each other. Jason indicated that she should continue.

'Are you ashamed of me that you have not asked me to come with you?' she asked in a small voice. Still it was impossible for her to beg.

'Do you want to be seen in the company of a man whose presence you find distasteful?' His eyes seemed to bore into her very soul. 'I naturally assumed you would prefer to remain here.'

'I—I have never been to London. I think I would find it exciting.' How breathless she sounded. He would refuse, of course. Why would he want her with him when he had a pretty mistress to accommodate him?

'Very well.' Jason shrugged his shoulders, the casual gesture betraying none of the exhilaration suddenly coursing through his veins. 'But there is a condition. When we return to Whispering Wood, you will sleep in this room in my bed.'

'As you wish.' It was done! She had committed herself. And it felt wonderful!

In two strides Jason had crossed the space between them and his fingers fastened over her shoulders. His face came close to hers, and the embers in those grey pools were now a roaring fire that made her knees grow weak.

'Don't play games with me, Melisande, or you will find yourself in my bed this instant, willing or not,' he said harshly. 'You've shown little inclination to share anything with me since our wedding night.'

'That was your choice . . .' she began, and he interrupted her.

'And you know why! Nothing has changed. If I take you with me, it means that you have agreed that our marriage will no longer be the farce it has been these past weeks. I'll brook no last-minute show of shyness, or whatever ruse you think to employ to keep me from you. None shall. Do you still want to come?'

Mutely she nodded, her gaze never wavering beneath

his stare. A heavy sigh escaped his lips. For a moment she thought he would kiss her, but he did not, and when he released her and drew back, she little realised the effort it cost him. But Jason knew if he touched those soft lips, possessed them as he longed to, he would have to possess her body too—and it would be too soon. He had a better way: he would take her to London. He would woo her as he knew she had always wanted—and win her, for now he was sure that she would not longer refuse him. And when they came home . . .

'So be it. Pack your most alluring gowns and your jewellery. I shall show you London in all its grandeur—and all its squalor, so that you will not want to remain there as your sister does but rather reside here at Whispering Wood where you belong,' he told her, his features once more masked by the smile that revealed none of his inner torment. How difficult it had become to restrain himself these past weeks. Thank God she had resolved the conflict between them! He had achieved victory far sooner than he anticipated, yet it brought him no satisfaction. That would come when he held her in his arms and she did not try to flee from him. Then he would be able to tell her everything—and to apologise for his manner.

Did she really belong at Whispering Wood, Melisande wondered, as she closed the door of her room behind her and crossed to the window. Drawing back the heavy curtain, she stared out into the darkened garden. The wind was sighing in the trees again—even the slightest breeze elsewhere seemed to intensify once one turned into the drive approaching the house. She could barely hear the sound of the river tonight. If she belonged—if she loved Jason . . . There was no doubt in her mind that she *did* love him! Why, then, did they not whisper his name to her as in the legend? She strained her ears—nothing . . .

It did not matter, she told herself fiercely as she climbed back into bed and eased Merlin to one side so that she could regain a little of her pillow. He was taking her to London. They would be together, and once they returned, she knew he would not hesitate to claim his rights as her husband. He had made that quite clear. It was what she wanted. Perhaps in her heart she had always secretly wanted him. So be it. When she returned to Whispering Wood, she would be his wife! Then she would hear the wind whisper his name. Then she would belong—accepted by house and husband.

'I am so glad you are coming with us,' Amanda declared when she heard the news the next morning. 'I knew he would relent in the end.'

'Relent?' Melisande queried, looking up from the selection of petticoats spread across the bed. She had lost no time in deciding what to take with her. She wanted to look her prettiest and make Jason proud of her, and so make up for their estrangement.

'He said you would come, but he was not going to tell you until the very last moment. I think you had made him angry over something. He did not say what, of course. He does not discuss his personal feelings with anyone. He never has.'

'Yet—yet you knew he had seen me at the ball here—and . . .'

'And taken a fancy to you? Oh, yes. I heard him discussing you with his mother. I shall never forget his words, because they were so out of character for him. Jason had never shown the slightest inclination to marry, and then his eyes alighted on—how old were you then? —thirteen . . .'

'What did he say?' Melisande begged, not caring that she had gone to him unnecessarily and begged him to take her to London. It had—or would soon—bring them together, and that was all that mattered.

'I listened outside the garden door . . . I was fascinated at the thought of the inscrutable Jacre Dacre smitten by a thirteen-year-old girl. Now, what were his exact words?' Amanda's smile was mischievous as she watched Melisande's face. 'I shall marry that girl. Yes, that was what he said. No matter how long I have to wait, I shall have her! I've been thinking about it lately . . . Isn't it romantic! Just like a fairy-taile. To have a man want you for five years . . . to be so patient . . . yet steadfast in his resolve. I am so happy for you both. I really am. I know I haven't shown it, and have been selfish and rude and involved in my own troubles. Yet I have none, and it's time I accepted that. Jason was right to come between Richard and myself. We would never have been happy. I realise now that I never loved him. I would have been miserable, and Jason, bless him, was wise enough to see it.'

'Why don't you tell him?' Melisande said, hugging her. 'I know he would welcome a show of affection from you—as it used to be.'

I shall marry that girl. No matter how long I have to wait, I shall have her! The words spun around in Melisande's brain. Five years! Just like a fairy-tale. Indeed it was! The kind of story she had loved to read and could lose herself in, shutting out the ugliness of the world. How beautiful the world was today, she thought, as she handed Rose several petticoats and started to select her shoes. Everything was beautiful, and she was suddenly very, very happy.

CHAPTER NINE

THE JOURNEY TO London was begun on a dull, overcast day with rain threatening to descend upon the travellers throughout the whole of the journey. A lame horse faced an unwanted overnight stay at an inn outside Oxford, and the next morning Melisande awoke to the sound of heavy rain pounding on the windows of her room, and was desolate. She had wanted her first glimpse of the city to be one of splendour and colour, so that she might see and understand what attracted so many people to its crowded streets. However, a few hours after they had continued on their way a weak sun broke through the grey clouds, and her spirits, like the weather, began slowly to lift.

From the seat opposite, Amanda and Jason watched her growing excitement with some amusement, but were careful not to allow it to show lest they diminished it. There was nothing exciting in London for either of them. Amanda had come to accept the shallowness of the friends that surrounded her whenever she stayed there and attended court, the lack of reality about the world in which she had once moved and thought was everything to her.

For Jason it was the home of *Moonwynd* and, as such, drew him back whenever necessary, but he had long ago ceased to be attracted to the bawdy atmosphere which prevailed at court and detested the intrigues and plots about the Queen. Elizabeth, as she aged, had grown even more difficult than she had been in her youth, when the fiery nature of her mother Anne Boleyn, coupled with the crude, often lewd characteristics of her father Henry VIII, had sent courtiers scuttling from her presence in fear of their lives. She was more unpredictable, more difficult when it came to retaining the loyalty of men who had once worshipped her and whom she had turned upon in her unbelievable vanity. As a queen, Jason acknowledged she was as good, if not better, at stratagems than a man would have been, but her intransigence—the very thing that had carried her and England through many difficult times with the Spanish, including the bitter and desperate fight with the Spanish Armada—now threatened to destroy all that once had been peaceful and serene. No one knew where they stood with her any longer. No, he had no taste for London, or the many things it had to offer. He was pleased that as soon as Whispering Wood had disappeared behind him, he longed to be back and could not return soon enough. If only Melisande felt that way, too. He had to show her London, show her the kind of life that some men and women revelled in. He would show her more: the narrow, cobbled streets filled with stinking refuse; the beggars who tore at heartstrings during the day, yet at night were miraculously cured of their ailments—limbs no longer broken or twisted, eyes that could see—in order that they could lurk in some dark alley and rob whomever passed by.

And then there was the bear-baiting pits which lined the River Thames, where lords and ladies rubbed shoulders with those same beggars and merchants and peasants, the latter hoping to improve their miserable existence by betting on a winning animal with the last coin in their possession—the very coin that spent elsewhere could have bought food or treatment for their family. It was an ugly world, and he did not want to dwell in it. Man's inhumanity to his fellow creatures often sickened him. Most certainly it angered him, and often he would return home in a black mood that took days to fade.

Would Melisande find the answer to her dreams here in this teeming city? Would her eyes alight on some handsome face, and he would see a hunger there not apparent when she looked at him? She wanted him, he knew it, yet she was denying it. Her sudden capitulation had taken him totally by surprise. He had been too exhilarated at first to think much on it, but now as the carriage drew nearer to *Moonwynd*'s anchorage, his thoughts were full of her, and of the silent promise she had made to him with her agreement to accompany him to the ship. He had deliberately kept his distance from her at the inn, sleeping on a hard chair while she took the bed. It was no hardship, for he had spent many worse nights on board ship without sleep—and he had *not* slept the night before. How could he, when she was so close, yet so distant from him? Not yet, he told himself again, smothering the urge to sit beside her so that he might feel her body against his as the carriage swayed and lurched over the uneven road. He had no shame where she was concerned. Over the past weeks he had used any excuse to touch her, to kiss her and try to ease the tension between them. It had melted away as if it had never existed, he thought in wonderment as she looked at him, her blue eyes sparkling with excitement. Never had he seen them shine so!

'Are we nearly there?' she asked.

'It will be almost dark before we reach the ship,' he told her, and instantly there was disappointment on her face. 'Don't worry. Tomorrow we shall start our tour of the city early, so you must get a good night's sleep.'

'How long can we stay? I want to see everything,' Melisande breathed, returning her attention to the outline of buildings in front of them. So many houses all cramped together. Goodness! How did people breathe?

'You shall, my sweet. I promise,' Jason murmured. 'Be patient.'

Patience! A virtue he had learned from his mother, bless her. Who, when he had told her what was in his heart that night many years ago, had merely smiled and not ridiculed him for a seemingly impossible wish. He stole a look at Amanda, who, bored with the dullness of the journey, was dozing, her fair head resting against the padded side of the carriage. Without the additional money he had spent on the conveyance to make it more comfortable, travelling would have been an abomination. He preferred to travel on horseback, for he was ill at ease confined within such a constricting space and had taken the precaution, as always when he journeyed away from home, of secreting weapons beneath the seats without the two girls knowing. He did not want either of them to be worried over the fact that every mile was potentially dangerous for them, in a time when highwaymen and footpads lost no opportunity to rob travellers.

One day soon he hoped to be able to confide to her his mother's dying words: he prayed it was not too late. Amanda had been more amicable of late . . . Melisande's influence, he acknowledged, grateful that she had not taken sides in the dispute and so caused further disruption. Perhaps, soon, he would be able to confide in his young wife also. The only two people he cared about in the world had been little more than strangers for so many weeks. The loneliness which had tormented him had, at times, been almost too great to bear. Was it over now?

When she awoke next morning, Melisande lay for several minutes not knowing where she was. The bed seemed to be moving beneath her! And then she relaxed, remembering that she was aboard *Moonwynd* and had slept in a bed almost as large as the one at Whispering Wood. And so comfortable! How long had she been asleep? Pushing aside the bedcovers, she ran to the latticed window and peered out, and a gasp escaped her lips. So many people! And ships! And women washing at the river's edge, spreading the laundry over the banks to dry in the sun.

It was a beautiful day. No sign of threatening black clouds to mar her excitement. Opening the window, she leaned her arms on the sill and listened to the gentle sound of the water lapping against the side of the ship. Above her she could hear someone singing . . . and an authoritative voice, immediately recognisable as that of her husband, giving orders. For an instant her heart ached as she thought of Lucy. How she wished she had thought to ask Jason if she could have come with them.

The wharves as far as she could see teemed with men who were repairing boats of every size and description. The houses were set quite close to the water, she saw, not envying the occupants when winter came—how cold and damp they must be, and in summer, all the odours of the water would pervade the homes. How different was Whispering Wood: the stream there was crystal clear, undesecrated by Nature or by man. Her nose wrinkled slightly at the smell of fish, and she saw some gutted remains floating past amid a pile of débris.

'Are you hungry?' Jason asked from the doorway. 'Come and have some food before we depart.' He had been watching her in silence for some while, enjoying the childish excitement radiating from her. Soon he would teach her what it was to be a woman, but this moment was hers, and he would do nothing to spoil it for her. Melisande was more than a little surprised when he caught up her robe, held it out to her, but made no attempt to take further liberties, as was his usual practice.

She followed him into the adjoining cabin, larger than the bedroom and furnished with solid oak. A table was laid with gleaming silverware, on which was a decanter of wine and a platter of sliced meats. For Melisande alone, someone had provided piping hot toast dripping with butter, and a bowl of fresh fruit. She noticed that Jason touched nothing while she ate, and lifted enquiring eyes.

'I have eaten,' he said with a smile, 'while you were still in dreamland. A sailor rises early.'

'Where is Amanda?'

'Still sleeping. It is only nine o'clock, and she is used to rising about noon.'

'Then she won't be coming with us today?' Secretly Melisande was pleased that they might be alone together and did not bother to hide it as she once would have done. The look Jason gave her made her heart flutter unsteadily.

'She has—other plans.'

As he relaxed in his chair, Melisande thought how easily he adapted himself to his surroundings. To look at him now, anyone would take him for a sea-captain in his leather jerkin and dark hide trousers, with knee-length seaboots which clung to his muscled legs. The white silk shirt accentuated the darkness of his features, and he looked almost piratical, she thought. Worthy of being in the company of Francis Drake, who, it was said, was little more than a pirate himself. Only his letters of marque from the Queen kept him above the law. Yet, without such men, would England be so great? How she longed to ask him about his adventures in far-off lands, but she did not deem it prudent. After the terrible way she had treated him since their betrothal, he might believe her questions arose out of some ulterior motive.

'May we go and see Priscilla while we are here?' she asked quietly. 'I know Father would be pleased to have news of her. She has not written to him since she left.'

'Did you really expect her to?' Jason asked. 'That one is concerned only with herself. Would you spoil our day before it has begun? But—if you must, a very, very brief visit. Is that clear?'

Melisande nodded. She had no wish to linger with her sister longer than was necessary. Nor would she allow Priscilla to spoil this very precious day. Her day—*and* Jason's day.

'What is that building over there, the white one that looks like a castle?' Melisande asked, biting into a crisp, green apple as she rose to sit on one of the padded seats beside the open window. Jason joined her, bending to follow her pointing finger.

'That's the White Tower. Where the Queen puts all the people she doesn't like,' he returned, smilingly. 'It has housed many famous people in the past. Now poor Walter Raleigh is entombed there. Such a man was not meant to be confided.'

'*The* Tower,' Melisande said awed by the battlements and crenellated walls. She had heard of the place, of course, who had not! King Henry had imprisoned there the wives who upset him, Anne Boleyn and Catherine Howard. And the Queen herself, when she had been the Princess Elizabeth, had lived many years within its walls, a prisoner of her sister, Mary. 'I do not think I want to see that too closely.'

'Where then shall we start?'

'Take me to the markets? I want to buy presents for Father and Lucy. Anything—everything, Jason,' she pleaded. 'How long are we here?'

'I should sail tomorrow on the afternoon tide. Time enough for you to have satisfied your curiosity, I think. Tonight, you shall listen to Will Shakespeare and his players again. Perhaps a visit to a bear-pit? A tavern on the waterfront? I know just the place, so that others may envy my good fortune when they gaze on you.'

'You are laughing at me,' she accused, turning her face away as he bent his head towards her. Only a day! She had brought enough clothes for a week at least, wanting him to be proud of her when they went out together. But a day was more than they had shared since their wedding. It was a beginning.

Pushing aside her loose hair, Jason brushed the nape of her neck with his lips. Instantly he felt her tense, and was about to draw back when he realised she was leaning back against him rather than straining forward, away from him. Turning her to face him, he tilted back her head and took her mouth with a heart-stopping kiss which seemed to go on for ever. Neither wanted to end it, and it was with great reluctance that he straightened, pleased by her response and more than a little aroused by her willingness.

'I think you should go and dress, or we shall not stir from this cabin the whole day,' he warned, wary of the sudden change in her.

'Wait and see what I shall wear,' Melisande ran into the bedroom, returning with a gown of deep burgundy silk in her arms. 'Do you like it?'

'You will turn every head if you put that on,' Jason chuckled, as he imagined her parading through the streets in such finery.

'It is not to your liking? What is wrong with it? Does the colour look wrong against my hair?'

'Not at all. I like it very much, but wear it tonight and find something a little less dazzling for our tour of the city.'

'Oh . . .' As she stared at the exquisite needlework on the stomacher, the heavy velvet underskirt and the rows of pure white lace that bordered the sleeves and hemline, Melisande understood.

'It pleases me to see you in fine clothes, but,' he added, a gleam in his eyes, 'I like you with—or without—finery.'

'I do not think I shall ever grow accustomed to anyone speaking to me as you do,' Melisande said, bright colour stealing into her cheeks.

'I am not anyone, my sweet. I am your husband. Go and change now; there is much to be seen.'

Melisande could not remember having enjoyed a day so much in all her life. The one brief, aggravating interlude when they visited Priscilla in her new home near Holborn was quickly forgotten as Jason whisked her away to see new sights. They should have forewarned her sister of their coming, she reflected, as they wandered down a cobbled street, not minding in the least the way merchandise was thrust beneath her nose for inspection. She had bought so much already, and Jason had not said a word to deter her!

Her sister had looked thinner, despite the gorgeous dress she had been wearing and the magnificent string of pearls about her neck. She had been on her way out on the arm of a middle-aged man whom she introduced, somewhat reluctantly, as Lord Pritchard. He was old enough to be her father, Melisande had thought, as she watched them walk away from the house, not liking the possessive way Priscilla clung to his arm, a permanent smile frozen upon her rouged cheeks. When Jason had asked after his brother, he was coldly told that Richard had been gambling for the past week, during which time he had not shown himself at home.

Neither Melisande nor Jason discussed the incident during the day, but when she looked into her husband's face, she knew what he was thinking. It was in her own mind too. She would say nothing to her father or to Lucy. Better they remembered her as she had been on her wedding day—beautifully gowned and adorned in jewels and satisfied with the catch she had made. How lucky *she* was, Melisande thought, as Jason's hand beneath her elbow steadied her as her foot stumbled on the uneven road.

'Where to now?' she enquired as he paused to look about them. They had been walking for hours—her feet thrust into neat leather shoes with bright red heels looked most elegant, but how they ached! And she was thirsty.

'I think it is time we retraced our steps and returned to *Moonwynd*. You will want to rest before we go out again. I do not want to waste one moment of this evening, so please do not fall asleep on my shoulder, my sweet,' Jason said, lightly touching her cheek with a ringed hand. As if she would! Did he not realise that she was looking forward to it as much as he? How could he? She had given him little reason, but tonight she would change all that. 'You are—different today,' he murmured, oblivious of the passers-by who had to step around them. He had eyes only for the lovely, so innocent, face upturned to his. How her cheeks glowed with colour and her eyes sparkled with a brilliance that could outdo any jewel; even the diamonds he had stowed safely away aboard *Moonwynd* until the time was right to return them to her. What had she been thinking of to give them to her father to sell? Thinking of others, as always. And Edwin—to try to sell them in Newbury, at the very jewellers he had purchased them from? They should both have known word would reach him sooner or later.

'I am happy,' Melisande replied, tucking her hand through his arm. 'And I am not in the least tired.'

'Well, I am, and I have some business to attend to before we start out again,' Jason told her as he turned her about. 'We have walked at least three miles from St Katharine's Hospital, where the ship is. You have bought up half of London on the way, and made me realise I am fast growing old. I shall welcome the peace of Whispering Wood after this excursion.'

'Old! You are not old . . . At least . . .' He was fourteen years her senior, with a great deal of experience in the world. What had she to offer him, except a love she was afraid to acknowledge lest he repulsed her.

'Thank you for the compliment—it was one, I trust.'

'Do you not like London, then?' she asked as they began to retrace their steps. He was right—they had come a very long way, and her legs were beginning to feel like lead. 'You do not want to live here, like your brother?'

'Live here, amid this noise? Attend court and watch how everyone fawns before the Queen and then plots behind her back? Never! I have lived in both worlds, and I prefer the country. The sea would take second place if I needed to make a choice. Is London not a disappointment for you?'

'No!' His eyes examined her face, and she smiled and gave a nod. 'A little, perhaps, but I would not have missed it for the world. But to compare life here to the one I have at Whispering Wood . . . This means nothing to me.'

'Then you would not mind if I did not present you at court?' Jason asked softly. He had intended to, and if she wanted it, he would, and would hate every moment she was being ogled by his so-called friends.

'Are you ashamed of me that you will not do so?' she asked in a hushed voice, and the hand covering hers tightened upon her fingers.

'The shame would be mine, in presenting you to people not worthy to kiss your hand—in opening the door to another world, one I do not think you would like, where wives cuckold their husbands daily and take great delight in it. Where husbands take and discard mistresses in the same manner as they would throw away a pair of old shoes. Where old men and women try to retain their youth by taking young lovers. Where to smile at a man, as you might, would mean you were willing to share his bed.'

'You make it sound horrible,' Melisande exclaimed, her vision of an elegant, intellectual court where she would be able to converse with people who shared her interests rapidly fading.

'On the surface there is beauty, as there are in these streets when you look about you. Do you not think the gardens over there are delightful? During the day they are. At night they will harbour footpads and men who would slit your throat for a single coin. Many of the fine houses we have passed are inhabited by people so deeply in debt that they frequently have to pawn the family silver or pewter in order to attend court. Life there is very expensive. And shallow. A friend one day could be an enemy the next.'

'I do still quite like London,' Melisande declared. 'It is so different. The people are—are exciting. Every face expresses something new for me. I know everyone in Kingsclere and they know me . . . but not here.'

'And it pleases you not to be known?' Jason chuckled.

'Yes, it does. I do not feel as if I am being watched —my every action assessed and deliberated about. I can go where I please, and am no different from any other woman in the street; I say what I like without the local gossip bandying it all over the village. If I were to walk down the road on your arm as I am now, everyone would be looking at us, speculating. Here, we are just two ordinary people out walking.'

'You will never be ordinary, Melisande. But you speak as if you feel restricted at Whispering Wood. Do you? Why? You are free to do whatever you wish, to go where you please. I have imposed no conditions on you at any time.'

'I know. I did not mean to imply that you had. It is just that I feel—feel so free here with you today. I think perhaps I have grown up a little in these past few days. I shall think differently when I return home, you will see.'

'So many men and women in this world are ambitious, yet you have neither ambition nor guile, or you would have accepted our marriage from the beginning.' A slight frown wrinkled Jason's brows as he looked down at her. 'That worries me, my sweet. You seek things for others and are prepared to sacrifice for them—your sisters and your father—never for yourself. Do no ambitions lurk behind those pretty, fascinating eyes? No desires of the heart to blind you?'

'But of course!' The look she gave him was wickedly provocative. 'My prince on a white charger. I shall always have him.' But now he was by her side, flesh and blood, not a shadowy figure in her dreams.

'Which I have denied you forever.' There was an odd note in Jason's voice . . . almost a tremor.

'My dreams are still my own, Jason. Do not take everything from me at once,' she murmured, lowering her gaze. Her heart belonged to him, and she knew she could not contain her secret any longer. Tonight she would tell him! She could not wait to return home!

By the time Melisande and Jason reached *Moonwynd* again, she was exhausted and paused only long enough to remove her shoes before falling upon the bed and sinking into a deep sleep. It was dark when she awoke. Someone had lighted a hanging lantern, and she lay sleepily watching it sway to and fro at the end of the bed. She had been dreaming of Whispering Wood, of standing at an open window and hearing the wind whisper Jason's name. The moment must happen! Amanda had said he cared for her. Her father believed it—and had he not said himself that he cared? Love had never been mentioned. Dare she hope it might happen for him as it had for her? Did it matter? She had enough for them both, and she would show him; then, perhaps, there would be truth and honesty between them for the first time since they had met again.

She lay remembering the many places he had shown her that day—and although London had not proved to be the glittering spectacle she had expected, she was glad to have seen it. She had watched shipwrights at work near *Moonwynd*, marvelled at the expertise of basket-makers and fanmakers, tasted the delights which came out of a hot oven, produced by master bakers, and marvelled at the intricate work being down in a small back street by Levantine goldsmiths. Every tiny street and alley held some delight for her. It would never have interested Lucy or Priscilla, but for her, it was a visit never to be forgotten.

Amanda, who came to help her to dress, found her elaborate descriptions amusing, for she had seen them all and considered them not worthy of a second thought. Markets were for selling things, she said with a shrug of her shoulders; what was exciting about that? Melisande realised that she had not seen them as she herself had.

'Tonight will be something to remember,' she said, fastening Melisande's gown. 'Fireworks, gaiety. And many young men . . .'

'Whom I hope you will keep at a respectful distance,' Jason declared as he came into the cabin, and immediately Amanda's mouth deepened into a pout.

'If you are going to start lecturing me again,' she began petulantly, and Melisande made an impatient gesture.

'Stop it, both of you! I will not have my day spoiled by your petty bickering.' Both looked at her in open-mouthed amazement, not used to hearing such a commanding tone. 'If you did not want her to enjoy herself, Jason, why did you bring her? Of course you did, because you know she will now use her head and not allow herself to be swayed by her heart. And you,

Amanda—why do you not admit to him that you have no intention of allowing your head to be turned by the first attractive man who looks at you? You don't want to be hurt again, do you? Or to hurt Jason, too, with your foolishness?'

'We stand justifiably rebuked,' Jason said, a smile deepening the corners of his mouth. 'I apologise, Mandy.'

'It has been a long time since you have called me that . . .' Amanda's lips trembled, and then with a soft cry she flung herself into his arms and kissed him full on the mouth. Melisande saw Jason's whole body stiffen with the shock of her action—that, or something deeper . . . something he kept secret. Why was it that when she saw the two of them together she felt they were so much closer than ward and guardian? The way he looked at her . . . The tenderness in his voice when he spoke . . . Over Amanda's shoulder he caught her questioning look, and she saw deep pain registered briefly in his eyes. There was more. But what? Would she never begin to know what was locked in his mind—his heart?

'We have both been rather foolish. Melisande has shown us how much it has affected our relationship. Let it end here, Mandy,' Jason said gently, his lips against her hair. After a moment she drew back, staring up into his face.

'I can choose my own friends again?'

'Have you not always done so?' It was a subtle reminder of what had taken place when he allowed her to go her own way. 'You should never have cause to be ashamed to tell me when you are attracted to someone. We used to be so open with each other until . . .'

'Until Richard,' Amanda answered, stepping back out of his embrace. 'I shall not make that mistake again. I know what I want now.'

'And what is that?' Jason enquired softly.

'To be like you and Melisande—happy, content. Trusting each other. You are so lucky—both of you!'

Bright tears glistened in her eyes, she turned and ran

from them. It was some while before either Jason or Melisande were able to move or to speak. Her words had touched them both in vulnerable places, for different reasons.

'I—I think everything will be all right between you now,' she said at length, and he nodded, moving forward to complete the fastening at the back of Melisande's gown. He was very adept, she thought. How many women had he had before her? How many beautiful, elegant women that he would not have minded being at his side at court? He did not want her there . . . to be seen by his friends . . . presented before the Queen. She had pretended that it did not matter, but it did! That would have been the climax to it all—his final acceptance of her as his wife. Then she could thrust aside Priscilla's comments with the contempt they deserved.

As Jason turned away towards the jewel-box that lay open on the bed, she allowed her gaze to admire the tall frame elegantly clad in a buff tunic with leather facings, a three-quarter cloak of a darker colour casually draped over his left shoulder. He wore a sword and dagger, despite the informality of the occasion. The sleeves of the doublet were slashed to reveal bright yellow silk that matched the lined cuffs of his leather gauntlets.

She felt her heart stop as he began to sort through the items there. She had not yet decided what to wear with the burgundy silk, and when he turned back to her, an eyebrow raised enquiringly, she said quickly, 'I thought the rubies, or the emeralds . . .'

'Where are your diamonds, Melisande? Nothing could better match the brightness of your eyes. Wear them tonight to please me.'

The diamonds! The ones she had given to Father for Lucy.

'I . . . Are they not there?' She joined him at the bedside, looking down at the assortment of beautiful stones gleaming in the lantern-light. 'I must have left them behind—how silly! But never mind, Jason. You choose for me, what I shall wear.'

Jason stared at her long and hard, his eyes narrowing at the tremor in her voice. The stones in his pocket should have been tossed in her face for her hypocrisy . . . whom had they been meant for? Her father? No, he had sufficient to keep him in comfort for many a year. Lucy? Of course, why had he not realised that sooner? For Lucy, so that her sister would not be forced into marriage. Did Melisande still consider herself an unwilling bride?

His fingers curled around the stones, and then came away empty. This was not the time. He would only provoke more conflict between them. In time she would tell him of her own free will. There would be no more coercion . . .

He selected a ruby pendant surrounded by diamonds, and fastened it round her neck. She quickly added matching earrings, relieved that he had not pressed the absence of the diamonds. Why had he remembered them out of all the pieces he had given her? Surely he could not know . . . His expression told her nothing as he stepped back to survey her appearance.

'The final touch.' He held out to her an embroidered mask, glittering with gold thread.

'Where are we going?' she asked, excitement rising in her. 'To a masked ball?'

'There is a firework display on the Thames tonight. The Queen will be in attendance, and I thought you would like to see it.'

So that was what Amanda had meant by gaiety, and many young men. It would be a time for flirting, for making assignations, for deception!

'Will you be wearing a mask?' she asked, and Jason shook his head.

'I have no need to hide my identity.'

'Nor I mine,' she returned, putting it aside.

'I am glad you said that.' He came close to her, his fingers reaching out to touch the mass of red curls draped in profusion over one shoulder. 'I like your hair this way, but best of all I like it loose . . . like tongues of hell-fire over your skin.' He kissed her with fierce, dominant ardour before escorting her on deck.

Amanda stood talking to a young man beside the gang-plank that joined ship to shore. A good-looking young man, Melisande saw as she drew closer, and then she recognised the face turned in her direction. Christopher Avery! He and Amanda! Could it be? Was that why she had been so willing to accompany Lucy on her secret trips to see him? She could not bring herself to be angry with the girl, for Lucy had no real interest in the young sailor except to use him to help her escape from an unwanted marriage. Now that was not to be, perhaps she would acknowledge that what she felt for him was solely friendship. If she did so, would his eyes alight elsewhere? As they were doing now?

'I leave my ward in your capable hands, Kit,' Jason said, halting before the couple. If he had any qualms about the decision, Melisande did not sense it in his manner. 'Lady Dacre and I shall be late back on board. See that you and Amanda are not. Do you understand me?'

'Perfectly, Captain. I hope you and your lady enjoy the evening.'

'We shall, Kit. Believe me, we shall.'

Melisande actually found herself blushing at his words, realising their implication, and was glad of the darkness to hide her embarrassment. A hand beneath her elbow, Jason guided her down the gang-plank and along the stonework to a flight of steps that led down to the water—and a waiting barge. Not as large as those floating past them, gaily festooned with ribbons and lanterns, but a small, intimate vessel steered by one of his own crew. Someone who would hear nothing, see nothing, she thought, as he gently handed her down and she settled herself on a cushioned seat. He had thought of everything, and how glad she was that he had. A moment later he eased himself alongside her and slid an arm about her shoulders so that she could lean back in comfort.

Where before she had smelt only the odour of rotten fish and refuse coming from the river, seen only the squalor and poverty lining the banks amid the hovels which many called homes, now everything was different. A slight breeze brushed her cheeks as she turned to look up at her husband, allowing herself to relax against him. The silver sheen of a full moon danced on the water, captivating her attention. In a barge ahead, someone was serenading his sweetheart with a love-poem, a badly written, badly delivered address of love that caused her to bury her head against Jason's doublet, trying hard not to laugh.

'Where is the romance in your soul, Princess?' Jason asked softly, his face bending closer to hers. 'I always used to find you with your head buried in a book of poetry.'

'Poetry, yes—but not this! Listen to him! The conceited ass! He should be telling his love how desirable she is, how lost he is without her, how life is empty when he does not hear her voice . . .' She broke off at the embers she had kindled in the depths of his eyes. Embers that became coals of fire, as she finished lamely, 'All he is speaking about is himself—how handsome he is, and how lucky she is to have him!'

Jason's free hand slid round her back, and his lips touched her cheek, her brow, her mouth, savouring it for a long moment before he said in a voice she had never heard before, 'Shall I tell you how desirable you are? So desirable that I wonder what I am doing here in this draughty boat when I could be in *Moonwynd*, making love to you in a comfortable, so very warm, bed. Shall I tell you how lost I am without you? How empty the days—the weeks—have been since we married and you turned your back on me? I deserved it in many ways, but not all, my sweet. Not all. I shall not speak of myself, only of you. How I love to watch the colour of your eyes change when you are angry . . . or thoughtful. When I see them I know what mood to expect—not that I can always deal with it! You are the most exasperating, delightful, argumentative, stubborn, lovable creature that I have ever encountered. And I hope tonight you will accept me for what I am: a man who would give you anything you ask. Be my wife, Melisande? Name your own price, if that is the only way I can have you. I have waited so long . . .'

'Five years . . .' she murmured, enjoying her surrender. His victory.

'You minx! What do you know of it?'

'Nothing . . . Only what you have hinted. Did you know Mother once told Father that I would marry you? He thought her mad.'

'Far from it! She knew what was in my mind that night I first saw you. She understood that I did not want to snatch a young girl from the cradle—so to speak. You were so innocent of life, and I—I had seen so much of it . . .' Jason's mouth found hers again, bruising it with a relentless pressure that made her wish they were aboard *Moonwynd* in privacy, not entwined in each other's arms aboard an open barge in full view of others.

'We are being stared at,' she whispered, catching a comment from a nearby boat.

Jason lifted his head and directed a glare across at the man who had uttered it, a derisive smile spreading across his face. 'What I do, I do openly—with my own wife. I do not hide behind a mask and seduce another man's wife.' The comment was loud enough to be heard, and pride engulfed her at his boldness. He did care! How could she doubt him now? Sliding her hands up behind his neck, she brought his mouth down to hers, her lips parting as they touched his, the sweetness of her kiss inflaming him beyond words as he pressed her down upon the cushions.

Melisande could not believe it! She had been presented to The Queen, and Elizabeth, replendent in white silk and ermine, her gown studded with breathtaking jewels, had rendered her speechless as she halted before Jason and Melisande and congratulated him on possessing a wife still modest enough to blush. And blush she had —to the very roots of her hair, while the Queen had smiled at her embarrassment before passing on, on the arm of some elegant courtier.

'You—you said you would not present me at court . . .' she began, and Jason looked across the table into her still very flushed cheeks and she grew weak at the look in his eyes. After the firework display was over, they had alighted from the barge on Bankside and joined the audience that sat and listened to a fascinating play by William Shakespeare. After the performance, he had presented his actors to the Queen who, in turn, was most gracious in her approval. She did not look arrogant or dictatorial, Melisande thought, upon her first glimpse of the tall, red-headed woman who approached. But as she listened, she heard a note in the somewhat mannish voice that could quell rebellion in her courtiers, and make ambassadors quake in their decorated shoes and scuttle back to their respective masters to tell of the virgin queen who would take no husband, give no thought to her own happiness, only to that of her people. England was her husband—the English people her family. Melisande did not envy her the role as monarch, great as it was—great as she had proved herself to be, but she felt for the woman and sensed a loneliness in her that would never be satisfied. 'Did you . . . Was this . . . I mean . . . Oh, Jason, you intended me to be presented, did you not?'

'Of course I did. I am proud of you, and I wanted everyone to see you with the Queen. It was all arranged weeks ago.'

'And you call me exasperating,' she declared, and he laughed at her indignation. 'Why was her approval so important to you?' Was it as Priscilla had said: that he needed the Queen's continued favour?

'Approval? What do I want with that? She has no cause to think me disloyal. If she commands me to go with Drake, she knows I shall go. If she asked me to go—perhaps. But, above all, she knows how dearly I love Whispering Wood. She knows that my ship and others like her in the near future will always be at her disposal. She knows, too, that more than anything I want to go home to live in peace with my bride.'

'Surely you have not told her all this?'

'I have a great friend in Francis Drake. Pirate that he is, he never forgets those who sailed with him. He has few friends, but I am one. He will always be close to me, no matter what is said of him. Upon the sea, one grows to assess character more clearly than on land. There are fewer diversions,' he added drily.

'I think the Queen is very lonely,' Melisande said softly.

'Wise words from a dreamer.'

'Why do you mock me?'

'Do I?' Jason leaned across the table towards her. He had brought her to a noisy tavern on the waterfront and astounded her by the number of people he had greeted as he led her through the downstairs room to a quiet room at the back, with a balcony which overlooked the river. It was a pleasant night, and the windows were thrown wide to allow a breeze to penetrate the smoky atmosphere that invaded the room, even with closed doors. What kind of place was this, she wondered, as a cheeky-faced girl had brought them wine, staring long and hard at the exquisitely gowned and jewelled woman sitting opposite a man she obviously had seen before —her manner proclaimed it. 'Did I not dress in white for our wedding? It was the closest I could come to your prince. I failed miserably, didn't I?'

'Perhaps if you had been yourself,' she began, and he interrupted her with an oath.

'I have never sought to be anything but myself. You did not want to know me. From the beginning you have disbelieved every word I have said.'

'It did rather sound like a fairy-tale,' Melisande reminded him. 'And there were you, telling me I should be a woman . . .' How could she not want to be one when she remembered how he had kissed her tonight, tormented her body and her mind with his words and caresses?

'Perhaps I have not succeeded in my quest,' Jason murmured.

'I concede defeat, my lord. I shall try to be all that you ask of me.'

He caught one ringed hand, lifting it to his lips. It was the wine she had drunk which made her feel so daring —so bold with her words and her looks, Melisande thought. Or was it because she now knew nothing could stop them from coming together? So much time wasted, and it was all her fault. Now she understood how her father had felt when her mother had died. She would feel the same if Jason were to be taken from her. She would be an empty shell; no one could ever fill her life again as he was doing.

'More wine, my lord? Perhaps you would like to go upstairs?' The barmaid was at his elbow again—Melisande had not even noticed her entrance—smiling down at Jason in a way that irritated her.

He caught her look, smiled in that same way that had always infuriated her with its self-confidence, and then said, 'My wife and I are quite comfortable here. Bring us a jug of your best red wine, and then do not disturb us again.'

'Oh, lawd! Your pardon, sir. My lady. I didn't realise . . .' The girl scuttled from the room as though pursued by the devil himself.

'I suppose it is rather strange for a husband to bring his wife to such a place,' Melisande murmured.

'It has been known, but not too often,' Jason chuckled. 'Now perhaps you understand why so many choose to be masked, concealing their identity while they take their pleasures.'

'A hateful way to live—it is dishonest!' Melisande declared. When the wine was brought and he poured her a fresh glass, she hesitated, then, spurred on by the glittering eyes watching her every move, she drank deeply . . .'

'My, how my princess has grown up of late,' Jason commented, as he tasted his wine. It was the best in the house, laced with brandy. He had supped it many times before, and knew from the way Melisande drained her glass that she had no idea of its potency. He should warn her; he did not want her incapable on such a night. And yet, he mused as he allowed himself the pleasure of enjoying her beauty, her nearness, her surrender, he could afford to be generous. She was his, and that was all he had ever asked for. Tonight, tomorrow, the day or the week after no longer mattered as they once had, for he knew she would come willingly to his bed. What had changed her mind? Yet he was content. That was something for any man to acknowledge in a lifetime. So many people pretended to be happy, faked satisfaction, lived dull, unfulfilled lives and dreamed of another more satisfying, but that was not for him. All he wanted sat across the table from him, and he would fight hell and high water to keep her by his side. 'What do you want to do now?' he asked, wondering in which direction her mind might wander. If it was in his power, he would fulfil her every wish.

Melisande raised her eyes and looked into his. Why should they linger here when *Moonwynd* awaited them? As though he had read her mind, Jason moved on to the seat beside her and took her in his arms. As they folded about her, so strong and possessive, she gave a soft sigh. It was not the wine, she told herself, it was because she wanted to. Had she not wanted to feel his body against hers from that first night, and been too stupid—too reticent—to acknowledge it? Had she done so, perhaps none of the problems between them would never have happened. If she had not heeded Priscilla's words on her wedding day, and indeed before, she would be his wife now. If her head had not been so full of fanciful dreams, she would have enjoyed more than just his company! The fault was hers.

'Think only of yourself. Be selfish. You deserve to be spoiled,' he murmured.

'Do I?' She was remembering his words spoken with such venom on their wedding night. She was prepared to obey that command if it brought them together, but how she wished he had not truly meant them! 'I have hurt you, I know that, in my ignorance—my foolishness—my . . .'

'Innocence.' Jason laid his lips against the rise of her breast, pulling away the fichu of lace modestly placed there above the low neckline. 'I accept that I was wrong—as you were. We both have much to learn. Let us do so from each other, my love. No more doubts. No more suspicions. Let us enjoy what God has given us . . . for the rest of our lives.'

'Jason—oh! Jason, take me back to *Moonwynd*!'

'Are you sure?'

'Yes, but there is a condition.' She raised her head and stared into the face that was suddenly wary. 'Promise me you will not sail with Drake. I do not want to lose you for a day—a week—let alone a year or more. I could not bear it.'

The cry was from her heart, and he held her tightly, unable to control the tremors that swept through him. This was no dream—for her or for him. She was the reality he had been thinking of for five long years. Perhaps, in a short while, he could make her forget her prince of fantasy. He had to succeed, or he had nothing!

He lost himself in the exploration of her mouth, her body. He wanted to take advantage of the rooms upstairs, to carry her there so that this magic moment would never end, but he contained himself. They were for others, and Melisande was his wife, and the comfort of *Moonwynd* awaited them. No matter how late they returned, he had instructed wine and food to be placed in the outer cabin, a warming-pan in the huge bed they would share. Tonight would be as no other. His patience would be rewarded. Dear God, do not let me disappoint her, he thought, as he drew back and lifted her to her feet. She swayed against him, not wanting the moment to end, either. Her head was swimming, her legs weak . . .

'I'll take you back to *Moonwynd*, Princess, and I accept your condition,' Jason whispered. He had committed himself unknowingly as she had done at Whispering Wood, taking the first step along a new road, prepared for whatever lay ahead. He felt very peaceful. Was this what it was all about? He loved her. He had always loved her. Was it enough? Would she be content with that? With one man, one love, until the end of her days, for that was as long as he would love her!

CHAPTER TEN

AS THEY DREW nearer to *Moonwynd*, Melisande sensed Jason withdrawing from her, almost as if he were afraid that, once on board, she would turn on him with searing reproaches for having been forced to marry him, more condemnation of his use of money to influence her father and have his own way. Once, perhaps, she reflected, as he helped her on to dry land again and they began to walk in the direction of the ship moored a short distance away. Not now. Not after this blissfully happy day. Not now that she acknowledged what was in her heart. Not now that she knew the meaning of love! He was careful about how he touched her now, she realised, as they stepped on to the deck of *Moonwynd*. How stern he looked—preoccupied, as though his thoughts were far removed from where they stood.

He had not been distracted when he had kissed her only a few minutes before the barge reached its destination. The hunger in his kisses had determined her resolve to deal tonight with the problem facing them and not wait until they returned to Whispering Wood. He was waiting for her to make the first move—he had demanded it as a condition of him accepting her as his wife. So be it! She would do as he wanted.

'Are you tired? You look as fresh as when we set out,' Jason said, opening the door of her cabin.

'A little,' she admitted. But not too tired to divest herself of the beautiful gown and put on something that would make her more appealing. Then she would go to him, and he would know she was sincere. What did it matter if he did not love her? Perhaps, in time . . .

'Good night then, my sweet. Sleep well.' His lips upon her brow were as light as a breath of wind, and then he had turned and made his way back on deck, as if he could not trust himself to remain in her presence a moment longer.

She was imagining things, Melisande told herself, closing the door firmly behind her and easing off her shoes. Jason Dacre was not the kind of man to lose control over a woman, certainly not an inexperienced country girl like herself. Inexperienced she might be, she thought, as she fought with the fastenings of her gown and at great length managed to extricate herself from it. But no longer foolish. Jason wanted her, and he would have her this night—he would have the woman she had sought to suppress out of fear and ignorance. Love had opened her eyes.

With sudden daring she tossed aside the nightgown she had been about to slip on, donning instead a deep blue velvet robe trimmed with fur. It left bare her shoulders, and as she looked at her reflection, Melisande was silently thankful that she had listened to Mistress Agnes and accepted the old woman's advice on the choice of her wardrobe. Even in this nightrobe she *looked* different—*felt* different. So sure of herself and what she was about to do. Was it the clothes or her newly-discovered love that made her so bold and gave her this abundance of confidence? She took great care with her hair, brushing it until it gleamed, and a smile playing about her lips, she arranged it casually over her shoulders. Like tongues of hell-fire had been Jason's description of it. What would he say when she presented herself at his door?

For a moment she wavered, and then a look of fierce determination masked her features. No, she would not turn back now! A knock on the cabin door sent her heart racing. Had he come to her? It was indeed Jason who entered and stood on the threshold, startled by the apparition that was waiting for him. For a moment Melisande was unaware of the other people who stood outside. She had eyes only for her husband, her breath catching in her throat as he advanced slowly towards her.

'I thought you might have retired . . .'

'No—not yet.' His gaze missed nothing: the slender curve of hip and breast beneath the velvet which clung to her lithe body, the long red hair covering her shoulders like a fire cloud, the heady smell of musk tantalising his nostrils, making what he had to tell her even more difficult.

'Melisande, prepare yourself for a shock. Lucy is here. She has run away from home.'

His words hit her like an iron fist, and he reached out to steady her as she swayed forward, gasping, 'Here! On board?'

He nodded, and stepped to one side, beckoning to the silent figures outside. She gave a cry as Christopher entered, supporting Lucy on one side, with Amanda on the other. Her sister's face was bruised, her dress ripped about the bodice and skirt, and she was barely able to walk.

'What has happened? Who has done this?'

'We have been able to get very little out of her. She will talk to no one but you,' Jason told her gravely. 'She will not tell us how she got here or when. Only that she was robbed earlier tonight in a back alley and all her money was stolen. Kit saw her watching the ship, but she ran away when he called to her. He chased her, and brought her aboard.'

'She ran from you?' Melisande asked in amazement, looking into the distressed face of the young man who helped her to lower Lucy on to the bed. 'Why?'

'He has betrayed me! Abandoned me! *She* . . .' Lucy's eyes turned in the direction of Amanda as she spoke, and the look in them was terrible—as though she hated the girl who not long ago had been a close friend. 'She has stolen him from me!'

'Hush, my dear, you are overwrought. Christopher will always be your friend—as Amanda will be,' Melisande assured her, noting the anxious glance Jason directed at her. Had her sister taken leave of her senses?

She had never loved Christopher, and the transfer of his affections to Amanda meant nothing to her. She was upset and tired and in need of comfort . . . and to talk, she suspected. To run away from home! Their father would be frantic. She did not have to say what was in her mind.

As she looked up at Jason, he said quietly, 'I shall send a messenger to Kingsclere immediately to inform your father that she is safe and well.'

'Thank you,' said Melisande. 'Will someone please fetch some water and clean towels.' Christopher turned on his heel and followed Jason from the cabin. 'Amanda, there is a robe in that trunk. Give it to me, please.'

Lucy shrank back as Amanda laid the garment across the bed and then withdrew towards the door, her lips quivering. Melisande quickly went after her, hoping to reassure her.

'She has been hurt, she does not know what she is saying,' she whispered. 'Please be patient with her.'

'She does not want him, let alone love him,' Amanda returned, fighting to keep the tears from her eyes. 'I do! This time it is no mistake. Oh, Melisande, I would not steal another girl's sweetheart. She told me herself he was free. What they have shared has been purely friendship, you must believe that.'

'I do, and you must not distress yourself further over her words. I shall find out what is behind this when she can talk more coherently. I think she is very confused . . . and frightened. It must have been a terrible experience for her. Tomorrow she will be her old self, you'll see. Go back to bed now and don't worry.'

How sure she sounded, Melisande thought, as she returned to her sister's side, but she was not. Lucy's strange behaviour frightened her more than a little. Why had she run away? What had passed between her and their father to send her scurrying from the house to London of all places? Was it because she knew Christopher was aboard *Moonwynd*? Had she intended to use him to take her away from whatever it was she feared? It was the only explanation she could think of.

'Lucy, dearest, sit up and let me help you to undress. This gown is ruined, but never mind, I have brought several.'

'Don't be nice to me, Sandy! I won't go back!'

'What has happened? Tell me,' Melisande pleaded.

'Father has something planned for my birthday. He told me. He was so pleased with himself. You know what that means, don't you? He has found me a husband.' Lucy said bitterly.

'No! No, you are wrong. He promised me . . .'

'Promised you what?' Her sister sat up, looking at Melisande curiously. There was an ugly bruise beneath her chin, where she had been struck when her assailant leapt at her from the shadows and felled her to the ground. More were visible on her wrists and arms and neck where she had struggled with him, desperate to retain the few coins she had taken with her. All to no avail. He had been stronger, rougher and more aggressive, and she had laid for over an hour in that dirty street until some brave person had ventured forward to see if she was still alive. Somehow she had made her way to where *Moonwynd* was moored—to see Christopher, the only person she thought could help her, holding another in his arms! He had never laughed at her love of the sea, although she knew that deep in his heart he could not accept that a woman could be as good a sailor as a man. Women were meant for the home, he had once told her laughingly. How she hated that confinement to a woman's future—the home, a family, a husband, with or without love! She could not—would not—consider it until she had discovered what else life held. She was capable, bright. Poor, but willing to learn. Why could she not go to sea as a man did? Christopher had laughed heartily when she suggested that! A woman at sea! Everyone knew a woman aboard ship was a bad omen —for sailors of long standing, at least. He had to admit that Lord Dacre had often taken his mother aboard

Moonwynd, and the ship had never sunk, but that was different!

He would never help her now, she reasoned. He was lost to her. Lost to the doe-eyes of Amanda Cummings. She hated him for that, yet in her heart she wished him well, for she was fond of him—as she would have been fond of a brother. He did not deserve her anger or her spite, yet who else could she direct it upon? She was alone, without money—at the mercy of Jason Dacre, who would return her to her father so that she could make a good marriage and leave him in peace for the remainder of his days. Foolish Melisande ever to have thought that they would have filled his loneliness. Only Jason's money could do that!

'What did he promise you, Sandy? Are you part of this?'

'Part of what?' her sister asked softly. 'Lucy, what has happened? Tell me, from the beginning, and at the same time let me get you undressed and into bed. You are shivering.'

Her face a tight mask of suspicion, Lucy allowed herself to be divested of her torn gown and underclothes and attired in the warm robe, settled into the comfortable bed. Despite all her misgivings, it was a great relief to stretch her aching limbs and relax amid the linen sheets.

'Sandy, if I am wrong . . . forgive me?' How could Melisande have been a party to her father's plans? She knew how she felt—how they both felt—about being married to strange men—unwanted wives, used for breeding. A horrible thought! 'Two days ago, Father called me into the study and told me he was planning a party for my birthday. Can you imagine how excited I was? A party for me! I really believed he cared—for a few minutes, at least.'

'He does care,' Melisande assured her. 'Somehow you have misunderstood.'

'Misunderstood what? Nothing was to be too grand for me. I could invite anyone I pleased. And then he said that, at the end of the evening, he would tell me something that would decide my future the way I wanted it. He has found me a husband, I know! My future the way I want it? Nonsense—the way he wants it! I would have no say. I hate him. I hate him!'

'Lucy, no!' Melisande gathered the quivering form into her arms, realising the terrible mistake that had occurred. Their father had been trying to convey that she would have her freedom, be a woman of means, no longer dependent on him—and Lucy, in her desperation to be free, had totally misinterpreted his words. 'Listen to me, please.' She hugged the trembling body. 'It is not as you suppose. Father . . . Father has agreed to give you some money. I spoke to him some while ago, and at last he is certain that you will never be happy until you are an independent young woman. Do you understand what I am saying? For your birthday, he is going to give you enough money to live as you wish—to go where you will. Lucy, my dear, dear sister, don't you understand the extent of his love? He is a lonely man now. He will be even lonelier when . . .' hastily she corrected herself '. . . if you go away. But he agreed with me that it must be done so that you can decide your own future. There is no husband! You will be free! Now, think on it, and then consider how he will feel, alone, without any of us. Can you not afford to be generous?'

'How is she? Give her this, it will warm her.' Jason's hard tones cut across her words, and Melisande drew back, wondering how long he had been standing behind her. He held out a glass filled with a dark liquid. 'Rum—a sailor's best friend,' he added, and she took it and held it to Lucy's lips. 'She should drink all of it. She needs to sleep, and forget what has happened.'

'Yes, drink it all, Lucy,' Melisande pleaded. 'Tomorrow I shall take you home, and we shall face Father together. He will tell you, as I have, that you have no need to fear for your future. It is in your own hands, my dear.'

'Let her sleep,' Jason said, stepping back. Edwin had

obviously not been very selective in his rhetoric, and Lucy had misunderstood the well-meaning gesture her own sister had instigated.

'No marriage? I am not to wed a strange man?' Lucy stared at them both in bewilderment, scarcely able to comprehend the words. 'The truth. You would not lie to me?'

'When has Melisande ever lied to you?' Jason demanded. Melisande was surprised at his hard attitude. Did he not care what her sister had suffered in mind and body? There was nothing in his face to betray his thoughts, as withdrawn from her now as that moment they had stepped aboard *Moonwynd*. He had known, she thought, unsure how or why she should suspect such a thing. But he had! The way he avoided her eyes confirmed it.

'It is no lie,' she said quietly, settling her sister beneath the bedclothes, but the moment she tried to move, Lucy started up, catching at her arm.

'Stay with me. Don't leave me! I don't want to be alone! I am so confused!' she cried.

'Don't distress yourself. I shall stay with you,' Melisande murmured, closing her mind to the plans she had made for this night.

'Safety in numbers, eh, my sweet?' Jason muttered, turning towards the door, and she blanched at the irony in his voice. Did he think she was deliberately using her sister as a way of avoiding him? Was he blind not to have noticed how she had prepared and perfumed herself? For him!

When Jason returned to the cabin several hours later, it was to find Melisande curled up in bed alongside her sister, Lucy's head cradled on her shoulder. For a long moment he stood staring into the serene face, a tight knot forming in his stomach as he thought of being held against her in that way. He was beginning to think Fate had decreed that they would never come together. Tonight he had hoped . . . But Lucy's inopportune arrival had ruined the intimacy between them. How precarious their relationship was. Would it ever be possible to wrest a successful marriage from the tumult of their lives?

With a wry grimace he returned on deck, knowing he would not be able to sleep. As *Moonwynd* slipped out towards the open sea, he stood with his back towards the shore, his face turned seawards. Had Melisande been able to see the expression on those shadowy features, she might have wondered at the pain and bitterness etched there.

The pitching of the ship as she cut her way through a heavy swell told Melisande they were no longer at anchor. She leapt out of bed in dismay and ran to the window. She could see nothing but angry, white-topped waves buffeting the sides of *Moonwynd*. The sky was grey and overcast, and the howl of the wind chilled her more than the knowledge that Jason had sailed early. Why? He knew she had intended to take Lucy home herself. What was he thinking of to subject her to a sea trip after all she had suffered? Lucy needed the comfort of her own home and her father's reassurance that he had not selected a husband for her.

Quickly dressing, she went on deck. The ship rolled and lurched beneath her feet, and she reeled along the deck towards the tall figure on the afterdeck, deep in discussion with Christopher Avery. The fierce wind whipped her hair into wild disorder, blinding her as it blew into her eyes. How could anyone enjoy this kind of life, she wondered, trying desperately to hold it away and continue her unsteady path towards her husband.

At that moment Jason saw her and left his companion to join her. Her look told him that she did not agree with his decision to sail on an earlier tide. He was prepared for that. 'I saw no reason why we should not leave early,' he said, anticipating her question. 'The sooner we get Lucy back to your father, the better. My business will not take long.'

'You knew it was my intention to take her home

myself,' Melisande retorted, once more angered by his apparent lack of concern. Did he consider the hiring of a sea-captain more important than her sister's safe and immediate return to Kingsclere?

'I could not allow that. The roads are dangerous for two young women. You are safer here with me: nothing can happen to you aboard *Moonwynd* or at Mousehole. I am responsible for your sister until I hand her back to your father. I have sent him word of where she is, so that he will not be caused further worry. I hope she is better this morning.'

'She is still sleeping . . .'

'Not any more,' Jason murmured, as something over her shoulder caught his eye. Melisande saw a smile touch the lean mouth, and turned.

Lucy had come up on deck. Her skirts billowing in the wind, she made her way towards them, far steadier in her progress than Melisande had been.

'She has a feel for the sea,' Jason added, as she paused to peer down at the foaming waves, laughing as spray was whipped up into her face. 'Kit was right, she should have been born a man.'

'Then she would have had no troubles to begin with,' Melisande retorted as her sister joined them. 'You should not be up here in the cold. I'll take you back to the cabin.'

'Let her stay,' Jason intervened. 'She can take the helm for a while, if she wishes.'

'May I really?' Lucy's face shone with excitement.

'We shall sail *Moonwynd* together,' Jason assured her, taking her arm. 'Won't you join us, Melisande?'

Mutely she shook her head and watched them climb to the afterdeck, where, under the amused eyes of many of the watching crew, she took the helm. Melisande wanted to join them, to try to recapture what she had shared with Jason the night before, but her stomach suddenly fluttered unsteadily, warning her how unwise it would be to linger on deck, and so she quickly turned and went back to her cabin.

'Things go well for you of late, Captain. I hear you have a new bride,' Mathew Armitage said, smiling across the well-scrubbed pine table at the silent man who sat facing him. They had been drinking together for the past two hours, celebrating the good news that had been brought. Captain of *Moonwynd*! What an honour! And to sail her alongside the flagship of Sir Francis Drake himself! He had not hesitated to accept. His wife was dead and his two daughters married, so there was no one to wait at home and worry; it was better that way. He could understand why Lord Dacre was not anxious to command the ship himself, having been married only a few short months.

'Well enough. Why do you ask?' Jason returned, lifting thoughtful eyes to the weatherbeaten face opposite. Broad shoulders were lifted in a shrug, and he added, 'Would you consider me a foolish man, Mathew?'

'Proud—stubborn—obstinate to a point of mule-headedness when pushed too far and you consider yourself in the right,' was the blunt answer.

'Which I am now,' Jason muttered, almost to himself.

'And a trifle too arrogant over certain things,' Mathew Armitage added.

'What things? Speak up, man. Finish the assassination of my character.'

Again a shrug, as the man reached for his tankard of ale.

'You alone can truthfully answer that. You have sown your wild oats along with the rest of us, but it was the innocence of youth, and you hurt no one by doing so. In fact, there was many a tear shed when you left port in the old days. But foolish, no! You have a good head on your shoulders.'

'Then why am I acting like a damn fool now?' Jason demanded with a scowl.

'Drinking here with me when you have other things on your mind? More important things? You could have sent me word, you know; you didn't have to come yourself.

I'd have ridden like the devil to see Drake, and well you know it, even if you hadn't put in a good word for me—which I suspect you have. What are you trying to prove? And to whom?'

'Myself, perhaps?' Melisande was resting when he had left the inn where they had taken lodgings for the night. A headache, she said, brought about by the pitching of the ship, and she had refused his invitation to make this visit with him. As spite for not being allowed to take Lucy home? he wondered, although he had to admit that she did look very pale. Perhaps she had told the truth. Tomorrow they would hire a carriage and return to Whispering Wood. There everything would be resolved once and for all. Yet again he was seized with this sense of foreboding—seemingly without reason. A few short hours, and she must keep her word. What could happen between now and then?

'No, you are sure of yourself, that's why men follow you. You give them confidence—the very thing you now lack. Why don't you go to her? Resolve whatever is between you. Don't allow the fire to go out.'

'It was never alight,' Jason answered wryly. 'At least not for her.'

'When you have achieved so much with so many women, you fail with this one!' Mathew exclaimed. 'You must love her very much. At last it has happened. Go back to your wife. If you don't, you are a fool!'

'Oh, Sandy, I feel so—so alive,' Lucy breathed. 'It is as though a miracle has happened to me. However did you get Father to agree to give me money for my birthday? No, don't deny it. It had to be you.'

'It was all his own idea,' Melisande returned, sitting up in bed. The ache in her head had lessened slightly, but there was still a vicious pain over her eyes. Thank goodness her stomach had ceased to be troublesome. How Lucy had laughed—yet not really unkindly at her discomfort—one sister abed, while the other had revelled in her new-found freedom, walked the decks of

Moonwynd as if she was indeed her captain, and made plans for her own future.

Melisande felt a little hurt at the way her sister spoke only of going to France, of leaving her father and all she had known in the past. As she listened to her, Melisande had thought how much she sounded like Priscilla, and instantly hated herself for making such a comparison. They were worlds apart. Yet, in truth, each in her own way was selfish.

'Must you leave Father alone so soon? Could you not stay awhile with him?' she asked, as Lucy continued with her excited chatter. Had she made the right decision? She was beginning to have doubts, yet if she had not given her father the money to make Lucy independent, he would have lost her. He would lose her anyway, she realised unhappily. Her good deed was not turning out at all as she had hoped.

'What does he want with me? He has been trying to be rid of us all for years,' Lucy replied, her mind still dwelling on the prospects Paris held for her. 'He loves Kingsclere, you know that, and he has his friends back now. He will not miss me.'

'He will,' Melisande insisted, wincing as a pain seared through her forehead. 'He does not want you to go. If you must, could you not go together?'

'Sandy!' Lucy protested. 'He would watch my every move—it would be impossible.'

'Not if you loved him—as I do. As you should.'

'Now you are reproving me. For what? You are annoyed because Jason has left you alone this evening. Come for a walk before we go to bed, and feel the wind in your hair, the sea-spray upon your face. It is exhilarating! Come and share my dreams for a little while, and perhaps then you will understand why I must be free.'

Free from what? Melisande wondered, as she climbed from the bed and found a warm cloak. It was not exactly the perfect night for walking on the beach, but she did need some fresh air after the stuffiness of the room. Perhaps Jason would have returned by the time they came back, and she could talk to him. How she needed to talk to him . . . before it was too late. They were becoming strangers again. He, smiling and sardonic, nothing like the kind person who had held her in the barge and been proud to present her as his wife in the tavern at Wapping.

And she? She was wondering if they would ever find that moment again. Wondering, if had she gone to him that night aboard *Moonwynd*, it would have meant as much to him as it would have to her.

Moonwynd was anchored in Mount's Bay, closer to Mousehole than Plymouth, where the fleet was gathering for the expedition of Sir Francis Drake and Hawkins, for it was just outside the village that Mathew Armitage had his small cottage. Jason had found lodgings for them all at a pleasantly comfortable inn perched high on the clifftops. Lucy had loved it immediately, for she could listen to the sound of the sea from her bedroom window.

He had left them to rest, indicating that he would be back for supper, but it was well past ten o'clock when Lucy and Melisande decided to take their walk and he had still not returned. They had eaten a light supper together—Melisande being able to consume only a small amount of freshly made chicken soup—and while they ate, she had allowed her sister to chatter on, for it helped to ease the ache inside her. Was he deliberately staying away? Drinking with friends, enjoying their company? It was not her fault that she did not like the sea as Lucy did. He had spent more time with her sister than he had with her during the short voyage . . . and it both hurt and annoyed her. And afterwards, when she considered it again, she was ashamed to be jealous of Lucy's friendship with him. He, too, loved the sea. He could understand her sister's passion, where she and her father could not. She tried not to feel hurt, but did he have to pay so much attention to another woman, even if it was her own sister? Love could be cruel! Wonderful! Destructive! How would it be for Jason and herself when they returned to *Moonwynd*? How she wished she could foretell the future.

The four ships that had set out from Brittany made good time across the Channel and anchored in the same bay as *Moonwynd*, although well out of sight, as darkness settled over the Cornish countryside. Longboats were lowered, men hastily, but carefully and quietly, clambered into them, and oars were muffled with rags so that there would be no tell-tale sounds as they dipped in and out of the water to alert the watch on the silent ship they passed. Quiet orders—orders in Spanish—were passed among the men as the longboats made the shore. All knew what they had to do, and revelled in the fact that they were about to avenge the past victories of El Draque against their people. Tonight England would know what it was like to have their homes in flames, their women and children slaughtered or abducted! Tonight they were the pirates and eager for a taste of blood. It was a bold venture, spurred on by desperation at the successes of the monster El Draque. Tonight they would avenge many wrongs—and force the great virgin Queen Elizabeth to her knees with their audacity! Tonight Spain would triumph!

With the same stealth, they left their boats and began to scale the cliffs, to find tiny, winding paths leading to the top. Armed, dangerous, every man, with no other notion other than to devastate homes and property, as El Draque had done to them. To show the great sailor he was not invincible. Yet there was more than one man among the six hundred who split up and set out on their individual missions—to Mousehole, Penzance and Newlyn—who questioned the reasoning behind such a raid. They might kill many English, but what would that accomplish? Women and children did not man the ships which El Draque would sail against the Spanish fleet. And behind in Spain they had families of their own—which made the killing task that much more difficult. Not all were seized with a blood-lust, there were those who were tired of having to fight an enemy who came and went like a will o' the wisp. Here one moment, gone the next, and always capable of doing so much damage to Spain.

While many pressed forward, eagerly bent on their task, others hung back, lingered on the beaches . . . tending to the longboats longer than was necessary before starting on their distasteful quest. These were the men Lucy and Melisande saw as they wandered idly along what had been until then a deserted stretch of sand. Her sister had been right, Melisande was pleased to acknowledge: they had been walking for the past half-hour, and her headache had completely disappeared. The wind in her face and hair was like a tonic. And the sound of the sea . . . Yes, it did bring her pleasure, although on board ship, she knew she would never have felt this way. It was a lonely sound, and yet not so! When she listened to it, she could almost have been reading her book of poetry . . . It was music in her ears, as the stream at Whispering Wood had been gentle upon her ears and brought her contentment. Now she understood what Lucy had been trying to tell her. She loved the words of the past written by men who had no doubt experienced the same kind of tranquillity as she was now doing. There was little between them, after all. And Jason . . . If only she could share some of this with him. Why had he not returned and walked with them on this pleasant stretch of sand—listened to the sound of the sea, heard the cries of the night-birds as she did, felt the emotion of the moment?

He would have laughed at her! He laughed at her books, her dreams. Oh, Jason . . . She whispered his name upon the wind, her eyes closed for a moment as she sought to bring him to her—if only in her thoughts. What is keeping us apart?

'Sandy, are the fishing-boats late home? There are men on the beach.' Lucy came to an abrupt halt as they rounded a jutting rock and came upon three longboats pulled up on the shore. Half a dozen men lounged near them, talking in low tones. 'They are no fishermen!' The gasp made Melisande strain her eyes to pierce the gloom and identify those ahead. Fishermen, no! Fishermen did not linger by their boats after a day's work. There were no nets, nothing to convey what they had caught. They were dressed normally, but something about the way they moved, constantly watched the cliffs above, made her uneasy.

'Lucy, stay here. I don't know . . . Perhaps they are not local men, but . . .' She broke off as one man started over the sand and his ankle twisted on a hidden stone. The expletive that broke from his lips made the colour ebb from her cheeks. 'They are not English!'

'What are you saying?'

'I—I am not sure, but . . . Could they be Spanish? It is nothing like I have ever heard before. Lucy, quickly, we must go back the way we came and tell someone.'

'Melisande, you are allowing your imagination to run away with you!' Lucy gave a laugh that brought three heads twisting round. With a harsh yell, they started towards the girls. Lucy gave a cry as she saw the pistols in their hands, and heard the exchange of conversation in a tongue so strange that she believed her sister immediately. 'Dear heaven, what are we to do?'

'Run!' Melisande urged, pushing her from their hiding-place. 'Run and warn someone. The Spanish are upon us. They must have heard of Drake's fleet gathering at Plymouth. Go . . .'

She pushed her sister out into the open and fled after her, praying every step she took that someone was awake in Mousehole at this hour. If they were not . . . And where else had the Spanish gone to? They must warn someone! Jason—oh, Jason! she cried as she ran. Where are you?

She heard muffled oaths behind them, which gave wings to her feet, and somehow they were ahead of their pursuers as they reached the cliffs and the narrow, tricky, uneven path to the top—and safety! Pushing Lucy ahead, she started up, gasping for breath, her feet slipping and sliding on the combination of earth and sand. Lucy, some way ahead, slipped and slithered back into her. Melisande managed to hold her steady without losing her balance, and they started up to the top again. The men behind were more experienced at travelling over uneven terrain and were soon gaining on them. Each time Lucy looked back, Melisande sensed the mounting horror in her expression. To fall into the hands of Spaniards! If they were not killed, they would be taken away and sold as slaves . . . The Spanish had no regard for human life! So many of their English prisoners had ended up on Spanish galleys, chained to an oar until the day they died. That would not be their fate, Melisande realised, as she heard the harsh breathing of a man close on her heels.

'For the love of heaven, run,' she cried. 'Warn the village. Go!'

She herself lost her footing and slipped several feet back into the arms of the Spaniard behind her. She raked at his cheeks with her nails, and was cuffed violently on one cheek with his fist. Her last vision of her sister was as she turned and looked back—and started down, her young face blazing hatred and defiance . . . And then she dropped into a black abyss which knew no pain and no fear . . . nothing but darkness . . . Somewhere in that blackness she heard a scream of terror . . .

Melisande recovered her senses to find herself lying face down in a longboat, where she had been dumped by her captor when he had been forced to turn and defend himself against the horde of villagers that poured down the path and along the sand. At their head, a dark-skinned man with eyes of fire wielded his sword mercilessly on those Spaniards in his path. He gave no quarter and fought like a madman, inspiring those who followed to follow suit.

The party that had attacked Mousehold lingered longer than their companions who had gone further to the town of Penzance, while other Spaniards turned along the clifftops to the village of Newlyn. They were the closest to the beach and their longboat, well within sight of their ship which would take them to safety. They had caught the English pigs asleep in their beds, and took great pleasure in inflicting as much havoc as possible. Houses were fired, churches fired and sacked. So unexpected was the raid that before the inhabitants of the village and town knew what was happening, most of the Spaniards were already withdrawing to the safety of the beach and the open sea.

Many men had already left their homes to join the fleet gathering in Plymouth, leaving wives and family at home. Women and children, who bolted doors and windows and sat huddling in fear lest they fall victim to the revenge of these Spanish invaders—as some did. Heavy with booty and trophies of their evening's work, they started back down the cliffs . . . speculating about the fate of the English woman who had fallen into their hands.

'Melisande, look at me!' Jason's urgent tones cut across her fading senses. She struggled back to reality, opening her eyes on to his taut, grim features. She had watched him fighting his way across the sand towards her, and the madness that had possessed him was almost as frightening as being captured by the Spanish. She was looking at a stranger, the man of action she had never known—action and decision. Everyone looked at him for orders, which came in a clear, firm tone and brooked no argument. So bold and so brave! He had saved her life. And Lucy's. If he had not come . . .

Where was her sister? She struggled to sit up, but a violent pain tore through her head and with a cry she fell back into Jason's arms. Lucy had been coming back along the path towards her when she had fainted . . .

'Don't try to move, my love, you have had a bad fright,' he whispered, bending his head to lay his lips gently against her cheek. How he was so controlled, when he wanted to kiss those quivering lips, he did not know. So close to death! He had almost lost her! Damn his stupid pride! While he had been drinking with

Mathew Armitage, she had been in the hands of the Spaniards! Alone, frightened, believing herself about to be abducted . . . Dear heaven, he had brought her nothing but pain and unhappiness since the day he encountered her again. It was as though their union was cursed by Fate itself. 'You are safe now. Everything is under control.'

How reassuring he sounded. Melisande lifted her eyes, and over his shoulder saw that the clifftops were alight with fires, and further to her left, a dull red glow rose into the night sky.

'What—what has happened?' Her voice was barely audible.

'Those are warning beacons. A little late, as it happens, but they have brought every available man out to fight the Spaniards. This was the last raiding-party. Their lust for plunder boded them ill, and many will not return to Spain to boast of this night. They reached Penzance, and the village of Newlyn is ablaze.' Jason gathered her close against his chest. His shirt had been almost torn from him, and her cheek rested on bare skin.

He cared! She felt it in his touch, heard it in his voice! How her head ached. Where was Lucy? She could not see her sister among the people gathered about the longboat where Jason had found her. Amanda was there, clad in her nightclothes, wet from sea-spray as she knelt at the side of Christopher Avery, binding the wound in his arm. Something was wrong. Jason refused to look at her, ignoring her question as he lifted her into his arms and turned towards the cliff path.

'Lucy!' she cried, her voice rising with anxiety. 'Where is she? She was with me when I fell. Have they taken her? Jason—tell me they have not!'

'No, my love. They did not take her,' came the quiet answer, in a tone deep with undisguised pain. Men in front of them moved back to allow him to pass, and it was then that they saw what they had been concealing.

Lucy lay at the base of the cliff. Someone had folded her hands over her heart. She looked so peaceful and serene that at first Melisande did not realise how still she was. So still that there could be no denying she was—dead!

'You say she was coming down after you . . .' Jason whispered, tightening his hold on her as he felt the tremors racking her body. 'She must have slipped and pitched over the edge. She did not suffer, I swear it. The fall . . . The fall broke her neck.'

The cry hurled from Melisande's lips tore through him with the keeness of a gleaning knife. She lolled in his arms like a rag doll, no colour in her cheeks, her eyes tightly closed. As he started up the path with his unconscious burden, men gently gathered up Lucy's lifeless body and followed him. No one spoke. There were no words to describe the grief they knew he was suffering—or that of his young, lovely wife. No words which could have washed away the pain. Only time would do that. Time, and the love they shared.

'Lucy! Stay!' Melisande started up in bed, her hands reaching out for the sister slipping once again from her in her dreams. For two days she had lain in bed at the inn and known no one, been unaware of the silent man who sat at her side throughout the hours of darkness—and those of light, too. She dwelled in a world where Lucy was still alive, dreamed of the birthday party she had been planning with her father. Of her sister's delight when she was presented with the money to set her free from the chains of an unwanted marriage. But always, when they presented her with that fabulous envelope, she did not take it, but began to draw back from them . . . fading as she did so until she was little more than a shadowy form in the brightly lighted room at Kingsclere. Melisande ran after her, calling her, begging her to return . . .

And then she would wake and find herself in a strange bed—and once again have to face the reality that her sister was dead! Not once had she been aware of Jason sitting in the shadows, listening to her ramblings, feeling the same pain as she did, sharing her loss, wishing he had died instead.

Strong hands on her shoulders gently but firmly pressed her back upon the soft mattress. Something cool was placed on her burning forehead. She felt the comforting pressure of someone's fingers curled about hers, and clung to them as she closed her eyes again and the dream returned. Why would Lucy not stay with her? There was no need for her to run away now. She was free—independent! Had she not allowed her jewels to be sold to make it so?

She was on the deck of *Moonwynd* again, staring down at the white-crested waves pounding against the bow of the ship. Jason should not have insisted that Lucy sail with them. He should have allowed them both to return to Kingsclere. They would have been safe there. 'You are safer here with me,' he had said. 'Nothing can happen to you aboard *Moonwyd* or at Mousehole.' He had been wrong. It was all his fault, as everything else had been his fault. Priscilla was unhappy in her marriage, Melisande was trapped within the confines of her own pride and stubbornness, and Lucy . . . Reality came without warning . . . Lucy was dead.

Jason drew back from the bed as she fell into an exhausted slumber, his lips a tight line. She blamed him for her sister's death, and in a way she was right. Had Lucy not been with them . . .

The words seared his brain, his very soul. His fault! Never would he forgive himself. Never would she forgive him! He slumped into a chair beside the window, staring out into the darkness. She had made up his mind for him. Drake's expedition had been postponed for several weeks due to the Spanish raid, and that would give him enough time to do what had to be done. He would hurt her no more.

'Melisande, my dear child, it is time you began to take more interest in yourself again,' Edwin murmured to his daughter as they sat at supper late one night, three weeks after Jason had brought her back to Whispering Wood and, in an agony of mind, had taken Edwin into the study and related what had happened at Mousehole. They had shared the pain and the grief.

But whereas, in the following weeks, during which Edwin was a guest at the house, not wanting to return to the solitude and loneliness of the big house in Kingsclere, he had begun to accept the terrible blow dealt to him, Jason could not, and retreated more and more into himself. Rising early, he would ride, then work about the estate until he was so tired that he could scarcely move. Even that did not help him to sleep or dim Melisande's words in his tortured mind. Nothing Edwin said could lessen his burden. And Melisande herself was no help to him. She was pale and lifeless, doing very little about the house, leaving all decisions to the steward Thomas.

Melisande raised her eyes to her father's face and managed a faint smile. How glad she was of his presence. He, alone, gave her some small comfort. He, alone, knew what she was suffering.

'Be patient, Father. I miss her so.' Her lips trembled. She darked not mention her sister by name, for it still made the tears start to her eyes.

'You should get out more,' Edwin insisted. 'Why do you not ride with Jason? You love to ride . . .'

At the far end of the table, Jason looked at her, and immediately she avoided his burning gaze. On his left, Amanda bent her head and whispered to him. After a moment, he nodded. The girl smiled shyly and placed her hand in that of Christopher Avery, who sat beside her. Since that night, they had been constant companions. She had nursed him through a fever which came upon him a few hours after the return to Whispering Wood, where Jason had insisted he stay until he had recovered from the wound in his arm.

Jason felt a pang of envy as they gazed into each other's eyes; this time, he knew it was no mistake. Amanda was truly in love, and it was returned with an ardour he accepted was genuine—and as passionate as that he had for Melisande. This time he would not interefere. They had his blessing.

'I think Melisande is going to be too busy helping me in the next few weeks, Lord de Vere. Jason has given me his permission to wed Christopher. Isn't that wonderful?'

'I allowed Edwin to share your secret earlier this evening,' Jason said casually, waiting for some reaction from his wife, but Melisande's expression gave away no emotion. It was as though she had closed a door again between herself and the real world. Had she retired anew to that of her dreams? he wondered. He had enticed her from it once with his kisses, but he doubted if she would allow it again. 'And he has an offer which may interest you.'

'Yes, it struck me the moment Jason mentioned the happy event,' Edwin said, a sudden glow stealing through him. She was a pleasant young woman who had greatly comforted him since his loss. Her compassion was boundless. 'As you know, I have a large, very large house in Kingsclere—so many of the rooms are empty. With my daughters . . .' He chose his words carefully, as Melisande's gaze rested on him and he watched the colour of her eyes change to a deep amethyst '. . . no longer in need of this old body to care for them, it will be a lonely place.'

'You can stay here, Father,' she interrupted. 'Can he not, Jason? For as long as he pleases.'

'If that is what he wants.'

'It is not, although I thank both of you for the kind thought. I am fond of the old house, Melisande. You know that. It holds many memories for me of your mother, and of you children when you were young. Memories that will never leave me as I grow old. But to get back to what I was proposing. Amanda, my dear . . . I believe your young man has given up his idea of going to sea?'

'I have, sir.' Christopher answered, and Amanda's

fingers tightened over his. The decision had been made without regret. He did not want his wife to grow old before her time, as his mother had done, waiting months, years, for him to return from the sea. Forced to have a baby all alone, rear it without a father . . . a man by her side to give her support and love. 'I shall not become a Pilot. I shall go back to the land. I'm a good farmer. Amanda and I intend to find us a small house somewhere with some ground . . . In a few years, I may even have my own sheep and cows. Who knows?'

'But you were to sail in *Moonwynd*!' Melisande said, as the conversation began to penetrate her dulled senses. Not going? To wed Amanda? 'You love the sea!'

'That I do, my lady, but I love Amanda more,' came the honest answer. 'I couldn't sail now, anyway; my arm won't be healed in time. It set me to thinking about what else I could do with my life, and I've made up my mind. I'm going back to the land. I love that, too. I wanted to be a Pilot because it would have made my mother so proud of me . . . my father, too, 'cause I know he's watching over me. But I think he'll understand why I've changed my mind. I'm good with my hands, and Lord Dacre has kindly said he will provide a few animals to start us off. We'll manage. You'll see.'

Yes, he would, Melisande thought as she looked into the determined young face. Amanda looked no less determined, no less enamoured of the prospect of becoming a farmer's wife. How love changed people!

'You will need somewhere to live,' Edwin continued. 'I should like you both to make your home with me. As I have said, there is plenty of room . . . and there are acres of land behind the house that have not been touched in years. It is yours to do with as you please. It will not be easy, but you are young and strong. There is one other matter . . . your mother. I believe she is not in the best of health?'

'Nothing a little extra warmth or food couldn't put right,' Amanda replied. 'Christopher and his mother have very little money, Lord de Vere. Jason has helped over the years, but when he leaves home . . .' Her expression became quite distressed as she considered the situation. 'She will have no one to care for her. Your offer is most kind and generous, but we—Kit and I—must consider what is best for her, too.'

'I would not have you do otherwise.' Edwin beamed at her. 'I have heard tales of your mother's venison pies, and her stews! Do you think she would consider coming with you and becoming our housekeeper? The cook I have has decided to go and live with her sister in Newbury, so I am in desperate need of someone. Now, what do you say to that, both of you?'

Lucy, oh, Lucy, if only you could be here to hear all this, Melisande thought, as Amanda and Christopher exchanged smiling looks. How happy he had made them, and in sharing his house, he would be sharing his heart, the love he had in abundance there.

'Say Yes,' she pleaded. 'You will be happy there, I know it. And Father will watch over you like a mother hen. Please?'

'Yes.' Amanda breathed. 'We accept. Don't we, Kit?'

'If—if you are sure . . .' Christopher looked from Jason's face to that of Edwin, unable to believe their good fortune. A huge house and land! And his mother, too. All of them together beneath one roof. It was like a miracle.

'That's settled, then.' Edwin raised his glass of wine, patting the hand Melisande laid upon his arm affectionately. The gesture told him he had her approval, too, and that was of the greatest importance to him. If only he could resolve what was wrong between her husband and her. 'Let us drink to the sound of laughter in my house again—and perhaps,' he added with twinkling eyes, 'the patter of tiny feet.'

Amanda blushed behind her glass as the toast was drunk. Jason drained his glass and rose to his feet.

'If you will all excuse me, I have some letters to write. There is a great deal to be done if you youngsters insist on being married at once. In the morning, Kit, you and I shall look over some livestock.'

'If we wait, you will miss the wedding,' Amanda said, rising to fling her arms about his neck and kiss him soundly. 'Thank you. Thank you! You are the most wonderful man in the world.'

'Why—why should Jason miss the wedding?' Melisande asked her father as Amanda and Christopher followed Jason out of the room. They were off to the garden, she mused, to sit beneath the rose-arbour and make plans for the future. How she envied them what they shared. She and Jason were like strangers: in his presence she was awkward and tongue-tied, and he seemed to go out of his way to avoid being alone with her. What had happened to them? She needed comfort, the touch of his arms, his lips. She could not bear this estrangement one moment longer. Yet how did she end it? There was no warmth in his expression when he looked at her, no gentleness in his voice. He was polite, but withdrawn—a stranger, like the one she had seen on the beach. Was that behind it? Lucy's death? They had not spoken of it, yet each sensed the other was thinking of it whenever they came together.

'Do you not know?' Edwin looked at her with a frown. 'He has said nothing to you?'

'Said what? I have no idea what you mean.' A flutter of uneasiness flickered through her.

'He told me days ago that he intends to sail with Drake. Are things so bad between you that you would allow him to be away from you for a whole year? My child, if he goes, you will lose him for ever.'

'Go? With Drake?' Melisande repeated, the blood ebbing from her cheeks. She swayed back into her chair, shaking her head in disbelief. 'Why?'

'That is for you to tell me. You do not share the same room. That is bad enough in itself. You have never accepted him as your husband, but I thought that would resolve itself with time. I was sure he was the right man for you.'

'He is. He is,' Melisande whispered. 'I don't understand. I want to be his wife, he knows that. I have promised . . .' Yet, since their return from Mousehole, he had not come to claim what he knew was waiting for him. He had not even entered her room at odd times as had been his custom. The usual banter was missing. The mocking smile, the suggestive remark. It was as though he had completely lost all interest in her. Had he? Had he come to the conclusion that she would not fulfil his expectations, after all?

'I think you should have these back, Melisande. I have no need of them now.' From his pocket Edwin took the diamonds she had given him to sell, and laid them on the table before her. 'I did sell them, but I was stupid enough to take them to the jeweller in Newbury where Jason had purchased them many years ago for his mother! They were recognised at once. He redeemed them and returned them to me, to give to you at an appropriate time. You are married to a very understanding man, my child. He did not reproach you in any way. He said he understood your love for your sister and what had been in your mind to act as you did. That is why it hurts him so now, that you blame him for her death.'

'I? Blame Jason?' Melisande gasped. 'Father, how can you say such a thing—it isn't true! It was not his fault she slipped. She was coming back to help me. It was my fault, if anyone's . . . I tried to make her go on . . .' She broke off, tears flooding her eyes. Blame Jason? *That* was the reason for his strange attitude, his reluctance to stay near her. He thought she could not stand the sight of him!

'Two nights ago, I sat with your husband and watched him get very drunk. I've never seen him lose his head with drink before. It took quite a lot to do it, mind. He talked as never before. How that man is suffering! Don't you remember what you said to him? You were prostrate with grief over Lucy's death, I admit, but to turn on the very man who adores you, who idolises you!'

'Father, you are talking in riddles. Everything about

that time is confused in my mind,' Melisande confessed, drawing him down beside her and clinging tightly to his hand. 'Tell me, I beg you. I remember the beach, and Jason lifting me from the boat . . . and then seeing . . . Lucy. After that . . . nothing. The ride home, you being here at Whispering Wood, Amanda's care . . . But Jason has hardly been near me or spoken to me. I thought he no longer wanted me.'

'The man is tormented with guilt—a guilt he does not deserve to have weighing on his shoulders. Apparently one night, at the inn and here, you cried out: "Your fault! Your fault! I wanted to take her home." Do you know what that means?'

'Yes. Dear heaven, how I have hurt him. I had no notion of it.' She bowed her head, her shoulders shaking with sobs. *She* had blamed him—albeit unknowingly, and unjustly. No wonder he could not bear to be with her. Such an ugly accusation hurled in the face of a man whose only fault was that he had cared for Lucy's safety—and her own. The roads were unsafe. He knew it, and so did she . . . But in her anger and bitterness and grief, she had put aside reason and saneness and, in doing so, had probably lost her husband!

'The separation may solve all your problems. A year is a long time,' Edwin murmured, stroking the red hair that had fallen over her face. 'Do you love him?'

'With all my heart.'

'Then go to him before it is too late. Give him your heart—and your love,' her father insisted, lifting her to her feet. Gently he wiped her eyes and patted the tears from her ashen cheeks. 'Allow nothing to stop you, do you hear? You will not have another chance.'

'Jason, may I speak with you, please?' Melisande had knocked on the door of the bedchamber, and then entered without waiting to be invited. Nothing, but nothing, she had vowed as she climbed the staircase, would prevent her from telling Jason how she felt about him. But as she closed the door behind her and he rose from the table at which he had been working, his cold manner was not encouraging. Gathering together all her courage, she added, 'As you are going away, there is much we should discuss.'

'Your father has told you, then? A pity, I wanted to break the news to you myself.'

'To soften the blow? Or were you going to wait until the last moment, the day before you departed, perhaps, so that the wound you inflicted would be deep?' she demanded, advancing into the room. He had discarded his coat and unfastened the front of his shirt to reveal the broad fair-haired chest. How she wanted to lay her aching head there, close her eyes and allow him to make love to her!

'You have given me little indication these past weeks that you are even aware I am alive, so my leaving will hardly cause you concern,' was his sharp retort.

'It is true, then, that you are planning to go with Drake? To leave me alone for a whole year. How can you?' Melisande halted before him, and in the candle-light he was startled by the brilliance of her eyes, bright as two magnificent sapphires. Was that anger in them? Whatever had possessed her to come to him now, like this? She did not care what he did or where he went. The farce was at an end, and he, for one, was glad of it. The nightmare would soon be over . . . One of another kind would begin aboard Moonwynd, as he lay alone in his bed and his thoughts were of her, as they always would be.

'Melisande, what is the meaning of this pretence? At least we can be honest with each other now. From the moment we met again, I have done nothing but bring you pain and unhappiness one way or another. You were right, of course. Had I not insisted that Lucy sail with us, she would be alive now.'

The clipped words hit her like a fist, momentarily throwing her off balance. And then, as she stared at him, she saw the pain deep in those grey pools and knew his brusqueness was a defence against her.

'You cannot blame yourself.'

'You blame me,' he flung back bitterly. 'My God! To have heard the words from your own lips . . .' Jason's tortured features betrayed the extent of his agony—agony he had kept within him, sharing it with no one until it had become too great too bear and the wine had loosened his tongue as never before that night with Edwin. He had unburdened his soul to the older man, and found relief until the next morning when he awoke, with an aching head and the knowledge that nothing had been resolved. Only he could do that. Nothing must stop him. 'I accept that you were right in your condemnation.'

'I was out of my head . . . I knew nothing of what I said,' Melisande whispered, stifling the urge to take his face in her hands and kiss the pain from it. 'Do you not understand? I do not blame you, but myself. Had I not begged Father to keep the birthday surprise a secret, she would not have run away. She believed he had found a husband for her, but I told her the truth. She was so happy, Jason. Happy, until the moment she died.' Tears coursed down over her cheeks. She could not contain them; did not want to. She needed the relief of tears. 'Perhaps I was unable to accept any blame. I do now . . . But then . . . I should not have turned on you. It was unjust and cruel, and I beg your forgiveness.'

'Nevertheless, I can only think of one way to alleviate further unpleasantness between us,' Jason replied. The sight of her tearful countenance moved him when he knew he must not allow emotion to rule his thoughts. 'If I go with Drake, that will allow you a whole year to decide what you wish to do. To remain at Whispering Wood as my wife—my real wife—or to return to your father's house. If you are not here when I return, I shall accept your decisions. If you decide to go, I would be grateful if you would not abandon your committments here until the last moment. I would like to know the house and estate are in good, capable hands.'

'If—if you return,' Melisande whispered. He had

thought everything out without a word to her. He was prepared for her to be gone when he returned! Was that why he had not kept her to her promise?

'Much as it would simplify matters, my sweet, I do not intend to have my head blown off,' Jason told her with a crooked grin. 'I shall come back—to what, is up to you.'

'You have thought of everyone today, haven't you?' she said, stepping closer to him. 'Amanda, Christopher —even Father. He told me it was really your idea for them to live with him when they are married. Everyone—except me!'

'I am in no mood to play games with you, Melisande,' he flung back. Did she think this was easy for him? 'What is it that I have overlooked?'

'My feelings in this matter. Am I not to be consulted on whether or not you should go away for a whole year?'

'I was given to understand that you would be overjoyed if my obnoxious presence were removed. If I stay, things would not be as they are now. I want you too much.' The words fell reluctantly from between tight lips. She was making him say things he had never intended she would hear—not now!

'Always you speak of want . . . never of love,' Melisande cried.

'Love! My God, woman, if you knew half my thoughts, you would blush for a whole year. Of course I love you! I have done since that first night I saw you here at Whispering Wood. A slender gazelle in a gown of green, with hair of fire. When I opened my eyes that night at Kingsclere and found you bending over me, you will never know how close you came to being hauled into my bed and more than soundly kissed! I knew then that if I allowed you to get away from me again, I would lose you, and so I used every means at my disposal to keep you within reach. I apologise for ever believing I could become the prince of your dream world. My ministering angel put me through hell. Look, but don't touch . . .' His grey eyes began to glitter, and the fluttering in Melisande's heart grew. Her own heart was beating so loudly she was sure he could hear it. Love her? He did love her! He had always done so! And had been afraid to tell her—afraid he would lose her with protestations of his passion. Unable to use words, he had tried to show her the depths of his love, but she in her pride and obstinacy had refused to accept the miracle that had taken place.

'That—that was your idea . . .' she stammered, drowning in the depths opening up before her eyes. She was being pulled down, deep down, unable to think . . . 'Not mine.'

'And a damn-fool one, which is the reason I must go away. If I don't, you'll find yourself in my bed—where you belong—by force, if that's what it takes, and then you would hate me—and I'd hate myself. I've tried to be patient . . . to give you time.'

'Yes . . .'

He blinked at her, not understanding the meaning of the single, softly spoken word.

'Yes, it's what I want, too,' Melisande whispered, swaying against him. His arms slowly, almost against their will, closed about her and the trembling grew as the warmth of his hands stole through her gown. 'I tried to tell you before, but it never came out the right way. I was coming to you that night aboard *Moonwynd*, but Lucy . . .' she hesitated, burying her head amid the down of fair hair. 'I love you so much!'

That was why she had been smelling so sweet, looking so tantalising, and he had thought it had been to torment him! Fool! Stupid blind fool!

'Is Lucy not between us?' Jason asked hesitantly.

Melisande raised her head and looked up into the drawn features. 'She never was. Forgive me?'

'Oh, my sweet little love! My foolish little love . . .' The words were lost on his lips as he found her mouth, bruising it with a fierce pressure that robbed her of breath, told her nothing separated them now, that nothing ever would again.

'I am cold, Jason . . .'

'Come to bed, then, and let me warm you,' he whispered the invitation.

Melisande lay very warm and very comfortable in her husband's arms in the afterglow of their lovemaking. He had taken her to the gates of paradise and opened them with his love, transporting her into a world of passion and fulfilment such as she had never dreamed possible for two people to share. All inhibitions vanished under his skilful guidance, his worship of her body.

'Are you asleep, Jason?' she asked softly, when he had not moved for a long time. In the candle-light, his face looked peaceful as never before, wiped clean of all tension and suspicion. Love had brought him peace, as it had her.

'I am not about to spoil this wonderful moment by falling asleep,' came the amused reply, and she snuggled against a bare shoulder with a laugh.

'You are very clever to have thought of having Amanda live with Father. He will never be lonely now. Clever—and thoughtful,' she added, not wanting him to misunderstand her choice of words. She would never again be careless in her judgment of him. 'I think she and Christopher will be very happy there. It is a lovely old house, and there is so much they can do with it. You do not fear she has made a wrong choice this time?'

'With Kit? No. Besides, I promised her I would no more interfere with her life.' Jason's lips trailed tickling kisses down over her bare arm to the rise of her breast and then up along the smooth line of her throat to the side of her mouth. 'And now she knows the truth, she understands why I prevented her relationship with Richard. But, of course, you don't know about that other skeleton in the family closet. I'm afraid it is another one which had to break loose.'

'What is it?' Melisande asked. She had always thought there was more to his close guidance of Amanda's conduct that he had ever revealed.

'Amanda is my half-sister. We had different fathers,

but shared the same mother. An indiscretion on her part, which happened while my father was away at sea. The child, when she was born, was given into the keeping of a childless family, close friends of my mother. When Father was killed—the couple had died several years before—Mother had her brought to Whispering Wood. She always hoped that one day I would be able to tell Mandy the truth. She has grown up enough for me to do that. It brought us closer together than I ever thought possible.'

'Oh, Jason, I am so glad.' Melisande sank against him, losing herself in the pleasure of his kisses, the hands which roamed her body, exciting every fibre with their touch. Suddenly she drew back from him, her head arched in an intense attitude of listening.

'What is it?' he asked, momentarily apprehensive.

A strange smile spread across Melisande's face. A look of total wonderment, of hearing, yet not believing, and then, as he watched her, he saw acceptance take the place of disbelief and gathered her to him again with fierce possessiveness, knowing that his wildest hope had come true.

'Listen!' she whispered, her lips against a dark cheek. 'I can hear the trees talking. Your name . . . they are saying your name, Jason.'

'I told you that one day they would.'

In Melisande's room, Merlin left his bed to jump on the pillow as he did every night, and stretched languidly, finding himself alone with no one to share it. Soft voices reached his alert ears, but he was too comfortable to get up again and investigate. Yawning, he stretched full length on the silken cover . . .